RICCARDINO

Andrea Camilleri was one of Italy's most famous contemporary writers. The Inspector Montalbano series, which has sold over 65 million copies worldwide, has been translated into thirty-two languages and was adapted for Italian television, screened on BBC4. *The Potter's Field*, the thirteenth book in the series, was awarded the Crime Writers' Association's International Dagger for the best crime novel translated into English. In addition to his phenomenally successful Inspector Montalbano series, he was also the author of the historical comic mysteries *Hunting Season* and *The Brewer of Preston*. He died in Rome in July 2019.

Stephen Sartarelli is an award-winning translator. He is also the author of three books of poetry, most recently *The Open Vault*. He lives in France.

Also by Andrea Camilleri

Inspector Montalbano mysteries

Short Stories

Other Novels

ANDREA CAMILLERI

RICCARDINO

Translated by Stephen Sartarelli

PICADOR

First published 2021 by Penguin Books,
an imprint of Penguin Random House LLC

First published in the UK 2021 by Mantle

This paperback edition first published 2022 by Picador
an imprint of Pan Macmillan
The Smithson, 6 Briset Street, London ECIM 5NR
EU representative: Macmillan Publishers Ireland Ltd, 1st Floor,
The Liffey Trust Centre, 117–126 Sheriff Street Upper, Dublin 1, DOI YC43
Associated companies throughout the world
www.panmacmillan.com

ISBN 978-1-5290-7334-8

Originally published in Italian as *Riccardino*

1 3 5 7 9 8 6 4 2

A CIP catalogue record for this book is available from the British Library.

Typeset by Palimpsest Book Production Ltd, Falkirk, Stirlingshire
Printed and bound by CPI Group (UK) Ltd, Croydon, CRO 4YY

MIX
Paper | Supporting
responsible forestry
FSC® C116313

RICCARDINO

ONE

The telephone rang as he was finally drifting off to sleep, ever so delicately, after what seemed like hours and hours of thrashing about in bed without success. He'd tried every trick in the book, from counting sheep to counting without sheep, from trying to recall the first book of the *Iliad* to dredging up the opening of Cicero's *Catiline Orations*. Nothing doing. There was no way. After '*Quo usque tandem, Catilina*', dense fog. This was an insomnia without remedy, as it was not caused by any excessive meals or onslaughts of nasty thoughts.

He turned the light on and looked at the clock: not yet five a.m. Clearly they were calling him from the station; something big must have happened. He got up lazily and went to answer.

There was another phone socket next to his bedside table, but he hadn't used it for quite a while because he'd become convinced that having to walk the short distance from one room to the next when woken up in the middle of the night gave him a chance to clear away the cobwebs of sleep still stubbornly clinging to the insides of his brain.

'Hello?'

His voice came out sounding not only ragged, but as though stuck together with glue.

'Riccardino here!' yelled a voice that, unlike his own, was shrill and festive.

He became irritated. How the hell could anyone be shrill and festive at five o'clock in the morning? And there was another detail that could not be ignored: he didn't know anyone called Riccardino. He opened his mouth to tell him to buzz off, but Riccardino didn't give him time.

'What happened? Did you forget we had an appointment? We're all here already, outside the Bar Aurora, and you're the only one missing! It's a little cloudy at the moment, but it's supposed to be a beautiful day!'

'I'm sorry, I really am . . . just give me ten, fifteen minutes . . . I'll be right over.'

And he hung up and went back to bed.

Sure, it was a dastardly thing to do; he should have told the truth and said they'd dialled a wrong number. Now, instead, they would spend all morning waiting outside the Bar Aurora for nothing.

On the other hand, to be fair, it simply wasn't acceptable for anyone to dial a wrong number at five o'clock in the morning and get away with it.

He no longer felt the least bit sleepy. At least Riccardino had said that it was going to be a nice day. Montalbano felt reassured.

*

The second phone call came in just after six.

'Chief, beckin' yer partin an' all, wha'? Did I wake yiz?'

'No, Cat, I was already awake.'

'Are ya rilly sure, Chief? Or are ya sayin' 'at jess to be p'lite?'

'No, Cat, you needn't worry. Go ahead and talk.'

'Well, Chief, Fazio called jess now cuz 'e wannit me to say 'e got a call.'

'So why are you calling me?'

'Cuz Fazio said to me be callin' yiz.'

'Me?'

'Nah, natchoo, Chief, Fazio.'

At this rate, the inspector would never manage to find out what had happened. So he hung up and called Fazio's mobile.

'What's going on?'

'Sorry we had to bother you, Chief, but somebody got shot.'

'Dead?'

'Yeah. Two shots, right in the face. I think you'd better come and have a look.'

'Augello's not around?'

'Have you forgotten, Chief? He went to his in-laws' with his wife and Salvuzzo.'

Montalbano realized bitterly that asking whether Mimì Augello was available for service was a sign of the times – or, rather, a sign of time in the singular: his own, personal time and the years now weighing on his shoulders. In the past he would have rigged the deck to keep Augello away from a case, not out of envy or to screw his career prospects, but just so he wouldn't have to share the indescribable pleasure of the solitary hunt with him. Now, instead, he would have gladly turned the investigation over to him. Of course if a case fell to him and he had no choice but to take it on, he would still dive right in, as he had always done, but these days, whenever he could, he preferred dodging it from the start.

The truth of the matter was that for a while now, he'd no longer felt like it. After years and years of practice he'd come to the realization that there was no one more brain-dead than someone for whom the solution to any problem was murder. So much for De Quincey and murder 'as one of the fine arts'!

Morons, all of them, both the retailers, who killed out of greed, jealousy, or revenge, and the wholesalers, who massacred in bulk in the name of freedom, democracy, or worse still, in the name of God himself. Sometimes they were shrewd, in fact, and even intelligent, as Sciascia had remarked, but still they always turned out, in one way or another, to be brain-dead.

'Where'd it happen?'

'In the middle of the street, about an hour ago.'

'Any witnesses?'

'Yes.'

'So they saw the killer?'

'Well, they saw him, as far as that goes. But nobody seems able to identify him.'

What else could you expect, on this fine island of ours? You can see, but cannot identify. You're present, but can't say anything definite. You saw, but only vaguely, because you left your glasses at home. Anyway, nowadays any unlucky wretch claiming that they recognized a killer as he was killing immediately finds his life ruined, not so much by the killer himself seeking revenge as by the police, judges, and journalists who will put him repeatedly through the mincer at the police station, in the courtroom, and on television.

'Did they give chase?'

'Is that some kind of joke?'

What else could you expect, on this fine island of ours? Yes, sir, I was there, but I was unable to give chase because one of my shoes was untied. Yes, sir, I saw everything, but I couldn't intervene because I suffer from rheumatism. Anyway, how brave do you have to be to start running, unarmed, after someone who's just shot someone else and has still at least one more bullet in his gun?

'Did you inform the prosecutor, the doctor, and Forensics?'

'Yes, everybody.'

He was stalling, he realized. But there was no dodging this one. And so he asked, reluctantly:

'What's the name of the street?'

'Via Rosolino Pilo, and it's near—'

'I know where it is. I'm on my way.'

*

By yelling and cursing and blasting his horn until his ears rang, he managed to carve a path through a crowd of fifty or so people who'd come running to the scene like flies to shit and were now blocking the entrance to Via Rosolino Pilo to anyone, like him, coming from Via Nino Bixio. The root cause of the blockage was a police car parked across the width of the entrance to the street, with patrol officers Inzolia and Verdicchio – known on the force as 'the table wines' – presiding over the scene. At the far end of the street, which gave onto Via Tukory, the 'wild beasts' – that is, patrol officers Lupo and Leone – were also standing guard. The police force's 'chicken coop', on the other hand – that is, Gallo and Galluzzo – were in the middle of the street with Fazio. Also visible in the middle of the street was a body lying on the ground. Not far away were three men leaning against a lowered metal shutter.

From windows, balconies, and terraces, old and young, women and men, toddlers, dogs, and cats looked down, leaning so far out they risked crashing to the street, all in hopes of getting a better view of what was happening. And amidst it all, a din of voices, calling, laughing, crying, praying, yelling, a great cacophony just like at the Festa di San Calò. And, as at the fiesta, there were people snapping photos and others filming the scene with those tiny little mobile phones that nowadays even newborns know how to use.

The inspector pulled up to the kerb and got out of the car.

At once a lively dialogue started up over his head.

'Look! Look! It's the inspector!'

'It's Montalbano!'

'Who? Montalbano? The one from TV?'

'No, the real one.'

Montalbano suddenly felt extremely agitated. Some years back he'd had the brilliant idea of telling a local writer the story of a case he'd conducted, and he had immediately spun it into a novel. Since hardly anyone reads any more in Italy, nothing came of it. And so, being unable to say no to that tremendous pain in the arse of a man, he'd gone ahead and told him about a second case, and then a third and a fourth, which the author then wrote up in his way, using an invented language and working from his imagination. And these novels, go figure, had become the biggest sellers in Italy and were even translated abroad. And then the stories made it onto TV and enjoyed extraordinary success. And as of that moment the music changed. Now everyone recognized Inspector Montalbano and knew who he was, but only as a fictional character on television. It was an unbearable pain in the arse, something that could have come out of a play by another local author, a certain Pirandello.

At least the actor who played him was excellent. He didn't look the least bit like him, and on top of everything else was a good ten years younger (the bastard!). Otherwise it would have been too much, and Montalbano wouldn't have been able to walk down the street without being stopped every two paces for an autograph.

'Can't we do something to make these people stop

ogling and enjoying the show? Even crows have more decency!'

'What are we supposed to do, Chief? Fire into the air?'

'And who are those guys?' Montalbano asked, gesturing with his head towards the three men sticking close to the metal shutter.

'Friends of the victim. They were with him when it happened.'

Montalbano looked at them. All in their thirties, all with crew cuts, all in grey sweatsuits, all rather athletic, and all with sun-baked faces. At the moment, however, their sporting air had dispelled, giving way to a kind of mannequin-like stiffness, probably due to fear and shock. Something occurred to the inspector.

'Are they maybe military men?' he asked, hoping.

If they turned out to be soldiers in civvies, he could bow out at once and pass the case to the carabinieri . . .

'No, Chief.'

The dead man was dressed the same way, except that the front of his sweatshirt had dark streaks and stains from the blood he'd lost, which had formed a puddle on the street. His face was gone, blotted out. And in his right hand was a mobile phone.

Only then did Montalbano, looking around, notice that there was a sign on the closed shutter: Bar Aurora.

He felt strangely certain – with a certainty as absolute as it was inexplicable – that the poor bastard who was shot was the same person who had called him on the phone before dawn by dialling a wrong number.

He walked over to the three men, who were huddling closely together as though cold.

'I'm Inspector Montalbano, police. What was the dead man's name?'

The three athletes were as though asleep on their feet, the pupils in their saucer eyes spinning round and round and up and down like marbles, and surely not seeing anything. They didn't move, didn't answer, and couldn't bring the person standing before them into focus.

'What was his name?' Montalbano repeated, patiently.

At last one of them, clearly making an effort, managed to bring his eyes to a halt on the inspector.

'Riccardo Lopresti,' he said softly.

'Riccardino?' asked Montalbano.

It was as if he'd said a magic word, as if he'd plugged in the cable feeding energy to the three.

Losing at once their spellbound immobility, they regained colour, heat, feeling, life, and the power of speech.

'Did you know him?' asked, lips trembling, the man who'd been the first to speak.

Montalbano didn't answer.

A second man started speaking in a low voice, almost as if praying:

'Riccardino, my God, Riccardino . . .'

The third man said nothing, but started weeping silently, his face in his hands.

A ray of sun, as sudden and sharp as a spotlight, lit up the inspector and the three athletes. Montalbano raised his head. The clouds had opened an eye; the morning gloom was dispelling. Riccardino had been right. It was going to be a beautiful day. Just not for him. But none of it mattered in the least any more.

At this point the airborne dialogue resumed overhead.

'Wha'ss happenin'? Eh? Wha'ss happenin'?'

'What are they doing?'

It was the people who lived in the same building as the Bar Aurora. Unable to see what the inspector was doing, since he was directly below them, they were asking the people in the building across the street to fill them in.

'The inspector's talkin' to three guys.'

'An' wha'ss he askin' 'em?'

'You can't hear nuttin' from up here.'

'But can't this isspector talk a li'l louder like he does on TV?'

'Audio!' commanded some idiot from a window.

'We wanna hear!' protested another.

They were acting as if they were watching TV, and so they wanted to enjoy full audio and video, as if they'd paid for a cable subscription.

Montalbano's balls went into such a vertiginous spin that he was afraid he would achieve lift-off at any moment. Fazio, who knew him inside and out, came over, feeling worried. The inspector made a snap decision.

'Fazio, I'm taking these three gentlemen to the station.'

'But when the prosecutor gets here—'

'When the prosecutor gets here you'll give him my sincere regards.' Then, to the three men: 'Come with me. We can't really talk around here.'

As they were walking towards the car, the overhead dialogue turned into a chorus of joy.

'He arrested 'em. He arrested 'em all!'

'Shit! He's really good, that Montalbano!'

*

Before arriving at the station, he stopped outside a bar and ordered the three men to drink a glass of cognac each. They obeyed, though grimacing in disgust. Apparently either they weren't in the habit, or it went against their code of sporting ethics. Whatever the case, to make up for it, the booze did wake them up a bit.

'Chief, ahh, Chief! The perfesser was lookin' f'yiz!'

'What professor, Cat?'

'Th' author perfesser.'

'If he calls back, tell him I'm not in.'

The guy had probably already got a whiff of death by murder, even if he did live all the way up in Rome.

The inspector had the three men sit down in his office, opposite his desk, then took a sheet of paper and a ball-point pen and asked the first one on the left:

'First and last name, profession, and home address.'

'Mario Liotta, surveyor, Via Marconi 32.'

The second man was named Alfonso Licausi, and he too was a surveyor, residing on Via Cristoforo Colombo; the third was Gaspare Bonanno, accountant, living at Piazza Plebiscito 97.

'And what about Riccardino Lopresti?'

Riccardino was employed at the Banca Regionale, with

a degree in business and economics, and he lived at number 3, Viale Siracusa.

'And now we can get started,' said Montalbano.

The three men, who seemed to expect the kind of interrogation you see in the movies, were surprised by the first question.

'How did the four of you become friends?'

The three men looked at each other, tongue-tied. A few seconds later, Liotta, who must have been a sort of spokesman for the group, replied.

'We met in first grade. We were all in the same class.'

'And you're all from Vigàta?'

'Yes, Inspector.'

'Are you all the same age?'

'We were all born in 1972.'

'Then what?'

'Then we started getting together outside the classroom as well and our families became friends. We never let each other out of our sight, even though we later ended up going to different schools. At any rate, we've been together ever since. You know what people call us? The four musketeers.'

'Because you all dress alike?'

'No, that's just the uniform of the Virtue and Labour Sports Club, which we belong to.'

'What particular sports do you engage in?'

'No single thing in particular. We work out a lot at the gym.'

'I like to swim,' said Montalbano. 'But not in a pool. In the sea.'

The three men exchanged a quick glance. So was this famous inspector just talking to hear himself speak? Or was he alluding to something they didn't grasp?

'Let's continue. Are you married?'

'Yes. Alfonso and I married Gaspare's two sisters, whereas Gaspare married my sister.'

'And what about Riccardino?'

'Excuse me, Inspector, but why are you calling him Riccardino, the way we do? Did you know him?'

'I met him a couple of times,' Montalbano said evasively. And he repeated his question: 'And what about Riccardino?'

'Riccardino, no.'

'He wasn't married?'

'He was, but to a German woman.'

Maybe there'd been a shortage of available sisters? 'Did he meet her in Germany?'

'No, he met her here in Vigàta. She's the younger sister of a woman who married a man from Vigàta.'

See? No matter which way you turn, there's always a marriageable sister who turns up.

'She'll need to be informed.'

The three looked at one another again. Liotta resumed speaking, but was a little unsure.

'Do we . . . do we have to do it ourselves?'

'I think it's best, no? You were friends, weren't you?'

The three squirmed in their chairs. Montalbano realized he'd stepped into a delicate situation.

TWO

Once again Liotta took it upon himself to answer the question. 'Inspector, Riccardino was like a brother to us, that's how close our friendship was; but we don't feel the same way about Else, his wife.'

'You don't get along with her?'

'I can tell you openly: she did everything humanly possible to try and separate us from Riccardino, to break up our beautiful friendship. Nasty gossip, insinuations, lies . . . Luckily, though, she never succeeded.'

'And what was the reason for her behaviour?'

'The reason, you ask! We never had any idea. Even our wives tried several times to get closer to her, but she never changed her attitude, not even a little. It was hopeless. You know, sometimes Riccardino, poor guy, was forced to make up excuses just so he could see us, like he had a secret lover or something!'

'She was probably jealous,' Gaspare Bonanno cut in. 'It's possible she couldn't bear our friendship because she felt excluded.'

'Do they have children?'

'Else and Riccardino? No,' said Bonanno.

'Where were you supposed to be going this morning?' Mario Liotta took the floor again.

'Well, since today's a holiday—'

Montalbano hesitated.

'It is? What holiday is it?'

'All Saints' Day, Inspector.'

How was it that this stinking job wouldn't even leave him in peace on holidays? He gestured to Liotta to continue.

'We'd planned to go on a long walk, all the way to Monte Lirato. Six hours in all, there and back. And we'd bought some panini to eat along the way. We were all supposed to meet at a quarter to five outside the Bar Aurora. Normally we're all quite punctual.'

'Why there, of all places?'

'Because it's practically equidistant from all of our homes. And since we weren't bringing our cars, it was the shortest—'

'So it wasn't the first time you met up at that bar.'

'No, in fact it was our customary meeting place, our "home base", so to speak.'

'And who knew about your planned excursion for the day?'

'Well . . . our wives, naturally.'

'Only them?'

'Everybody knew, Inspector. Yesterday, for example, we told our friends at the sports complex. Why should we keep a perfectly normal walk through the countryside secret?'

'Tell me what happened this morning.'

'Gaspare and I met in Via Bixio, and the moment we came out onto Via Rosolino Pilo, we saw Riccardino, who'd arrived before us. And so we started talking.'

'Do you remember what you talked about?'

'Well . . . mostly we were worried about the weather. I thought it was going to rain, but Riccardino was hopeful and claimed it would turn out to be a beautiful day. After a while, seeing that Alfonso was running late, Riccardino gave him a ring and he replied that he'd be there within fifteen minutes.'

Alfonso Licausi gave a little start in his chair, raising his head with a sudden jerk, and looked confusedly at Liotta. But he said nothing.

Licausi's reaction set off alarm bells in Montalbano's head. Why hadn't he said that Riccardino had never called him? It would have been the most natural reaction, but it didn't happen. And this convinced Montalbano that, for the moment, it was best not to reveal what had actually happened.

'You said that Mr Licausi was running late. How late was he running when Riccardino called?'

The three looked at one another, in a silent, quick consultation.

'About ten minutes,' said Liotta, answering for them all.

It tallied. Indeed it was just a few minutes before five when the inspector was woken up by Riccardino's call.

'Did any of you manage to hear what he was saying when he was speaking over the phone?'

'You know how it is, Inspector, when people talk on their mobile phones. They usually step aside for a little privacy. Well, Riccardino, as he was dialling, walked a few paces away from us, stepped down from the pavement, and went almost into the middle of the street. We heard him talking, but we couldn't understand what he was saying.'

'Maybe you can tell us, Mr Licausi,' said the inspector, his expression as innocent as a cherub's.

'I don't know what my friends are talking about. I want to formally declare that I never received any phone call from Riccardino,' Licausi replied firmly and harshly, though he'd turned as pale as a corpse.

'What?!' Liotta reacted, half-confused, half-angry. 'What are you saying? Riccardino told us he'd spoken to you! And he repeated what you said to him! Isn't that right, Gasparì?'

'That's right,' confirmed Bonanno, himself confused.

'I'm telling you he did not speak to me, and you must believe me!' Licausi retorted, raising his voice. Then, as though something had just occurred to him, he added:

'Why do you want to drag me into this?'

Ouch. For one thing, they'd all instinctively stopped speaking proper Italian and started talking in Vigatese, which no doubt meant that they were reverting to their longstanding common idiom. Secondly, what was it that Licausi didn't want to be involved in and feared that his friends were luring him into?

17

'Now, now,' said Montalbano, pretending not to understand. 'Calm down. I'm not trying to drag you into anything.'

Licausi didn't even look at him, but just sat there in silence and cast his eyes down at the floor.

'Please continue, Mr Liotta.'

'As Riccardino was talking on the phone, a big motorcycle came out from Via Bixio and its driver was wearing a full helmet.'

'It was a Yamaha 1100 road bike,' Gaspare Bonanno cut in.

'And so? Does that make a difference?' asked the inspector, who didn't know the first thing about motorcycles.

'It's a very powerful motorbike, almost as fast as the racing bikes and not at all easy to drive. On top of that, you hardly ever see that model around here.'

'Let's continue.'

'The man on the motorbike pulled up outside the bar and left the engine on. I thought he was going to get a pack of cigarettes from the machine outside. He put one foot on the pavement, took off his big gloves, and reached inside his jacket with one hand.'

Montalbano looked at him with admiration.

'My compliments. It's hard to find witnesses who remember a killing in such detail.'

'My friends tell me I have an excellent visual memory. At that moment, Riccardino, who was still in the middle of the street, called out to us and said that Alfonso would be there in fifteen minutes. Mario and I then turned around, taking our eyes off the motorcyclist, and . . . and then we saw Riccardino fall to the ground.'

'That's an important point for the investigation,' said the inspector. 'How much time passed between the end of the phone call and the killing of Riccardino?'

The answer came at once.

'Very few seconds. I think I already said that. Riccardino had just finished telling us what Alfonso had said to him.'

Deep inside, Montalbano heaved a sigh of relief. The question he'd asked was of no importance to the investigation; it concerned his own conscience. He'd been worried that Riccardino died because he, Montalbano, had told him to wait there for a bit longer. But in fact the killer was already there and ready, and would have fired his gun even had the inspector told Riccardino that he'd dialled a wrong number.

'Didn't you hear the shots?'

'No, we didn't hear anything. The motorbike's engine was as loud as a heavy machine gun . . . It was hard to make anything out.'

'And what happened next?'

'The man on the motorbike sped away so fast that he spun his wheel. And he passed so close to the pavement where I was standing that I reached out instinctively with both hands to keep him away and actually touched his jacket.'

'What direction did he drive off in?'

'He went straight up to Via Tukory and then turned right.'

'Did anyone by any chance get the licence number?'

Liotta looked at Bonanno and Bonanno looked at Liotta. They said nothing, but understood each other perfectly.

'No,' said Liotta, the spokesman.

'Too bad,' the inspector commented.

'About the licence plate?'

'No, about the fact that you didn't see the man on the motorbike as he was shooting.'

'Are you saying that in your opinion it wasn't the motor-cyclist who killed Riccardino?'

'The thought never even crossed my mind. All I'm saying is that you two cannot be absolutely certain that it was the motorcyclist who fired the shot. In a court of law your testimony would be worthless.'

'So why did he drive away?'

'He might have got scared, Mr Liotta, because he saw somebody fire a gun. But it's only an unlikely conjecture. That motorbike . . . had you ever seen it before?'

Another silent consultation. 'No,' said Liotta.

'Who called the police?'

'Not us. Riccardino was the only one with a mobile phone . . .'

'What did you do after the motorcycle drove off?'

Only Liotta answered.

'I went up to Riccardino to see whether . . . but I immediately realized that it was hopeless . . . His . . . his face was gone . . . It was just a big jumble of . . .'

He couldn't go on. He gulped a few times. His mouth must have been completely parched.

'And what about you?' Montalbano asked Gaspare.

'I honestly don't remember. I think I just froze. I was, like, paralysed.'

'And you, Mr Licausi?'

'It had already happened by the time I got there.'

Maybe it was the tone he used in saying this, but Liotta and Bonanno turned and stared at him.

'I would like to set straight this business of the phone call once and for all,' he said darkly. 'I repeat: Riccardino never called me, and therefore I can't have spoken to him.'

'But if—' Gaspare began.

'But why are you denying that Riccardino called you?' Liotta interrupted him.

'Guys, stop busting my balls with this, OK?' Licausi said, sounding irritated and almost threatening. And he'd also gone back to speaking Vigatese.

'But do you mind telling us what interest you could possibly have in denying the existence of a perfectly innocent phone call?' Liotta insisted.

'And do you mind telling me what interest you could possibly have in insisting it took place?' Licausi said angrily, rising to his feet.

Interest: a word one would never expect to be used in true friendship.

Indeed, it seemed to be emerging that the three men were not quite so hand in glove with one another as they wanted everyone to believe. Hadn't Liotta said they were called the four musketeers? And wasn't the Three Musketeers' motto 'All for one and one for all'? Or maybe they were just trying to pass a hot potato? Whatever the case, it was now clear that they had something to hide. Not clearing up the misunderstanding over the phone call had been a shrewd move on the inspector's part, and he was now gloating inside. But it was important to avoid the scuffle that was brewing.

'Mr Licausi, please sit down. We're not at the gym here, and there's no free-form wrestling allowed.'

He sat down without a peep.

'Let's see if we can shed a little light on this business of the phone call, which seems to have you at odds with each other. Can you, Mr Licausi, tell me what time it was when you arrived at the appointed place?'

'Right after Riccardino was killed. I can say this with assurance because I was coming out from Via Tukory and very nearly got run over by a Yamaha 1100, which I then found out was being driven by the killer.'

'Where do you live?'

'In Via Cristoforo Colombo.'

'Did you come on foot like the others?'

'Of course.'

'So, if my calculations are correct, coming to Via Pilo from Via Cristoforo Colombo, and walking rather fast, it would take you at least fifteen, twenty minutes. Is that correct?'

'Yes, sir. It takes me fifteen minutes.'

'And do you know what that means?'

'It means that when Riccardino called me, if indeed he called me, I was already out of the house.'

'Exactly. And yet somebody did answer the phone. Couldn't it have been your wife?'

'At the moment I'm on my own; my wife is on holiday at San Vito Lo Capo.'

'Do you have any children?'

'Yes. A little girl, three years old.'

'Well, if that's the way it is,' said Montalbano, 'then there can only be one explanation. Riccardino dialled a wrong number and talked to someone else.'

'Oh, come on, Inspector!' Gaspare intervened stubbornly. 'Riccardino would have immediately realized that it wasn't Alfonso at the other end!'

'Then there's another possible explanation,' Montalbano conceded. 'Riccardino called someone else, spoke to this person, and told the two of you that he'd been speaking to Mr Licausi.'

'But why, for the love of God, would he have gone through such a song and dance?' asked Liotta, raising his voice.

Montalbano's answer made his blood run cold. 'That, I don't know. But maybe the three of you do.'

And this, too, was an excellent move on his part, intended to widen the rift – which was still underground but ready to surface – that was forming between the three musketeers or whatever they were. And indeed Liotta, Bonanno, and Licausi fell silent. And exchanged long, wordless glances.

The time had come to throw down his ace. Which he

did. The more noise he made, the more he stirred the waters, the better. Maybe something would come floating to the top.

'Unless Riccardino himself was called,' he said half under his breath, as though absentmindedly.

An electric shock seemed to jolt the three. 'But we would have heard the ring!'

'Not necessarily. There are plenty of phones that can be set to vibrate instead of ring. And there are others that give a weak signal before ringing . . . Riccardino may have heard or felt the incoming call and then pretended that he had dialled.'

'But why would he do that? And who would ever call him at that hour?'

This time it was Gaspare Bonanno asking the questions.

'His wife, for one. Or someone else trying to warn him.'

'Warn him of what?' yelled Liotta.

'How should I know? Maybe of some imminent danger.'

'And why would Riccardino not have said anything to us about this danger?' Liotta asked.

'And why would he have told us something that wasn't true?' said Bonanno, seconding him.

Like a good Jesuit priest, Montalbano threw his hands up and raised his eyes to the heavens, as if to say that the true reasons for human actions were known to the Lord alone. But then it was Licausi who answered Liotta's and Bonanno's questions.

'The inspector is surmising that maybe Riccardino didn't trust us,' he said.

In a flash Montalbano removed his Jesuit cassock and donned the offended, aggrieved face of someone who's been treated unjustly.

'I am merely making abstract conjectures, Mr Licausi, stuff based on nothing. Do you really think I'm the kind of man to draw specific conclusions from such uncertain hypotheses?'

He must have put on a good act, because Licausi looked confused.

'I'm sorry, I apologize,' he said drily.

The inspector decided that it was time to take the question of the phone call off the table. By this point he'd milked it for all it was worth and got some results. He slapped himself on the forehead.

'How stupid! There's a perfectly easy way to find out who Riccardino called! How did I not think of it earlier?'

He picked up the receiver.

'Cat, get me Fazio, would you?'

While he was waiting, he reviewed in his mind the lie he would tell the three men. Which was that the Forensics lab had called the number recorded in Riccardino's mobile phone's memory, and a man had answered, saying that he was woken up at five o'clock in the morning by a caller who'd dialled the wrong number, and that, to avenge himself for the rude awakening, he'd told the caller that he would be at their meeting in ten minutes. Which is exactly what he himself had done. And if one of the three men happened to ask how it was possible that Riccardino didn't realize that it wasn't his friend's voice at the other end, there were a hundred potential answers he could give.

'Hello, Fazio? Listen, are the Forensics people in yet? Good, I need you to ask one of them to check what the number was for the last phone call the victim made on his mobile phone, and then—'

'Already taken care of, Chief.'

Montalbano smiled to himself. If Fazio already knew that Riccardino had dialled his own home phone number, the improvisation they would have to perform would be easier.

'So it's already been taken care of,' he repeated for the benefit of his audience.

Licausi, Liotta, and Bonanno just sat there, as taut as bowstrings, on the edge of their chairs.

'And whose number was it?'

Fazio lowered his voice.

'Are those three gentlemen still with you, Chief?'

'Yes.'

'Then I can't talk.'

Montalbano was convinced that Fazio didn't want to say over the telephone that the number belonged to the inspector's landline. So he gave him a hand.

'Does it belong to someone we know?'

Fazio's reply threw him off.

'No, Chief.'

What could that mean? But he, Montalbano, was indeed the recipient, however mistaken, of the final phone call Riccardino made in his life!

'Are you sure about that?'
'Absolutely.'
No point insisting.
'OK, thanks. Get back to me as soon as you've finished.'

THREE

But Fazio had something else to tell him.

'Chief, while we're at it, I also wanted to let you know about a tragic scene I witnessed.'

'And what was that?'

'Some moron phoned Riccardo Lopresti's wife and told her that her husband had been shot, and where. So the poor woman raced to the scene. Luckily Dr Pasquano was around. The poor woman was crying like Mary at the foot of the cross.'

'And where is she now?'

'One of our men took her home. She'd come with her sister.'

'Thanks again.'

He hung up and looked silently at the three men, who looked back at him in turn, also silently.

Moments later, Montalbano said:

'I'm sure you gathered that the Forensics lab dialled the number they found in the phone's memory.'

Here a long, suspenseful pause was in order, and, as if following a script, he supplied it.

Then he let fly a few words, stressing every syllable. 'As I'd assumed, Riccardo dialled a wrong number.'

And he told them the lie he'd prepared. The three swallowed the bait, and the inspector thought he could read an expression of relief in their faces.

'See? He *didn't* call me!' Licausi said triumphantly.

'Do you do that often?' Montalbano asked him.

The other became immediately defensive.

'Do what?'

'Come late to appointments.'

'Never. My friends can attest to that.'

'But that wasn't the case this morning.'

'This morning . . . my alarm clock didn't ring. That does happen sometimes, you know.'

'Of course it does. Oh, and another thing. Somebody has informed Mrs Lopresti that her husband was murdered.'

This time the expression of relief on the three men's faces was clear as day.

'So we no longer have to . . . ?' Liotta asked, seeking confirmation.

'No,' Montalbano replied curtly.

Now he needed only to apply the final touch to the drama he'd been staging since he first realized there was something fishy between the three bosom buddies.

He immediately changed script and character. Putting

on a distracted air, he looked around the office as though seeing it for the first time in his life, bowed his head to his chest, and murmured to himself:

'Well, well, well . . .'

The three looked at him as though spellbound. The expression of relief now gone, they were starting to look a little worried. Montalbano picked up his ballpoint, removed the cap, examined the tip very carefully, put the cap back on, and put it down again.

'I don't think there's anything left to say, correct?' he said all at once, rising to his feet.

Taken by surprise, the others did the same, looking dazed.

'Naturally,' the inspector continued, 'you'll have to repeat your declarations in front of the prosecutor.'

He gave a little smile out of only the left corner of his mouth, as he'd once seen Humphrey Bogart do in a movie, then extended his hand first to Gaspare Bonanno and then to Alfonso Licausi.

'Have a good day,' he said.

And he sat back down, leaving Mario Liotta standing there with his hand extended and ready to shake the inspector's.

'No, you, Mr Liotta, I want you to stay another five minutes. It won't take long, but there are two or three things that need to be cleared up. Your friends can wait for you outside the station.'

Licausi and Bonanno were left so stunned by what he'd asked of Liotta that they couldn't even manage to start moving towards the door of the inspector's office. And so Montalbano repeated gruffly:

'I said have a good day.'

The two men finally turned their backs and left the room. Meanwhile Liotta sat back down, stiff as a board. Since his friends hadn't closed the door behind them, the inspector got up and shut it.

Already flummoxed, Liotta grew more nervous and worried.

Montalbano sat down and picked up the receiver. 'Catarella? For the next five minutes I don't want to be disturbed by anybody. Got that? I mean it.' Perfect mise-en-scène.

Liotta's heart rate must have increased. Surely he was wondering what it was the inspector needed to ask him surrounded by such secrecy. Putting the receiver down, Montalbano picked up the ballpoint, removed the cap, stared long at the tip, put the cap back on, and put it back down.

'Well!' he said.

Was he referring to the dubious testimony of the three bosom buddies?

Or did it simply mean he felt uncomfortable not knowing exactly how a ballpoint pen worked?

Uncertain, Liotta became even more agitated and began to squirm in his chair.

'Could you tell me how many times a year you and your friends go on these lovely long excursions through the countryside?'

Liotta reacted as if the inspector had asked him whether he knew the exact distance, down to the last millimetre, between the Earth and the Andromeda galaxy.

His brow beaded up with sweat.

His face spoke clearly: *But what's that got to do with anything? What's he getting at?* But his mouth only managed to stammer:

'Well . . . I don't . . . er . . . but who . . . um . . .'

'On average, of course,' the inspector generously conceded.

At last Liotta was able to articulate a few words with a full meaning.

'Well . . . you know . . . it's not like we ever kept track . . . but, at the drop of a hat . . . to make a rough guess . . . I'd say maybe twelve . . .'

'Really? Are you really sure?' asked Montalbano, putting on an expression of extreme surprise.

The man was equally surprised by the inspector's surprise.

And frightened at the same time. It was entirely possible that Italy had some obscure law allowing only a certain number of walks per year, beyond which it became a crime. And he didn't know it.

'Wh . . . why? I don't understand what—'

'That means once a month. You realize that, don't you?'

'Yes, but I don't see what importance—'

'I'll decide what's important, if you don't mind.'

'I'm sorry, I didn't mean to—'

'No need to apologize. On the contrary. You've been

very cooperative with the law, doing your duty as a citizen. An exemplary one, I might add. My compliments. It takes a lot of courage, you know.'

'To do what?' asked Liotta, utterly at sea.

'To testify, as you are doing. What a sad fate most witnesses suffer in our part of the world! Among the cases I know, one has been forced to move to Switzerland under an assumed name, since they threatened to kill his wife and children, and another was killed in a mysterious car accident . . . Well! Never mind . . . One last question, can you tell me what size . . .'

He trailed off, looked at the ballpoint as though hypnotized, reached carefully out with one hand as though afraid he might get bitten, touched the pen twice lightly with his fingertips, then withdrew his hand.

'. . . what size shoe Riccardino wore?'

Liotta gawked, opened his mouth, closed it, reopened it. 'For . . . Forty-four.'

'How do you know?' Montalbano snapped, in the tone of an asshole cop in an American movie.

'Be . . . be . . . cause we wore the s-same size shoes . . .'

'And his head?'

'Wha . . . what do you mean?'

'What do you mean, what do I mean? What size hat or beret, or cap, did he wear on his head?'

'I don't know.'

Montalbano lowered his eyelids and looked at him through the narrow slits.

'How odd. You know his shoe size but not his hat size.

Or do you perhaps know his hat size perfectly well but don't want to tell me because you're now scared after everything I've just said about witnesses? So, are you becoming reticent on me now?'

Liotta, who by this point had been reduced to the state of a doormat, threw up his hands disconsolately and said nothing.

'OK, no problem. Thanks just the same. You can go now. Have a good day,' said the inspector, dismissing him brusquely.

Liotta was so fried by this point, so numb in the head, that he didn't grasp Montalbano's words.

'Wha . . . ? I'm sorry, what did you say?'

'I said you can go now.'

Montalbano did not stand up, did not hold his hand out to him. There was a hissing sound when Liotta rose to his feet. Apparently the seat of his trousers had become so wet with sweat that it stuck to the imitation leather of the chair he was sitting in.

The inspector watched him stagger away like a drunkard. And as soon as he opened the door, he fired another jab at him that hit him like a shot in the back.

'You disappoint me, Liotta.'

Liotta lurched, struck square between the shoulder blades, but managed to drag himself out into the hallway, where he vanished.

Now, when his friends anxiously pressed him on what the inspector had asked him in their secret session, could Liotta really tell them the truth? Which was that

Montalbano had wanted to know what size shoe Riccardino wore and how many times they walked over the course of a year?

No one would ever believe it.

And if he made up some lie, it would be even worse. Seeing the shape he was in after coming out of the inspector's office, his buddies would have been convinced he was lying to them.

And the rift between them would grow even more.

You're still pretty sharp, Montalbà, he congratulated himself.

But as he was reviewing himself, he began to feel a powerful sense of unease that had nothing at all to do with the murder of Riccardino, but with his own behaviour towards Liotta.

So what? You put on an act, staged a drama like a thousand other times in your career! What's so unusual about that? he wondered.

Nothing unusual at all, he answered himself.

Hold on a second. There is something new here, something different.

Namely?

Namely that when, on official duty, you play the part of a specific character to mess with the head of the person you're interrogating, at the same time you're watching yourself, observing yourself, judging yourself, and you appreciate yourself or you don't.

You are at once an actor and a spectator of what you're doing.

And so, if you played your part well, the other Montalbano, the one watching the play, compliments you.

And that pleases you, just the same way an actor is pleased by the compliments the audience pays him.

At first this pain-in-the-arse doubling never happened to you; the whole business started when the stories you told that author were broadcast on TV.

You caught the bug, Montalbà.

Without wanting to, you began competing with the actor. Simple as that.

But, you see, it's an unequal, pointless competition, because while the TV shows are watched by millions, you have only yourself as audience.

And the actor will always be better than you for at least two reasons: first, because the actor knows what will happen next, while you are always forced to improvise; and, second, because he studied acting, and you studied how to become a police detective.

You know what your only choice is, Montalbà?

Your only choice is, whenever they broadcast the programme bearing your name, to turn the television off, leave the house, and go to the cinema and watch Donald Duck.

*

'Chief! Ahhh, Chief, Chief!'

'What's wrong, Cat?'

'I tink I'm atween a rack and a bad place, Chief!'

'Why, what is it?'

'Wha' it is izzat on one en' o' the line 'ere's yiz tellin' me ya don' wanna be distoibed, an' on 'e other en' o' the line 'ere's 'Izzonner the C'mishner 'oo wants a talk t'yiz poissonally in poisson an' oigently in oigency.'

'No need to get upset. You can put the commissioner through to me.'

'But have you gone mad, Montalbano?' was Bonetti-Alderighi's opening.

More than a yell, it was a howl.

'I wouldn't know, but maybe, why not?'

'Trying to be witty, Inspector?'

'I wouldn't dare. Anyway, trying to be witty with you, sir, would be like talking Finnish to Australian aborigines.'

'Can't you see what kind of nonsense you speak? What the hell have Finland and Australia to do with anything? Now keep quiet and listen. You have just done something gravely wrong, got that? Unheard of! I'm inclined to believe that you did it without realizing just how outrageous your little initiative was, but, unfortunately . . . What, don't you have anything to say for yourself?'

'Mr Commissioner, allow me to remind you that, just now, you told me to keep quiet. If you'll please explain to me what impure act I've committed—'

'Impure act?! Learn to speak proper Italian! You removed three eyewitnesses from the custody of Inspector Toti!'

'Removed?'

'Yes, sir, removed! Those witnesses were supposed to remain at the scene of the crime, available for questioning by Inspector Toti! Whereas you . . . Anyway, it behoves me to inform you that you are henceforth dismissed from this investigation. Is that clear?'

'Perfectly, Mr Commissioner. May I ask a question?'

'Go ahead.'

'Who is Inspector Toti?'

'Enrico Toti is—'

'The one-legged infantryman who hurled his crutch at the enemy, no? You know, the First World War hero?'

But as he was asking these questions he became worried. Maybe he was taking things too far; the commissioner might well realize he was mocking him. Luckily, however, Bonetti-Alderighi considered himself too superior a man to imagine that anyone would dare make fun of him.

'Don't be silly, Montalbano! Do you realize how old that Enrico Toti would be if he were still alive today?'

There you go: it was like speaking Finnish to an Australian aborigine.

'I really wouldn't know, sir. I've never been very good at maths.'

'Never mind, Montalbano. Inspector Enrico Toti is the new chief of the Flying Squad. And a very able young functionary from Lombardy.'

He hung up without saying goodbye.

But how was it that these chiefs of the Flying Squad changed every couple of weeks?

And how was it that these young and able functionaries from Lombardy, Piedmont, Veneto, and Friuli somehow, the moment they set foot on Sicilian soil, always got their arses handed to them in their first investigation?

At any rate, the inspector wasn't bothered, deep down, by the phone call. Once upon a time he would have had a fit and raised the roof to hang on to the case. Now, instead, he was happy to let them mess it up.

✢

'Fazio? Are you still there? Come back to the station; the commissioner just called to inform me that the case has been turned over to somebody named Toti from the Flying Squad. What kind of guy is he?'

'With all due respect, he seems to me like someone to be avoided. Just now he started yelling like he was out of his mind. The audience on Via Rosolino Pilo even applauded.'

'Was he pissed off because I brought the three witnesses in to the station?'

'That's exactly right. He wants them here, at the scene of the crime.'

'So? Let him go and get them. Do you have their names and addresses?'

'Yes, Chief. We already went. But they weren't at home.'

'That's impossible! They left here well over half an hour ago!'

'I don't doubt it. Problem is, they didn't go home. Mrs Bonanno told us her husband called her to tell her they'd decided to take their hike to the mountain after all, to commemorate their friend Riccardino.'

'Look, all you have to do is send a squad car out on the main road—'

'No, they're nowhere to be seen around the main road

or in fact along any of the roads leading to the mountain. Inspector Toti suspects that, thanks to you, they've gone on the run.'

*

It all became immediately clear. Apparently the three bosom buddies needed to go to a secluded place, far from prying eyes, to talk among themselves in peace and get to the bottom of what happened during his interrogation of Liotta, which seemed to have shaken them up.

*

Another half an hour went by before Fazio returned.

'Did you find them?'

'You've got to be kidding! We finally left, but Inspector Toti's still on the scene, waiting for two cars to arrive from Montelusa, so they can start hunting for the three men. Who he now calls "the fugitives". What do you think of that?'

'Tell me something, Fazio. Why didn't you want to tell me over the phone that the last call made on Lopresti's mobile was to my landline?'

Fazio's jaw dropped.

'What are you saying, Chief? You mean Riccardo Lopresti phoned *you*?'

'He misdialled. Instead of calling Alfonso Licausi, he called me.'

And he told him the whole story. Fazio looked more bewildered than ever.

'But, Chief, the last call made on Lopresti's mobile phone wasn't to your home number.'

'Then who did he call?'

'Liotta.'

'Liotta?! Are you sure about that?'

'Absolutely. I called myself. The guy from Forensics saw the call in the memory and passed the phone over to me. So I dialled the number and a woman answered the phone and said: "The Liotta home, who's calling?" So I hung up. And now my question is: what need did Lopresti have to call Liotta, when Liotta was just a few steps away from him?'

Montalbano thought about this for a moment before answering.

'You know what I say? That apparently Riccardino didn't want to talk to Liotta.'

'So who did he want to talk to, then?'

'To the woman who answered, Liotta's wife. And he didn't even want to talk to her, which he couldn't have done anyway with her husband standing right there; he just wanted to send her a prearranged greeting, maybe just a ring. What I think happened is this: Riccardino ends his phone call to me, thinking I'm Alfonso Licausi, and tells his friends that Alfonso will be arriving in about ten minutes. As he's speaking, he lowers the hand holding the mobile phone down to his side and, without using the other hand or looking at the device, dials the number to Liotta's place. It wouldn't be so hard to do, and he must have done it many times before. And a second later, he gets shot.'

'Which means . . .'

'Which means that Riccardino was doing it with the wife of one of the musketeers.'

Fazio looked confused. 'What musketeers, Chief?'

'Never mind. The whole business concerns Inspector Toti alone from now on.'

'Right. What should I do?'

'I don't understand. Are you supposed to be doing something?'

'Chief, should I tell Inspector Toti that Riccardo Lopresti's last phone call was to Mrs Liotta or not?'

'The commissioner assured me that Toti is a very capable man. So he should be able to find out on his own. But do whatever your little heart tells you to do.'

'Then I'll just keep quiet,' Fazio decided.

FOUR

What with one thing and another, lunchtime arrived. And since he didn't feel very hungry, he decided to go to Enzo's trattoria on foot, hoping the walk would stir up a little appetite. He decided, moreover, to take a longer route along less frequented streets, to avoid the tremendous hassle of having to dodge motor scooters and to breathe some slightly less polluted air.

When he entered the restaurant, the television was tuned to TeleVigàta. The murder of Riccardino had made a great many waves, and everyone apparently was anxious for the latest news on the investigation. The people in the dining room who knew Montalbano raised their heads to look at him and greet him, nevertheless wondering how the inspector could find the time to eat out instead of doing his duty.

'Hello, Inspector. Today I've got couscous the way God intended it to be made,' said Enzo.

'So why are you waiting to bring me some?'

On the television the newsman was talking off-camera

ANDREA CAMILLERI

as images of Via Rosolino Pilo appeared on the screen. Once the people at their windows and balconies realized they were being filmed, they waved their hands or handkerchiefs in the air in greeting.

Where Riccardino's corpse once lay, there was now a silhouette traced in chalk on the street. What the hell was the purpose of those silhouettes, especially after hundreds of photos had been taken from every perspective, including those of the dead body? Over the course of his long career, Montalbano had never been able to answer this question.

'. . . since the Forensics lab found no empty cartridge cases at the scene of the crime, we can assume that the killer used a revolver . . .'

Then the images vanished and in their place appeared the purse-lipped, chicken-arse face of Pippo Ragonese, the channel's chief commentator. And at the same moment Enzo set a dish of couscous in front of him.

'Today, during the initial investigation into the barbarous killing of Riccardo Lopresti, a rather strange and, to say the least, alarming incident occurred. Inspector Salvo Montalbano, whose often reckless and irresponsible decisions are unfortunately nothing new, literally removed three witnesses from the custody of Inspector Enrico Toti, the new chief of the Montelusa Police Flying Squad, to whom we extend our most heartfelt wishes for a successful outcome on his first case. Montalbano took the three men to the Vigàta police station, before setting them all free. The three witnesses, whose names we will not reveal for the moment, have now gone missing and cannot be found. Inspector Toti then promptly began a manhunt which we sincerely hope will soon bear fruit and set right any damage the rash and irresponsible initiative of Inspector Montalbano may have caused. I take this opportunity to remind Mr

44

Montalbano that the serious, daily activity of a police inspector who is required to respect the law himself before forcing others to respect it is one thing, and a TV movie in which a fictional character of the same name obeys only the laws of the imagination, and not those of the human race, is another thing entirely. We wouldn't want our Inspector Montalbano to have any mistaken notions concerning this clear distinction.'

Of all these words, Montalbano heard only a few, but only as sound, not as meaning. He had succeeded in concentrating so hard on the scent and flavour of the couscous that he was able to blot out all sounds and voices of the world outside. After the couscous – which Enzo had made with a good dozen species of fish – it would have been theoretically impossible for a human being to eat more fish. But his long walk had achieved the desired effect, and in fact the inspector scarfed down four roast mullet as a second course.

When he got up from the table, he determined that he would be unable, with all that cargo inside, to take his usual stroll along the jetty to the lighthouse. His only hope was to drag himself to the station and flop down like a dead weight on the office sofa.

Naturally, the moment he turned on his side, he dozed off.

*

The door crashed hard against the wall, a bit of plaster fell to the floor, the inspector leapt to his feet, and Catarella begged his pardon, saying his hand had slipped. The usual ritual, in other words. Montalbano had never managed to get used to it when awake, so imagine when he was half-asleep. He took a deep breath to avoid the urge to jump on Catarella and pummel him with his fists, and then asked:

'What is it?'

'Chief, a lady woman jus' come in wantin' a talk to summon atta station an' since yer the only summon atta presently present moment inna station I tought—'

'What does she want?'

'She says summon busted 'er watta pipes.'

Montalbano flew off the handle.

'And she comes to us about it? And you dare to wake me up for this rubbish? Tell her to go and find a plumber!'

'Chief, I did tell the lady to go an' fin' a plummer, bu' she sez the pipe is fixed now.'

'Then what does she want?'

'She wants a riport the truck driver.'

'What truck driver?'

'The one 'at broke her pipes, an' 'en 'e even made 'er a 'ndecent preposition.'

'You mean proposition, Cat.'

What to do? Tell her to go and break another pipe, or remind oneself that the police must always serve the citizen?

'Did she tell you her name?'

Catarella turned as red as a bell pepper and rubbed his hands along the seam of his trousers, embarrassed.

'Yessir, Chief,' he said.

'And so?'

46

'Chief, I don' wanna repitt it cuz iss too 'mbarrassking.'

The inspector was curious. What indeed could the lady's surname be if Catarella refused to say it? And so, just to satisfy his curiosity — and certainly not because of the woman's broken pipes or the sleazy truck driver — he made up his mind and said:

'OK, you can show her in.'

Easier said than done.

The fiftyish woman who came in must have weighed twenty stone, was laden with gold — earrings, bracelets, brooches, necklaces, rings (which no doubt was why Catarella, impressed with all the glitter, had called her a 'lady woman') — and of such extensive circumference that she was unable to pass through the doorway, of which only half of the double door was open. She was in danger of getting stuck.

Montalbano leapt to his feet, raced over to her, threw open the other half, and, to avoid any collapses or avalanches, sat the woman down on the little sofa, which, under the strain, began to groan and creak perilously.

Once the mass of her glutei had spread out so far as to risk spilling over the armrests, the woman prudishly pulled the hem of her skirt down over her knees, tidied her hair, which was done up in a beehive coiffure somewhat reminiscent of the Leaning Tower of Pisa, delicately adjusted her earrings, bracelets, necklaces, brooches, and rings, then sighed and looked at the inspector, who only then felt the need to speak.

'What can I do for you?' he asked.

'I am Miss Augustina Facca, but everyone in town just calls me Tina.'

Facca. That must have been the reason Catarella was too embarrassed to repeat the name. He'd heard wrong, as he always did.

'Do you work, signorina? And if so, where?'

'I work at home. I'm a clairvoyant fortune-teller.'

'Do you tell fortunes with cards or a crystal ball?' the inspector asked with the utmost seriousness.

'With cards.'

'But don't you need a crystal ball to see the future?'

'No.'

'All right then, tell me what I can do for you.'

A deep breath and emphatic shake of the head. The Tower of Pisa leaned frightfully, while the earrings, bracelets, and all the other knick-knacks tinkled and rang like a pinball machine.

'It's insane! The stuff of madmen! You've got to believe me, Mr Commissioner, it's enough to drive a woman crazy!'

'Excuse me, signorina, but I'm not a commissioner.'

'You're not? Then what are you? A captain?'

'Yes,' replied Montalbano, just to dispense with the question.

'Well, let me tell you, Mr Captain, sir, that I live on the ground floor at number 2, Via Saverio Cucurullo.'

'Where is Via Cucurullo?'

'In Borgonovo.'

Every time he happened to pass through Borgonovo, a district at the west end of Vigàta, the inspector closed his eyes, even when at the wheel. Some ten or so small, repellent apartment blocks, built according to plans clearly drafted by an architect with a drinking problem and, more importantly, unable to choose between Gaudí and Le Corbusier . . . In order not to offend either, he'd taken a bit from each, and inexplicably, the buildings, all five storeys high, were crammed one against the other and connected by little streets so narrow that only one car at a time could pass between them. All around, on the other hand, was open countryside. Or, more precisely, a vast rubbish dump for everything imaginable: refrigerators, cars, toilets, bathtubs, carcasses of dogs and cats, leaky oil drums, rags, indefinable liquids, and maybe, just maybe, atomic reactors no longer usable.

And, if you looked hard enough, you would surely find a few human corpses buried under it all. The whole place stank so bad that birds, when they accidentally flew over the mess, shrivelled up at once and fell dead to the ground.

'So, tell me, what good things are happening in Via Cucurullo?' the inspector asked breezily, just to liven up the conversation a little.

'Good things?' the clairvoyant fortune-teller asked in horror.

'Well, bad things, then.'

'Everything!'

Montalbano didn't know what to say.

'Everything?'

'My good captain, the drunkards come here to vomit, the whores and their clients come to fuck, the lowlifes come and shoot themselves up with drugs, the hoods come to cut each other up with knives and fire their guns. Isn't that more than enough? And then there's that damn truck.'

'What does this truck do?'

'It comes and goes.'

What else is a poor truck supposed to do other than load, unload, drive off, come back, and leave?

'It seems to me that, all things considered, that truck driver is the only one doing what he's supposed to be doing.'

'That's what you think, Captain. But can you explain to me what he's coming to do every single night at twelve thirty, give or take a minute or two?'

'Maybe he's going to the dump.'

'Nah. There's no entrance to the dump on that side. The road ends, 'cause there's a wall.'

'Maybe he's going to see a woman.'

'Nah. Not enough time.'

'Why not?'

''Cause five minutes later he turns around and leaves. That's not even enough time to unzip his trousers, know what I mean?'

A refined, elegant observation.

'Absolutely,' said the inspector. 'Does he come by every night?'

'Monday, Tuesday, Wednesday, and Thursday.'

'Has this been going on for a long time?'

'Let's say about a year,' offered the fortune-teller.

'Let's,' the inspector accepted. 'But my officer also said something about a broken pipe . . .'

'OK, let me explain about that, Captain. The truck can barely fit down my street, and right in front of my place there's a sharp turn at the corner of the building, so he's got to manoeuvre to get by. Last night, when he was doing his manoeuvre, he crashed into the corner, right where my water pipe passes, and broke it. And he even got stuck there. Couldn't move forward or back. And so I ran out, saw the damage he'd done to the corner of the building, and I told the goddamn son of a bitch of a truck driver that he had to pay me for some new plumbing. And you know what that great big piece of shit said to me? He said that, since I was standing there with my mouth open, I would make better use of it by playing a little sonata on his skin flute! To me, he said that! To me, an honest, upright woman! A lady! That fucking pestilential arsehole of a man!'

'And what happened next?'

'Next, after smashing up half the corner, he managed to get by. Then I waited five minutes for him to come back and called Mr Filippo Nicotera, who's a saintly Christian man and a plumber, and in about two hours he fixed the piping.'

'And now you want to file a complaint against the truck driver?'

'I want him to die in prison!'

'Did you get the licence-plate number of the truck?'

'I'm not too good with numbers.'

'Listen, signorina, is Via Cucurullo long or short?'

'It's just six small buildings, three on each side.'

'And nobody else who lives on that street has anything to say about this truck that comes by every night?'

'Nah. Nobody else gives a fuck, my good captain. Except for that saintly man, Filippo Nicotera.'

'Does he live in the same building as you?'

'Nah. He lives in building six, the last one on the block. From his bedroom window he can see where the truck stops.'

'Is Mr Nicotera married?'

'Nah. He's a widower,' the fortune-teller replied, sticking her tongue out and moistening her lips.

The gesture, clearly a conditioned reflex just like that of Pavlov's dog, was a revelation to Montalbano.

'Has Mr Nicotera by any chance ever invited you to his place to show you what the truck driver does?'

Signorina Tina blushed, smoothed the Tower of Pisa out a little, and quickly touched all of her gold finery.

'I went there just once. But don't get the wrong idea. Mr Nicotera is a devout Christian and I am a woman of exemplary conduct.'

'I haven't the slightest doubt about that, believe me. And what did the truck driver do, that time you saw him?'

'He got out of his truck carrying a kind of parcel, which he set down on the ground, and then he took a wooden crate he had in the cabin of the truck, leaned it against the wall, picked up the parcel, climbed up on the crate, leaned all the way forward to put the parcel down behind the wall, then climbed down, picked up the crate, got back in the truck, and drove off.'

'Have you ever seen the truck driver's face on other occasions? I'd like to know if it's always the same person.'

'Yes, I have. One evening this driver needed to relieve himself, and before getting back in the truck to start up the engine, he went over to the street lamp. And so me and Mr Nicotera got a good look at his face. It's always the same guy.'

She didn't realize that, with those words, she was admitting that there had indeed been more than one nocturnal visit to the saintly man's bedroom.

'Is he someone you or Nicotera know? Someone you've seen elsewhere?'

'Nah, never.'

'Now, tell me the truth: haven't you ever gone to have a look at that parcel? To see what it's about, how much it weighs, that kind of thing?'

'Me? Never! I never poke my nose into other people's affairs!'

'How about Mr Nicotera?'

'But how could that poor saintly man ever manage? Aside from the fact that his left leg is kind of twisted, he would have to climb over a wall that's almost five foot high, and the people living in his building might see him.'

'Well, maybe with your help . . .'

'But the parcel isn't there any more!'

'So somebody takes it away?'

'Yessir.'

'Wait a second. Are you telling me that the truck driver leaves the package there around twelve-thirty, and the next day someone else comes and takes it away?'

'Nah. It's not anyone else, it's always the same driver. Got that?'

'Let me get this straight. This driver, at twelve-thirty a.m. on the first four days of the week, comes by—'

'Making an infernal racket, Captain. Just imagine, it makes the whole *trabacca* shake—'

'It makes what shake?' asked Montalbano, who'd never heard the word before, or perhaps had forgotten it.

'The bed. And it gets so bad sometimes that it makes the little baby Jesus I got over the bed fall and—'

'We can talk about that later, please. So, after leaving the package, the truck driver returns the following day with the truck and—'

'Nah, nah. He doesn't return with the truck, he comes in a car that makes an even more infernal racket than his truck. He comes back around seven in the evening, picks up the package, and leaves.'

'And did you recognize the driver?'

Fazio appeared in the open doorway. 'Can I come in, Chief?'

'No,' said the inspector. 'I'll buzz you in five minutes.'

The story the fortune-teller was telling him was beginning to pique his curiosity.

'Listen, signorina, when the truck comes by at half-past midnight, is it full or empty?'

'Empty. Which is why it makes all that noise. Since the

street is full of potholes, the truck rattles and shakes all over, and my *trabacca*—'

'Right, right, I got that. Tell you what. Are you free tomorrow afternoon?'

'Nah. But I could free myself up.'

'Then let's say I'll come to your place tomorrow afternoon, but, naturally, I'll give you a ring first. Could you give me your number?'

'Didn't I already say I'm not too good with numbers? You can find my number in the phone book.'

'Could I also talk to Mr Nicotera?'

'When you call me tomorrow, I'll give him a call.'

'All right, then . . .'

But the clairvoyant fortune-teller didn't move.

'Is there something else?' asked Montalbano.

'What? Aren't you going to get me to file a complaint?'

'Look, it's as if you've already done so. That's why I'm coming to see you tomorrow.'

The woman adjusted the Tower of Pisa.

'I just got an idea. Instead of coming in the afternoon, why don't you come around midnight? That way we can go and pay Mr Nicotera a visit and you can have a look at the person driving the truck.'

She punctuated her offer with a mischievous little smile that left Montalbano feeling terrorized.

A nightmare scene unfolded before his eyes: the clairvoyant fortune-teller and the saintly Christian man rolling around naked on the latter's bed.

He declined the offer.

'It's better if I come first to see the route the truck takes.'

'All right, if you say so . . .' said the fortune-teller, with a sigh of disappointment.

The manoeuvre of rising from the little sofa proved to be an arduous one, in that Signorina Tina, on her first attempt to stand up, lifted the sofa itself with her, its armrests clinging to her haunches. A solution was reached when Montalbano, on her second attempt, grabbed the back of the sofa and pressed down on it with all his weight.

FIVE

Once the woman was gone, he called Fazio. 'Do me a favour and shut that half door.'

Fazio hopped to it, as he was keen to talk to the inspector and wearing a little grin that seemed to indicate he was enjoying himself.

'You certainly look pleased about something. What is it?'

'Did I tell you that Inspector Toti got really pissed off because you released the three witnesses?'

'Yes, and I also heard about it on TV. And so?'

'Well, in the twinkling of an eye he unleashed a big commotion of cars coming and going to the countryside in search of the three.'

'And did they find them?'

'Yeah, Chief, they did.'

'So where were they?'

'At the house of Manzilla, the lawyer, who's a friend of theirs. They went straight to him for advice when they left here. The lawyer invited them to stay for lunch, and they learned from the television that they were being sought by the police.'

'Then why did they say they were going to hike to the mountain anyway?'

'At first they did want to do that, but then they changed their minds.'

'And what did they do when they learned that Toti was looking for them?'

'The lawyer was furious and phoned the commissioner and said he would file an official complaint against Inspector Toti because, by his actions, he now has everyone far and wide thinking that the three men were accomplices to the murder. You yourself know that whatever the TV says is the gospel truth.'

'And then what?'

'Then the lawyer said that his three clients were available to the prosecutor and the police, but only on condition that Inspector Toti was taken off the case. And you want to know the best part? Manzilla, who's sly as a fox, before phoning the commissioner, called in a bunch of journalists so they could listen to the exchange over the speakerphone. And they went to town and recorded it for the TV.'

'What was the commissioner's reaction?'

'He said that while it's true that Inspector Toti may have carried things a little too far, the primary responsibility was yours.'

'Mine?!'

'Yes, yours. And he closed by saying that he would never

in a million years replace Inspector Toti simply because a lawyer demanded it.'

'Good. For a minute I was scared.'

'Of what?'

'That they might take the case away from Toti and give it back to me.'

Fazio shook his head.

'I'm worried about you, Chief. You seem different to me.'

'To me too.'

*

Darkness fell. He was about to leave the office to go home when the telephone rang.

'Chief, ahh, Chief! Iss the sackerstan of the Biship of Montelusa wants a talk t'yiz poissonally in poisson.'

'Put him on.'

'Inspector Montalbano? This is Father Bartolino, the secretary of the Bishop of Montelusa. His Excellency would like to meet you.'

He'd never met or even seen the Bishop of Montelusa. Whatever the case, with priests it was always best not to get on one's knees right away.

'All right. I'll try tomorrow to—'

'Not tomorrow, Inspector. His Excellency would very much appreciate if you could come to the bishop's office this evening. He begs you with all his heart to do him this favour.'

Well, if he put it that way, that changed matters. 'Then all right. At what time?'

'His Excellency Partanna will expect you at nine p.m. sharp.'

Of course the Bishop of Montelusa would be named Partanna! But why, upon hearing the secretary utter the name, had a sudden light come on in the dark and dusty warehouse of his memory? And anyway, what, he wondered, could Bishop Partanna possibly want from him? Weighing his options, he decided that it was best to inform himself before showing up.

'Fazio!'

'What is it, Chief?'

'Do you by any chance know if we're presently involved in anything Church-related?'

'In what sense?'

'In the only sense in which we could be involved. Are we, for example, engaged in any investigation involving a priest, nun, mother superior, friar, bishop, cardinal, cardinal *in pectore*, deacon, Franciscan tertiary, sacristan, or even an altar boy?'

'No, Chief.'

'How about the carabinieri?'

'You know what they're like, Chief! Even if they're working with the Pope, they're never going to come and tell *us*!'

'So what should I do, in your opinion?'

'What's the problem, Chief?'

'The bishop wants to see me this evening in Montelusa, at nine o'clock, and it's already a quarter past seven. What should I do, eat first or afterwards?'

'You're better off eating afterwards. And you probably ought to go home and put on a nice suit and tie.'

'Oh, what a pain!'

*

The bishop's office was almost attached to the cathedral, which stood on top of the hill that the town climbed in terraced streets. Montalbano left his car at the entrance to Montelusa – he didn't feel like driving all the way up; there were too many one-way streets he didn't know, and he was afraid of getting stuck in a labyrinth of tight little passageways like a fly in a spider's web.

He began to scale the hill ever so slowly, through dark narrow backstreets tailor-made for deadly ambushes and up slippery staircases good for breaking your neck on. When at last he arrived outside the great door of the bishop's office, he was out of breath.

He looked at his watch. Two minutes to nine.

A problem immediately arose. The great door was locked, and as hard as he searched by the dim light of a faraway street lamp, he was unable to see any intercom or buzzer or doorbell.

There was only a massive lion's head knocker.

Was it possible the bishop's office hadn't yet been modernized?

He raised the cast-iron lion's head with some effort, then let it drop.

The boom, a sort of cannon blast that rumbled long

within the bishop's office and surely woke the living and the dead, terrified him.

He turned partly around, in the grips of an irresistible desire to run away.

The echo hadn't yet faded when he heard a voice in the street.

'Inspector Montalbano?'

A rather young-looking priest was calling him from about ten yards away. Behind him was a band of light beaming from an open door.

'It's this way, Inspector. The great door hasn't been opened for a good fifty years. Here's the regular entrance.'

And so he'd managed to look like a fool. He hoped he wouldn't mess it up again during the course of his meeting with the bishop.

'I'm Father Bartolino. It's a pleasure to meet you. Please follow me.'

That part of the bishop's office looked rather like a modern government building, and indeed had exactly the same squalid, depressing anonymity, heightened by fluorescent lighting, as a modern government building.

Montalbano, having expected dark corridors lined with crucifixes, Madonnas, and ancient portraits of bishops giving him dirty looks, felt a little disappointed.

'Let's take the lift,' said Father Bartolino.

The control panel had four lighted buttons on it, two with letters, one with a number, and the last with a little sky-blue circle with nothing written on it. The letters were B and G, meaning basement and ground floor; the number was I, meaning first floor; and the sky-blue circlet, the one Father Bartolino pushed, apparently indicated a supernal, celestial sphere in which the bishop's apartment was located.

Once the gate outside the lift opened, Montalbano found himself in the sort of dark corridor he'd been expecting earlier. The darkness was just barely interrupted by a few dim wall lamps that somewhat unconvincingly allowed half glimpses of crucifixes, Madonnas, and paintings of scary bishops and cardinals with sallow faces straight out of the Holy Inquisition.

After he'd taken two steps, he stumbled on an invisible carpet and would certainly have broken his head against a sixteenth-century chest had Father Bartolino not caught him as he fell. With some effort, the inspector managed to stifle a curse that in such a setting might have damned his soul to eternal hellfire.

After they'd been walking for some ten minutes through pitch-darkness, the priest knocked on a massive door, opened it, stuck his head inside, murmured something, pulled his head out again, and turned to the inspector as he opened the door wider and took a step aside.

'You can go in.'

Montalbano went in and the door closed behind him.

Ouch. What could it mean that not even the secretary was allowed to be present at their meeting? Isn't a secretary the person who knows all his boss's secrets?

His Excellency Bishop Partanna rose from a stately armchair behind a desk covered with books, notepads, and a computer, which was on but then promptly turned off.

'Do you surf?' asked the bishop.

What kind of damn question was that?

'Well, I do like the sea. I often swim and swim for—'

'I meant surf the web,' His Excellency interrupted him. Blunder number two.

'To be honest, I . . .'

They shook hands. His Excellency Bishop Partanna must have been about the same age as him. Slightly taller, neither stout nor lean, he had nothing priestly about him, neither in his manner of speech nor in his movements.

'Please sit down. And let me turn on a few more lights.'

As Montalbano sank into a comfortable black leather armchair, the big room brightened.

The walls were almost entirely covered by wooden bookcases bursting with old tomes and ancient binders. In the uncovered spaces hung paintings in the sorts of genres one might expect: Annunciations, Nativities, Crucifixions, Depositions. But one picture in particular caught the inspector's attention: a portrait of a bishop so hideous that it frightened you to look at him. If you ran into him in the middle of the night, you might very well have a heart attack.

'Pretty ugly, eh?' asked His Excellency, sitting down in an armchair beside Montalbano's and indicating the painting with his head.

'Well . . .' the inspector said noncommittally.

'He was an ancestor of mine. My great-grandfather's

brother. His name was also Partanna, Vitangelo Partanna. Pirandello described him perfectly as a skeleton in a frock.'

The bishop squeezed his eyes shut, trying to concentrate, then quoted:

'"*Tall and bent over his wretched gauntness, with neck stretched forward and tumid lips jutting in the effort to hold his shrivelled face up straight, and cruel, dark eyes over a hooked nose . . .*" Do you know the story?'

'Yes. I think it's called "The Defence of Mèola".'

That was why, when he'd heard the surname Partanna mentioned at the station, a little light had come on in his brain. But what was the present-day Bishop Partanna getting at?

'I wanted to get to know you poissonally in poisson, as Catarella would say,' the bishop began with a little smile. 'You know, I've read those books that have been written about you, and I've seen a few of the television episodes. Not bad at all. But a fictional character is one thing, and a real person something else.'

Montalbano felt like getting up and hugging the man. But he said nothing and didn't move.

'Can I get you anything?'

'No thank you, your excellency.'

'Then I'll get straight to the point. This morning I received what for me was some very painful news,' the bishop declared, turning serious.

What was there to say? Montalbano limited himself to giving him a questioning look.

'The violent death of Riccardino.'

So he also called him Riccardino!

'Did you know him?'

'I certainly did! About twenty years ago I was their religious instructor.'

That 'their' could only be referring to the four musketeers.

'So you also know his friends?'

'Of course. They were inseparable. Very good lads, too, you know. And to think they witnessed the ruthless murder of a friend who was more than a brother to them . . . They came to see me, all four of them, not even a week ago.'

'It's true, it was a very brutal . . .'

But the bishop's thoughts had already turned elsewhere. 'Could I ask you a question that will certainly surprise you?'

'Of course.'

'Why did you take the three boys to the police station? Apparently, from what people are saying, you shouldn't have.'

'It seemed best . . . to remove them . . .'

'From what?'

Montalbano explained the situation that had developed in Via Rosolino Pilo, with all the rowdy, vulgar people shouting and showing no respect for anyone or anything but their own shameless nosiness. As he was speaking, the bishop stared at him fixedly, never once taking his eyes off him.

'. . . I questioned them, told them to remain available to us, and then released them,' the inspector concluded.

'So when you dismissed them they hadn't been accused of anything.'

'No, nothing at all. They were, and are, just witnesses.'

'And they were free to go wherever they wanted?'

'Of course. We know how to reach them.'

Silence fell. Then, in a soft voice, His Excellency said: 'Alfonso Licausi is my nephew. He's the son of my sister Angelina, who's six years older than me. Mama died giving birth to me, and Angelina became my surrogate mother. When, today, she heard the news about what happened, and that it involved Alfonso, she felt unwell, and we had her taken to the hospital.'

'I see,' said Montalbano. 'I'm very sorry, but I do hope that with Alfonso now back home, your sister will feel reassured. In any event, as I'm sure you know, I was dismissed from the case after the opening salvos.'

But he didn't want to give the bishop the impression that he was cravenly taking himself out of the game.

'I do want to tell you in all sincerity, however,' he continued, 'that had the investigation remained in my hands, what you have just told me, that Alfonso Licausi is your nephew, would not in any way have influenced—'

'I'm well aware of that,' the bishop interrupted him. 'And I didn't ask you to come here with the idea of obtaining any sort of special treatment. Apparently my ancestor,' he said, looking over at the portrait, 'Bishop Partanna, was quite a schemer. I didn't inherit that defect.

Or virtue, given the times we live in. No, I wanted simply to ask you about the strange behaviour – and "strange" doesn't quite say it – of your colleague, Inspector Toti.'

Montalbano didn't like the turn the conversation was taking. Better nip it in the bud.

'Excuse me, your excellency, but I don't feel comfortable expressing judgements on the actions of my colleagues.'

'I'm not asking you to pass judgement. I'm quite careful not to. I merely want to know whether Inspector Toti technically had any reasonable motive for acting the way he did. I'll explain. Did he have any reason to suspect that Riccardino's three friends were involved in his murder, and thereby to order search parties, as if they were fugitives?'

It was a precise question that required a precise answer.

'At the moment he entered the scene, Inspector Toti was not in a position to suspect anything. The investigation had barely begun, to say the least; we hadn't really gone any further than identifying the body and taking our first specimens of evidence.'

'Then why, in your opinion, did Inspector Toti act so recklessly, so clamorously, so rashly? Without, apparently, even taking the possible consequences the least bit into account? Nowadays, unfortunately, saying that someone is under investigation is the same, in the eyes of the public, as him already being convicted. So you can only imagine what they must think if you also add that the person is being sought because he can't be found! Can you possibly explain to me why someone would behave so irresponsibly?'

Montalbano was in perfect agreement with the bishop's

argument, but he preferred to put up a diplomatic front, and said:

'Well, in the meantime he'd got all upset when he found out that the witnesses were no longer at the scene . . .'

'But that in no way justifies—'

'Also, since the three men couldn't be reached, he thought they must have fled. He just got a little carried away . . .'

'By the circumstances?'

'No, I would say by appearances. It happens often, you know.'

'You don't believe in appearances, Inspector?'

'My job forces me not to. If I did believe in appearances, I wouldn't be a very good policeman.'

'So what do you believe?'

'Well . . . For example, I believe in what's there but can't be seen.'

'Could you explain?'

Montalbano thought about this for a moment.

'You know that famous photograph of Tiananmen Square?'

'The one of the young man stopping a tank all by himself? Yes.'

'Well, your excellency, with those very words you are showing me that you let yourself be persuaded by appearances.'

The bishop looked at him, not knowing what to say.

'You said the young man "stopped" a tank. But in reality the youth is unable to "stop" anything at all, and the tank can't come to a stop all by itself. The tank, in fact, was stopped by the soldier driving it, who we don't see because he's inside it. Well, what's of interest to me is that soldier inside, who's invisible but who nevertheless exists in that moment, disobeying his orders, and engaging in an act at least as courageous as that of the youth standing in front of his tank.'

'That's an excellent explanation,' said the bishop. Then, after a moment's silence: 'They arrested him, you know.'

'Arrested who?' asked Montalbano, worried that Enrico Toti might have had another brilliant idea.

'The soldier driving the tank in Tiananmen Square. They shot him almost at once; such insubordination could not be tolerated. I informed myself on the matter. And, as you can imagine, it was extremely difficult to get an answer, and it took a very long time. But, as you can see, I too, at the time, did not let myself be taken in by appearances. I was and am very interested, perhaps even a little more than you, in what is there but cannot be seen.'

This bishop had quite a sophisticated mind. The inspector would have to watch his step.

His Excellency Bishop Partanna waited a moment for Montalbano to answer, but since the inspector remained silent, he said with a grin:

'Thank you.'

'For what?'

'For having spared me the facile retort that I'm interested in what is there but cannot be seen for the simple reason that such, in essence, is my job.'

SIX

As soon as he arrived in Vigàta, Montalbano noticed that the display window of the first bar on the main street was brightly lit up with all the sweets of the dead. Unable to resist, he stopped the car and parked, but did not get out.

He sat there thinking of a time when the dead used to leave presents on the morning of the second of November.

Shortly after his mother died, little Salvo Montalbano had gone to live at the home of an aunt who was married but had no children. His father lived in another town, but not a Sunday went by without him coming to see his son. Salvo's aunt and uncle loved him. Once, on the morning of All Saints' Day, the day before the Day of the Dead, his father came by while little Salvo was still asleep. Oh, the joy of being woken up by Papa! Even fifty years later, he still carried the emotion of that awakening inside him, still felt the thrill so intensely that it became as painful as a wound.

His father told him that he'd come back to town, even though it wasn't Sunday, because on the following day, the

Day of the Dead, they were going to go together to the cemetery and pay a visit to Mama. And he explained something that Salvo didn't know: that on the night between the first and second of November, the dead came down from heaven bearing gifts for all the little children who'd been good and not misbehaved. All one had to do was get a basket and put it under the bed. While everyone was asleep, the dead would come in and fill the basket with toys and sweets. But the dead also liked to play tricks: after filling the basket, they would take it and hide it somewhere. And so, as soon as you woke up, you had to go and look for it.

'What would you like Mama to bring you?'

That made sense. Because, for both his father and him, it was logical that the only person who could bring presents was her.

'A tricycle.'

That evening, after they'd finished eating, his father said to his aunt:

'Go and get a basket.'

The aunt returned with one.

'Something bigger.'

So Mama really was going to bring him a tricycle!

After his aunt tucked him in, Papa came to kiss him good night.

'I'm putting the basket under your bed. But now you must sleep. I mean it.'

And little Salvo obediently closed his eyes.

But something immediately occurred to him. If he was

able to stay awake, he would be sure to see his mother. He could remember nothing about her, save for a sort of golden light in motion, like spikes of wheat in the sun, lightly tossed by the wind and rustling gently.

Why did he have to be the one to lose his mother? He could never understand why.

His aunt had told him that the good Lord had decided to take her, for no reason, because that was his will. And so he'd decided no longer to pray to this Lord. Why pray to someone who does just whatever he feels like doing?

'Remember to say a prayer for your mother before you fall asleep,' said his aunt.

And when he felt sleep coming on, he said softly to the good Lord: 'I won't pray to you even if you cast me down into hell.'

At any rate, he swore to himself that he wasn't going to miss that night's opportunity for anything. At last he would be able to see Mama again. He promised himself he would remain awake. And he was not afraid. What's to be scared of, if the ghost is your mother? One concern did trouble him, however. If Mama realized that he wasn't in fact asleep, it was possible she would go back up to heaven without letting him see her. He therefore had to pretend to be asleep, like cats do when it looks as if their eyes are closed but they are actually counting the stars in the sky.

He managed to hold out for a short while as his eyelids began to flutter, but then, all at once, without realizing it, he plummeted into sleep.

*

'Salvù, come on, get up.'

There followed a breathless search all through the house, with Papa and Uncle and Auntie following behind, eager to share the joy of his surprise. At last he found the basket when he opened the big wardrobe in the dressing room. Out of the basket came a flaming red tricycle, entirely surrounded by sweets: marzipan fruits that looked just like the real thing, apple branches, mulled-wine *mostaccioli, carcagnette, tetù, biscotti regina* . . . and there was even a little sugar doll done up like an infantryman.

Later in the day, they all got in the car and went for a drive in the country.

He'd been given permission to bring his tricycle along. While the grown-ups were praying at Mama's grave, he started racing his tricycle up and down the cemetery's crowded lanes, coming across a great many little children playing, like himself, with the presents the dead had just brought them: scooters, pedal cars, little trains, toy rifles, tiny aeroplanes, dolls. And they called to one another and swapped gifts for a while, changing the day of the dead into a day of celebration.

But not him. He just kept on pedalling and repeating: 'Thank you, Mama, thank you, Mama . . .'

And he cried and laughed all the while. That was the last time.

The following year, the presents appeared under the Christmas tree instead. Maybe the dead could no longer find their way home.

*

He got out of the car, went into the bar, and ordered a large quantity of pastries and sweets. He was un- decided whether to buy a sugar doll as well, a gaudy, thick-thighed ballerina, but in the end felt too embar- rassed and, to compensate, bought two giant ricotta-filled cannoli.

✻

While sitting out on the veranda, wisely alternating between *biscotti regina* and *tetù*, *carcagnette* and *mostaccioli*, taking every so often a little sip of sweet Malvasia wine, he thought back on his meeting with the bishop. He needed to de- cipher its true meaning.

His Excellency Bishop Partanna apparently wanted to know what he thought of the way Toti had acted. But whether he'd given it his approval or criticized it, what, in fact, did the bishop have to gain either way? What im- portance could the opinion of a police detective not involved in the case possibly have?

No matter which way he looked at it, the bishop's desire to speak to him seemed to make no sense.

But that, in fact, was what worried him: the apparent senselessness of it. He'd never known a priest to say or do anything without there being a meaning and purpose behind it.

He was about to go to bed when the telephone rang. It could only be Livia. Two days earlier they'd had a serious little squabble over where to go for their Christmas holiday. Livia had suggested Johannesburg. For Montalbano this was like a cudgel blow straight to the forehead, which made him stagger.

'Johannesburg? But what the fuck are you thinking?'

'Stop using obscenities, Salvo, or I'll hang up!'

'OK, OK. Sorry. But can you tell me why the f— I mean, for what reason we should go to Johannesburg?'

'Because we've never been there before.'

'Well, as far as that goes, we've never been to Bangkok or Singapore, either.'

'All right then, we'll forget Johannesburg and go to Singapore.'

'Livia, try to be reasonable! We have barely five days' holiday, and we'll be spending three of them inside aeroplanes!'

'Where would you like to go, then?'

'To be honest, I don't feel like going anywhere. Just come here and stay with me in Marinella, and we'll spend five days in peace.'

'In peace?! As if I didn't know you! You would go off to the police station every day, and I—'

'OK, OK. I'll come to Boccadasse instead.'

'Sure, go ahead. But I've already decided: I'm going to Johannesburg.'

In conclusion, Livia had told him not to call back until he'd made a decision: either Johannesburg or Singapore.

And he hadn't yet made up his mind.

As the damn telephone kept ringing and ringing, he finally decided to answer.

'Hello?'

'What's happening, Salvo, were you sleeping?'

He immediately recognized the Author's smoke-shredded voice.

'No, but I was getting ready for bed.'

'I need to talk to you. It's rather important.'

'Listen, I'm really tired. This isn't a good moment, if it's something important that requires some thought.'

'Is it all right if I call you back in a couple of days?'

'Sure, fine. Goodbye.'

The memory of his squabble with Livia, coupled with the phone call from the Author, put him in a bad mood. He dawdled about for a little while, then lay down on the bed. Since he didn't feel sleepy, he started reading a novel, *The Skating Rink*, by a South American author, Roberto Bolaño, whose writing he liked.

When he reached page ten, a sudden reflux of acid, burning like a tongue of fire, shot up from his stomach and into his throat. He barely managed to keep the regurgitation from exiting his mouth. Apparently the *tetù*, marzipan, *biscotti regina*, ricotta cannoli, and Malvasia had merged in his stomach in a blend remarkably similar to corrosive sublimate. He sprang to his feet and raced into the kitchen, where he gulped down a heaped tablespoon of bicarbonate of soda.

It proved useless. He still had a treacherous night.

*

He arrived in the office late, because he hadn't managed to fall asleep until just before dawn.

'Chief! Ahh, Chief, Chief!'

'What is it, Cat?'

'Hizzoner the C'mishner jess call jess now! An' 'e talked to me poissonally in poisson!'

'Oh, really? What did he want?'

"E said ya gotta come ammediately to me!'

Montalbano, who was still a bit numbskulled from his bad night, felt lost.

'OK, here I am, right in front of you.'

'Nah, nah, Chief, not me bu' him, him bein' him.'

Montalbano gave up.

'Cat, you have to speak more clearly.'

'Awright, Chief, I'll do it step by step. So, anyways, the tellyphone rings, I pick up, an' I says, " 'Ere's Vigàta Police," bu' a verce cuts in an' says, "This is the Commissioner," an' so I says, "Atcha soivice, sah!" an' en 'e ast a talk t'yiz, an' I answer 'at yer not onna premisses. Follow so far?'

'Yes, go on.'

'An' so, 'e, 'e bein' 'im, Hizzoner the C'mishner, 'at is, 'e says to me – an' 'iss izza direck quoke: "As soon as he gets in, tell him to come immediately to me" – an' 'ass th' end o' the quoke. D'ya get it now?'

'Perfectly, Cat.'

*

All that was left for him to do was to get back in the car and drive to Montelusa.

As much as he didn't like meeting with Hizzoner the C'mishner, he felt at peace, and his conscience was clear.

Bonetti-Alderighi had no reason whatsoever to be angry at him. Unless he wanted to hash over yet again the business of the three witnesses he'd taken to the station.

But that was unlikely. By this point it was water under the bridge.

*

Naturally, the first person he ran into in the waiting room was the chief of the commissioner's cabinet, Dr Lattes, who hurried through with a binder under his arm.

'*Carissimo!*' he said in greeting to Montalbano. 'How nice to see you again! You look to be in splendid form!' he added, unable to contain his enthusiasm, gripping the inspector's hand forcefully and bringing it to his chest. Not for nothing was he called 'Lattes e Mieles'. In reality he didn't give a damn about Montalbano, but all the play-acting was part of his nature.

'And the family? Everyone doing well? The children?' Lattes continued implacably.

The inspector had told him more than a hundred times that he was unmarried, but the man had become fixated on the idea that he was married with children, and there was no making him change his mind.

Montalbano decided to try another way of getting the idiotic notion of the non-existent family out of his head once and for all.

'My wife left me,' he said, donning a pained expression and then dropping his head and staring at his toecaps.

Lattes seemed shaken; he took half a step back and opened his eyes wide.

'Really?'

'Yes. She lost her head over a Tunisian, a Muslim. And you know what, on top of everything else? An illegal immigrant!'

'My God! My God! And what about the children?'

'She took them with her to Hammamet.'

'And is that what you came to discuss with the commissioner?'

'No. It was him who summoned me.'

'Was it? I wonder why he didn't say anything to me . . .'

Montalbano threw his hands up.

'I'll go and find out what this is about,' said Lattes, knocking on the commissioner's door and going in.

What could it mean that the commissioner hadn't informed Lattes? There were only two possible answers: either the commissioner had forgotten to tell him, and therefore he was being called in for some negligible nonsense, or else he was being summoned over something so unpleasant that the commissioner didn't feel like telling even Lattes about it. In the latter case, it must concern an extremely sensitive matter.

Lattes returned with a slight frown on his face.

'He wouldn't tell me why he wants to see you. Anyway, you can go right in. He's waiting for you. But you have my deepest sympathies, believe me.'

'For what?' asked Montalbano, confused.

He'd already forgotten about the lie he'd told him about his wife running off with the Tunisian.

'For the sad situation of your family,' Lattes explained, walking away and shaking his head.

*

At first glance, the commissioner seemed to be in a bad mood. At second glance, likewise.

'Close the door and come in,' said Bonetti-Alderighi.

The inspector obeyed. The commissioner did not tell him to sit down, but continued studying the documents he had on his desk. Montalbano realized that he was trying to humiliate him by letting him stand there without coming to his assistance. And so he decided to get on his nerves. First he started coughing violently, recovered his breath, then coughed again, cleared his throat as if he had a bad cold, pulled a handkerchief out of his pocket, and then blew his nose so hard that it sounded like the trumpet on Judgement Day. The commissioner gave him a withering look.

'I'm sorry, sir,' said Montalbano, 'but I think I've got a touch of the flu. I'm told it's going around and is highly contagious. I think I even have a little fever.'

And he opened his mouth, as if to sneeze. The commissioner, who was a health nut, turned pale and wheeled his chair back a few feet, out of the range of the imminent sneeze.

Which never came.

And so the commissioner began. 'I called you here to tell you . . .'

Montalbano, who was starting to enjoy the game, opened and closed his mouth like a fish.

The commissioner froze.

'It won't come,' said the inspector, as if to excuse himself.

'I'll be quick. Try to hold it in,' said the commissioner. 'I called you in to inform you that, from today, you'll be handling the case. And now you can go.'

Montalbano opened his mouth again. This time in shock, not because he was faking a sneeze. Just to be safe, however, the commissioner wheeled his chair still further away, until the back was touching the wall.

'What case?'

'Montalbano . . . I guess the flu . . . Come on, have you forgotten? I'm talking about yesterday morning's murder in Vigàta!'

'I have to handle the case myself?'

'Who else, if not?'

'What about Inspector Toti?'

'Forget about Inspector Toti. He has other things to do. He's already taken the trouble to send you a copy of his report. You'll find it back at your station. And you must get in touch with Prosecutor Tommaseo.'

Montalbano could not, for the life of him, figure it out. Why had the commissioner changed his mind overnight? What could have happened? Maybe Toti had pulled another one of his supreme fuck-ups?

'Are you surprised?' the commissioner asked.

'Well, to be honest, I wasn't expecting . . .'

The commissioner's attitude changed. He brought his

chair closer to the desk, ready to brave any and all sneezes, and looked the inspector straight in the eye.

'You're a very good actor, Montalbano.'

Had he realized that the whole flu thing was a put-on?

No, it wasn't possible. So what acting was he referring to? 'Still, you should know,' the commissioner continued, 'that if I've made this decision it's because I was put in a position where I couldn't say no.'

'But, Mr Commissioner . . .'

'And sooner or later, I'll make you pay for all this.'

For all what? Was he raving?

'Listen, Mr Commissioner . . .'

'I don't need to listen to you for another second. All your words could do at this point is confirm the terrible opinion I have of the way you go about things. You can go now.'

Feeling numb, confused, dazed, zombified, in a trance, and, above all, feeling defeated in his duel with Bonetti-Alderighi, Montalbano turned his back to his superior and headed for the door, which he opened. As he was leaving the room, he heard the commissioner say sarcastically:

'And don't forget, when you see him, to give His Excellency Bishop Partanna my sincerest respects.'

Then everything became clear.

SEVEN

His exchange with the commissioner had dispelled all desire to eat, and so, instead of heading for Enzo's, he decided to go straight home to Marinella. He would make up for the skipped meal that evening.

He couldn't get out of his head just how badly he'd come off.

He'd felt completely lost in that office, unable to react the way he should have.

The shame of it! The rage!

When he got home, he gulped down two glasses of water, one right after the other, because his agitation had made him thirstier than a refugee in the desert. Opening the French windows to the veranda, he took several deep breaths of sea air.

It didn't really feel like November outside. The colours and mild air seemed more like those of a late-September warm spell that had been delayed along the way and was showing up only now, two months late.

He unplugged the telephone, settled in on the veranda,

found a cigarette, and lit it. And, head now clear, he started thinking.

First of all, there was no doubt that the commissioner had every reason in the world to be angry at him. If he normally treated him like a dishrag as, so to speak, standard procedure, then imagine this time, when he knew he had a good reason to do so!

Surely he'd received a phone call or two from Rome, ordering him to take the case away from Toti and give it back to him, and Bonetti-Alderighi had been unable to say no. And just as surely the person calling from Rome had made certain to specify that they were doing this as a favour to the Bishop of Montelusa. But how had Partanna managed so quickly to talk to someone so high up that he'd been able, just like that, to reshuffle the deck to his own liking?

No sooner had he formulated the question than he started laughing.

What? Had he forgotten that priests had been running the country for centuries?

Until not so long ago, they'd done so quite openly, under the auspices of the Christian Democratic Party. Then, when things started taking a bad turn, and the political class was drowning in an unusual wave of arrests and convictions for kickbacks, bribery, corruption, graft, pork barrels, and the like, the priests merely covered the faces of a few surviving Christian Democrats with blue handkerchiefs and sneaked them into the brand-spanking-new party now governing the country.

And wasn't the current Minister of the Interior one of these former Christian Democrats?

Whatever the case, the commissioner was dead wrong to assume that it was he, Montalbano, who had set the whole manoeuvre in motion. The inspector decided that the first chance he got, he would set the matter straight with his superior. He could not let this stand.

But what interest could Partanna possibly have in bringing him back into the game?

Could it really be only because Toti had made too many waves by overstepping his bounds?

These reasons seemed rather weak to him. Because in that case the bishop would simply have phoned the commissioner directly and asked him to tell Toti to move more cautiously and watch his step.

And that would have been the end of that.

No, there must be another reason. But try figuring it out! If the brain of a simple priest is, as we know, more twisted and contorted than that of a non-priest, then imagine what kinds of labyrinthine convolutions, meanders, and zigzags must make up the thoughts of a priest who had succeeded in becoming a bishop.

At any rate he could only conclude that, mutatis mutandis, the ball had been kicked back to him. *Sàvuta 'u trunzu e va 'n culu all'ortulanu.* Send the shears flying and they'll always find their way up the gardener's arse.

In another era, getting a case back after having had it taken away would have been cause for great satisfaction. Now, however, the idea of starting all over again unnerved him a little, and he felt a bit like someone who's stuffed his gut with antipasti but knows that the bulk of the eating has yet to be done.

He tried to recall the names of the three sportsman witnesses, the three musketeers, but couldn't. He'd suppressed them. All he could remember was the name of the murder victim, Riccardino. Hardly enough to start an investigation. There was no getting around it: he would have to read the scribbles that Toti had left for him. Take the first step. But he really didn't feel like it.

He sighed, cursed, got up, went into the bathroom, took all his clothes off, and stood in the shower for a good half an hour.

*

'Chief! Ahh, Chief, Chief!'

'What is it, Cat?'

'Issa 'annarable proxecutor wuz lookin' f'yiz four times! An' 'e says as how 'e's necessitated a talk t'yiz poissonally in poisson an' oigently wit' oigency! An' 'e ast yiz to call 'im soon as ya got to the affice.'

'Cat, I'm not gonna call him, but if he calls again, tell him I haven't come in yet and you don't know where I am.'

'So tha'ss how ya wan' me to respon' to the proxecutor?'

'Yes, Cat, just like that. And tell Fazio to come into my office at once.'

'I'm impossibilitated, Chief.'

'Why?'

'Cuz Fazio's betooken hisself absent, Chief.'

'Then call him on his mobile phone and tell him to get here at once.'

✳

In the middle of his desktop was a slender brown folder on the cover of which stood out a small piece of paper attached with a clip. Written on it were the words: *From Inspector Toti*. Also on the desk, but on the right-hand side, a tottering stack of papers to be signed towered almost three feet high. To the left, on the other hand, he saw a smaller stack about six inches high of scattered papers he had yet to read. His heart sank. Dejected, he propped his elbows on the desktop and set himself up with his head firmly wedged between his fists, eyes mildly agape, staring into the infinite void. This was what he used to do when, as a little boy, the teachers gave him too much homework. Not knowing where to begin, and especially having no desire whatsoever to begin, he would abandon himself to contemplating the white wall before him.

All at once, with a boom like a bomb blast, the door flew open and crashed against the wall. Montalbano leapt out of his chair, and Catarella appeared in the doorway, looking embarrassed.

''Scuse me, Chief, my—'

'Aaahhh!'

Montalbano's leonine yell froze Catarella. Out of the corner of his eye, the inspector had seen the stack of papers on the right first lurch to one side, then list perilously, then begin to slide onto the floor. The equally leonine leap he made to prevent an avalanche achieved the following result: his extended hands, instead of stopping the descent of the top end of the stack of papers, violently seized it right in the middle, sending dozens of sheets flying and fluttering across the room.

Montalbano felt too weary even to get angry.

'Now you're going to get down on all fours, pick up all the papers, and put them back in order on my desk.'

'Yessir, Chief . . . Sure . . .' Catarella stammered, getting down to work.

'What did you want to tell me?'

'Ah, yah, righ'. Fazio can't be ritched.'

'What do you mean?'

''Is mobble phone is toined off, Chief.'

'All right, I'm going to have a coffee.'

*

When the inspector returned, Catarella had just finished reconstituting the tower, which now looked a little more stable. 'It stands on iss own now, all by isself,' said Catarella, proudly admiring his handiwork.

'All right, then, you can go now.'

Catarella withdrew in reverse, upper body bent forward in a half-bow like a courtier of the Celestial Empire. Montalbano made a snap decision. He was ready to put up with anything to postpone the moment when he would have to open the folder with Toti's report in it. Extending his right hand, he reached out and grabbed the sheet of paper at the top of the pile, put it in front of him, and started reading it as he uncapped a ballpoint pen to sign it.

*

Fazio straggled back about two hours later, by which point Montalbano, right arm half-paralysed, had managed to dispatch about a quarter of the stack. The moment he saw him enter the room, he gave him hell.

'What kind of damn stupid way to behave is this, Fazio?'

'Why, what did I do?'

'What? You leave in the morning and return in the evening without leaving any notice as to how you can be reached? Does that really seem like the right way to proceed?'

'Chief, if you'll allow me—'

'Don't say "if you'll allow me"! I hate that expression!'

'Chief, if I may . . .'

'OK, go ahead.'

'This morning, as soon as you left to go to the commissioner's office, the folder you have in front of you was delivered here. The man from Montelusa explained that it was from Inspector Toti, who sent it because the case was being handed over to you. And so, not wanting to waste any time, I took the liberty of reading it myself.'

'Oh, really? And what does it say?'

'Hot air, Chief.'

'Thanks, Fazio. You've saved me a lot of time,' said Montalbano, picking up the folder and tossing it into the waste-paper basket. 'Then what?'

'Then someone phoned saying that last night, when he looked out of the window of his house in the Sparacio district, he saw something burning. So this morning he decided to go and see what it was from up close. And found the remains of a large motorcycle. A Yamaha 1100, almost certainly the one used by the man who shot Lopresti.'

'So there was just the remains of the motorbike?'

'Yeah, nothing else.'

'No helmet, no jacket, no gloves?'

'No, nothing at all, Chief.'

'Tell me something. How did it take you all day to go to the Sparacio district and come back?'

'Can I sit down?' Fazio asked instead of answering.

Montalbano nodded.

'The motorbike's licence plate was still legible. So I informed Forensics and then returned here. It didn't take me long to find out that the owner of the motorbike, Giacomo Collura, resident of Fela, on the morning of October the thirtieth, had reported the theft of the bike the night before.'

'That was to be expected. Standard procedure, I would say. Did you do anything else?'

'Yes. I went to the gym.'

The inspector stared at him. 'Since when have you—'

'No, no, no, Chief, what are you thinking? I went to the gym the murder victim used to go to, where the three musketeers go. It's called the Virtue and Labour Sports Club, and it's attached to the church of Sant'Antonio.'

Montalbano looked at him in admiration.

'But where do you get all this incentive? Do you know I can't even remember their names?'

'Chief, you'll have to forgive me, but, knowing you well as I do, I wrote up a little outline for you,' said Fazio, pulling a folded-up piece of paper from his pocket and laying it down in front of him.

Montalbano didn't even look at it. Instead, he looked deep into Fazio's eyes.

'What does that mean, what you said just now?'

'What did I say?'

'You said that, knowing me as well as you do, you made a little outline for me. What do you mean? That you consider me so senile that I can't even remember what I did yesterday?'

'But, Chief, you just told me you can't even remember the witnesses' names! Do you really want to know why I was so busy all day?'

'Yes. Tell me.'

'Because you're losing all interest in this job. I can't help but notice. I've known you for too long, Chief. It's not senility, it's exhaustion. You're burnt out, Chief. And so I'm just trying to spare you the trouble of doing the initial sifting, the most painstaking, boring part of the job.'

Without saying a word of thanks, Montalbano took the sheet of paper, unfolded it, and began to read.

Riccardo Lopresti
Born in Vigàta, 12 April 1972
Lives in Vigàta, Viale Siracusa 3
University degree in business and economics
Manager of the local branch of the Banca Regionale
Married to Else Hohler
No children

Mario Liotta
Born in Vigàta, 2 February 1972
Lives in Vigàta, Via Marconi 32
Surveying degree
Employed by the Cristallo Mine of Montereale
Married to Adele Bonanno (sister of Gaspare)
No children

Gaspare Bonanno
Born in Vigàta, 7 May 1972
Lives in Vigàta, Piazza Plebiscito 97
Accounting degree
Employed by the Cristallo Mine of Montereale
Married to Ida Liotta (sister of Mario)
Has one son

Alfonso Licausi
Born in Vigàta, 14 May 1972
Lives in Vigàta, Via Cristoforo Colombo 2
Surveying degree
Assistant manager of the Cristallo Mine of Montereale

Married to Maria Bonanno (sister of Gaspare)
Has one daughter

'Interesting,' commented Montalbano. 'And from this we see that the only exception was Riccardino.'

'I'm sorry, Chief, but why do you call him "Riccardino"?'

'I don't know, it just comes out that way.'

'So how was he an exception?'

'Getting shot and killed isn't enough of an exception for you? At any rate I was referring to the fact that he was the only one who didn't work at the salt mine. So, what did you find out at the gym?'

'It was closed, Chief. In mourning for Lopresti. But the caretaker and his wife were there, cleaning up.'

'Did they tell you anything about the musketeers?'

'Nothing of any importance. "He was such a good man, such a fine man, was Signor Riccardo, always ready to lend a friend a hand" . . . But I got the impression . . .'

'What kind of impression?'

'That the caretaker's wife wanted to tell me something . . . but not in her husband's presence. I'm going back there tomorrow, and I'll try and see if I can talk to her alone.'

'"Zit awright to come in?"'

Appearing in the doorway was Catarella, making a salute with his hand clenched in a fist.

Apparently he'd been about to knock in his usual fashion and only realized at the last second that the door was already open.

'Speak, comrade.'

'Chief, 'ere's a poisson o' the female pirsuasion onna phone.'

'What's her name?'

Catarella blushed.

'Chief, I'm too 'mbarrised to say 'er lass name. Iss a bad woid. She came yisterday, 'member? The one 'ooz pipe got busted.'

Fazio looked in alarm at Montalbano. Tina Facca, the clairvoyant fortune-teller!

Catarella vanished, and a moment later the telephone rang.

'Captain! Signurina Tina here. What's happened, aren't you coming?'

'I'm terribly sorry, signorina, but I really can't. Shall we say tomorrow evening around six?'

'Nah. I got a client. Shall we say seven?'

'Seven's good for me.'

'OK, but don't stand me up, I mean it.'

'Not to worry,' said the inspector, hanging up.

'Mind telling me about this business of the pipe?' asked Fazio.

'I'll tell you later. Do you know when Riccardino's funeral is?'

'Day after tomorrow, ten a.m. At the church of Sant' Antonio.'

'Therefore tomorrow, which is a working day, the three friends will be at the Cristallo mine. Do you know what their hours are?'

'They're in the administrative section and keep normal office hours. They start at seven in the morning and finish at five-thirty in the afternoon. You want to go and talk to them?'

'I wouldn't dream of it. I only wanted to know if they would be out of our hair tomorrow morning, because I want to meet their wives.'

'Maria Bonanno is at San Vito Lo Capo, you know.'

'I know, but she's sure to be back tomorrow night to go to the funeral the following morning. Which means that tomorrow morning I'll content myself with the German girl and Adele Bonanno, Liotta's wife. I'm hoping to find out why Riccardino rang her phone a few seconds before he got shot.'

'What need is there to go and ask her, Chief? Surely the two were lovers.'

'I'd go easy on that score. How do you really know that's the case? It would appear to be true, I agree. But we can't just go by appearances.'

As he was saying these last words, the smiling – and troubling – face of Bishop Partanna appeared in his mind, upsetting him. He banished it and continued:

'I'll give you an example. Let's say Riccardino knows that Mario is quarrelling with his wife. Since he's their friend, he wants them to make up. And so he secretly dials the Liottas' home phone number so the two can talk to each other.'

'Then why do it secretly?'

'Because if he'd known, Liotta would have prevented him.'

'Then why didn't he pass the phone to Liotta when he got through?'

'He didn't have time. He got shot.'

Fazio seemed unconvinced.

'I'll give you another example. Since he dialled the number without looking, he may have dialled incorrectly. Maybe he wanted to talk to someone who—'

'Excuse me, Chief, but that really seems far-fetched to me!'

'Oh, yeah? But hadn't he just dialled a wrong number when he called me instead of Licausi? Maybe he was one of those people who spend their lives dialling wrong numbers!'

Fazio looked at him with suspicion.

'But, Chief, do you know anything at all about Liotta's wife?'

'What are you thinking? Of course not.'

'Then why are you defending her as if she was the Blessed Virgin herself?'

'Do me a favour, Fazio.'

'Sure, Chief.'

'Forget what I just said. I was just blathering, saying the first things that came into my head. To get my brain up and running. Have you been wondering why the commissioner gave the case back to me?'

'Yeah. And I got the answer in town. They say it was Bishop Partanna's wishes.'

Shit! Everybody knew about it already!

'And so they also told you that the bishop intervened?'

'Yeah. Because Inspector Toti pissed off the three witnesses. And one of the three, none other than Alfonso Licausi, is the bishop's nephew. But did you really not know any of this?'

EIGHT

As soon as he was sitting down on the veranda in Marinella, he started gazing at the sea, which quickly turned rough. In the twinkling of an eye, it ate up half of the beach, with the waves making a furious racket. And little by little, that rage of nature began to infect him, and his conversation with the commissioner came back to him word for word.

If he didn't get it out of his system in a hurry – if he didn't somehow eject the blob seething inside him – quite likely he would never be able to get to sleep. But how? Who could he talk to? He certainly had to talk about things, that was clear. And the only person with whom he could confront the whole issue was Livia, though there was still the problem of their quarrel over where to spend their damn holiday. He weighed his options, stood up, went into the house, and dialled her number in Boccadasse.

'Hello,' Livia said at once.

'Salvo here.'

No reply.

'Hello? Livia? This is Salvo.'

Nothing. He thought they'd been cut off.

He always got terribly shaken up, indeed frightened to death, when the phone line was cut off as he was talking. He would feel for a moment as if any communication, not only with the person he was speaking to, but with all of creation, had become utterly, absolutely impossible.

He hung up and frantically redialled the number. Busy.

Want to bet that Livia, as soon as she heard that it was him, had spitefully left the phone off the hook?

He tried again, more upset than ever. This time the line was free.

'I don't like the way you're acting,' he said as soon as he heard someone pick up.

'And I don't like the way you're acting either,' replied a man's voice with a Genoese accent before hanging up.

Another man?! There was another man in Livia's apartment? Things were taking a really bad turn this time. He called back.

'Hello?' said Livia, sounding a little irritated.

'Who's that man there with you?'

'Wh . . . what man?' asked Livia, confused.

'The one who answered the phone!'

'There's no man here with me.'

'But I just spoke to him!'

She was flat-out denying the truth!

'Listen, since you seem to care so much, let's do this.

I'm going to go down into the street now, grab the first
passable man I find, bring him home with me, and then
you can call back and I'll have him answer the phone.
Would that make you happy, idiot?'

To judge from the tone of her voice, she seemed sincere.
He suddenly felt doubtful: and what if the second time
he'd called he'd dialled a wrong number?

'Well, when I didn't hear you any longer, I thought we'd
been cut off . . . and so I redialled, and I must have dialled
wrong . . . It happens. Speaking of which, the case I have
currently on my hands actually began with somebody dialling a wrong number . . . to my own house . . . Are you
still there, Livia? Hello?'

'I'm here.'

'Why don't you say anything?'

'Because it's not up to me. You have to do the talking.'

'Come on, Livia, don't joke around. I've been talking for
the past half hour! What would you like to know?'

'Before we continue this conversation, I want to know
what you've decided about our holiday.'

'You . . . you mean Johannesburg?'

'Yes, exactly. Johannesburg.'

Livia may have been born in Genoa, but she was more
hard-headed and tenacious than a Calabrian. On the other
hand, now that he thought about it, what would it cost
him just to say yes and then, at the last minute, announce
that he couldn't go? Just the price of an airline ticket, the
hotel reservations, and the penalty. The fact was, he really
couldn't see himself strolling among the Boers or whatever

the hell they were. So he closed his eyes, counted to three, and spat out the lie.

'OK, Livia. We'll go to Johannesburg.'

He was expecting an exclamation of joy, but was met only with a long silence.

'Livia, are you there?'

'Yes.'

'Don't you have anything to say?'

'I have one thing to say, Salvo. If, this time, you tell me, one day before departure, that you can't come, I swear, I will—'

'Come on, Livia! What are you thinking? I'm telling you that, after giving it some thought, I realized that it would be wonderful to see Johannesburg. You have no idea how curious I am to see what the Boers are like, you know — what do you call them? — the Afrikaners . . . But, for now, let's drop the subject, OK?'

'OK. Tell me what you've been up to lately.'

He told her about Riccardino's murder, Enrico Toti's idiocy, and the intercession of the Bishop of Montelusa. And he also told her that the commissioner was convinced that it was he, Montalbano, who had appealed to the bishop to get the case back.

'So what?' Livia said at the end.

'What do you mean, so what? Do you know that not only the commissioner, but everyone in town thinks I'm protected by the bishop?'

'And is that such a burden to you?'

'Yes. A terrible burden.'

'Then that could be easily remedied.'

'Oh, yeah? How?'

'Tomorrow morning you arrest the bishop's nephew. That way, the commissioner will take the case away from you again, and everyone in town will realize that there's nothing between you and the bishop. Quite the contrary.'

'Livia, mind if I ask what the fuck is goin' tru dat li'l noggin o' yers?'

'Don't use obscenities with me, and don't speak Vigatese!'

'I'm sorry. But you're not taking me seriously!'

'I can't take you seriously, Salvo. When have you ever cared about what people think about you? When have you ever taken public opinion into any kind of consideration? It's clear you're getting old.' And she added a little cackle.

'What do you find so funny?'

'I was just thinking that your TV alter ego, who's younger than you, has for his part remained true to himself.'

A knife to the heart would have been less painful. 'Speaking of which, Livia, don't you mind seeing an actress apeing you on TV?'

'No, why do you ask? Anyway, she doesn't ape me at all. And let me remind you that it wasn't me who went and told that writer all my personal stories and yours. So why should it bother you now?'

Better cut this short straightaway, to avoid further complications.

'I'm sorry, but someone's knocking at the door, surely someone from the station.'

And he hung up without wishing her a good night. The

phone call had put the finishing touches on his fit of pique.

He searched for and found a bottle of whisky that had just been opened. Sitting back down on the veranda, he started drinking straight from the bottle.

*

Viale Siracusa was part of a residential complex of single-family homes that bore the name, inevitably, 'The Two Pines'. The access road was broken up by a horizontal iron bar painted red and white, which opened and closed electronically. To the left of the bar was a glass booth with a bicycle leaning up against it. Inside was a man reading a newspaper. When Montalbano's car pulled up in front of the barrier, the man did not move. He didn't even look up. The inspector honked his horn. Same result. The poor bastard must have been deaf.

Another car pulled up behind Montalbano's, a brand spanking new BMW. The security guard must have recognized the rumble of the engine, because he got up immediately and ran out of the booth. Therefore he wasn't a poor deaf bastard, but simply a bastard. The man, who was wearing a uniform that looked exactly like that of an American police officer, leaned down to Montalbano's window to speak. 'Pull over to the side and let the *commendatore* through,' he commanded him.

'Not on your fucking life.'

'Excuse me, what did you say?' said the man, bending further down.

He was a sort of walking wardrobe of about forty and carried a large revolver sticking half out of its holster.

Montalbano didn't have time to reply before another car came racing up and stopped behind the *commendatore*'s BMW. It immediately started honking wildly.

Cool as a cucumber, Montalbano got out of his car and, looking the security guard straight in the eye, said:

'Listen to me, you fucking wannabe American, either you raise that bar or I'm going to stick the barrel of that gun of yours up your arse. The choice is yours.'

'Can I ask at least where you're going?' the guard enquired, having suddenly turned meek as a lamb.

'To the house of the widow Lopresti.'

'Wait and let me announce your arrival by phone.'

'What, do you think you're the archangel Gabriel or something? Just open the gate and don't you dare touch that phone, if you know what's good for you. Just tell me how to find her house.'

'The second street on the right, the fifth house on the left.'

Following the man's directions, he turned onto the second street on the right, pulled up at the fifth house, parked, and got out.

The name on the intercom buzzer was Arturo Tripodi. Hm. He rang.

'Who is it?' asked a woman.

'This is Inspector Montalbano, police. I was looking for Mrs Else Lopresti.'

'She doesn't live here. You've made a mistake. When

you're coming from the entrance, you should have taken the second street on the left.'

He got back in the car and drove the whole way back in reverse, until he reached the fifth house. This time he was right on target. Over the intercom buzzer next to the entrance gate was the name: *Dr Riccardo Lopresti.*

The little garden in front of Riccardino's house was a real surprise: a highly orderly thicket of roses of varying colours, the sort of garden one sees only in glossy photos in gardening magazines.

He rang the buzzer. No answer. Then he realized that it wouldn't take much to open the small, locked gate. Once inside, he went down the little walkway through an inebriating scent of roses, arrived at the front door of the house, and rang the doorbell. There was no answer. But the front door, too, was easily opened with a little push.

He found himself in a large living room that looked quite tastefully furnished.

'Mrs Lopresti! Signora Else!'

Silence. Maybe the signora was upstairs, in her bedroom, and couldn't hear. He walked through the living room, arrived at the foot of an elegant wooden staircase that led upstairs, and called out a bit louder:

'Signora! Signora Else!'

And where did the weapon whose barrel was suddenly pressing hard against the nape of his neck come from? How was it that he hadn't heard a thing – not a footstep, not even a rustle? But there was no point asking himself any questions. The fact was that someone was pointing a revolver at his head. It was best not to move or say anything, and wait for the other to speak.

But the other person did not speak. He turned the revolver around in his hand, and with the butt he struck the inspector hard in the head. Before closing his eyes and passing out, Montalbano got a glimpse of who'd struck him: it was the fucking arsehole of a security guard. And he even had time to think that the other Montalbano, the one on TV, probably would not have fainted, but would certainly have reac . . .

*

He woke up face down on the sofa in the Loprestis' living room. Beside him was Galluzzo, applying hot wet compresses to his head.

'How ya feelin', Chief?'

He didn't answer, but merely turned his upper body a little. The security guard was sitting in an armchair with his head in his hands. Fazio, who was standing with the phone receiver to his ear and the guard's revolver stuck in his belt, was yelling and cursing:

'I want an ambulance here immediately! I can't wait half an hour, understand?'

Montalbano turned his head even more, so he could take in the entire living room. He didn't see any dead or injured. Therefore Fazio must be calling the ambulance for him. He sprang to his feet, but a stabbing pain made him sit down again.

'Don't you dare call an ambulance for me!' he ordered.

'But, Chief, you were hit really hard! It's better for them to have a look at you at the hospital.'

'Put that phone down immediately.'

Fazio obeyed. The security guard was surveying the scene. His face was swollen, his upper lip split, and one eye wouldn't open.

'And what happened to him?'

'Nothing, Chief. He fell down the stairs,' said Fazio, his face as innocent as a seraph descended from heaven.

'Did he call you?'

'Yes.'

Apparently when Fazio and Galluzzo arrived and discovered that it was the guard who had struck Montalbano, they must have rained a torrent of punches and kicks down on him. 'I didn't realize you were a co— a policeman,' the guard said thickly, having trouble speaking because of his broken lip. 'I thought you . . . an' so I grabbed the bike and came here . . . and then I called the police. You've got to forgive me, Inspector. It was an honest mistake.'

'Where is Signora Else?'

'In Palermo, at the airport. She's gone to pick up Wo . . . her father, who flew down from Hamburg for the funeral.'

Montalbano himself was having trouble talking. It felt like someone was pounding his head with a hammer.

'All right. There's nothing left for us to do here,' he said, leaning against Galluzzo and standing up.

At that moment they all heard the ambulance arriving.

'And what do we do now?' asked Fazio.

'We can't send it back empty,' said Montalbano. 'The only solution is for you to shoot yourself in the balls and get treated for it.'

✳

He still had half a morning's work ahead of him. According to what he'd decided the previous day, he should now be going to pay Adele Liotta a visit. But his headache not only wasn't going away, it seemed to be getting worse by the minute. He certainly wasn't in the best condition for dealing with a woman who, if she really had been Riccardino's mistress, would use every feminine wile in the book to defend herself and keep him at bay. To save what remained of the morning, he would be better off going to the bank where Riccardino was manager and finding out what they had to say about him.

The branch office of the Banca Regionale was located in the central square, right next door to the bar that made the best ice cream in town. Montalbano went in and ordered a double espresso. The barman didn't understand and set two demitasses down in front of him. Oh, well. The inspector drank first one, then the other.

The barman looked at him uncomprehendingly.

'If you'd told me, I would have put it all in one cup.'

'No, no,' said the inspector. 'This is the way I like it. And when I order a quadruple coffee, I want it in four little cups.'

The armoured revolving doors in banks all seemed to have something against Montalbano: either they wouldn't open, or they would trap him inside. The one at the entrance to the Banca Regionale must have been in a good mood, because it let him through on the first try.

The room was full of people. He went up to window number one, which was free, and leaned down to speak to the clerk. But he didn't manage in time, because a hand grabbed his jacket and forcefully pulled him away.

Montalbano turned around and found himself facing a priest of about sixty, livid with rage and shooting flames from his eyes.

'You didn't take a number!'

He had a blaring voice rather like the fire department's siren, and everyone turned around to stare at them.

'But I—'

'No, ifs ands or buts! You must take a ticket with a number and not try to cheat!'

Montalbano then brought his lips up to the guy's ear and whispered: 'Careful, priest! I'm a protégé of Bishop Partanna.'

The priest recoiled. A worried-looking man of about fifty came out of a door.

'What is going on?'

'Nothing, sir, nothing, just a simple misunderstanding,' the priest said promptly.

'I am Inspector Montalbano, police. I would like to speak to the manager.'

'Please come with me.'

Montalbano followed him into the office, as the priest kept staring at him. The fiftyish man introduced himself:

'I'm the chief cashier; my name is Sergio Caruana. Management has given me the task of temporarily replacing poor Lopresti. You're here concerning the investigation, I assume?'

'Yes.'

They sat down, Caruana behind the desk, Montalbano in one of the two chairs facing it.

'So you knew him rather well – Mr Lopresti, that is.'

'Well, I knew him as the bank manager, at my place of work, but . . .'

'But?'

'We weren't friends; we never met in private outside the bank.'

'Why not?'

'Inspector, I'm fifty-two years old. Mr Lopresti was just over thirty. He had a different lifestyle, full of physical activity and sport, whereas I—'

'I understand. How long had Lopresti been manager of this branch?'

'For three years. Before that he'd worked at the provincial branch in Montelusa.'

'And is everything . . . all right around here?'

The cashier looked at him questioningly.

'I'm sorry, in what sense?'

'Let me ask you a direct question: do you think that the murder of your branch manager may have had anything to do, even in the most unlikely fashion, with his actions as a banker?'

'I would rule that out. The late branch manager was an

ambitious young man; he wanted to make a career of it. By honest means, however. He didn't make any stupid mistakes.'

'Isn't it possible that this desire not to make mistakes might itself be a mistake sometimes?'

Caruana understood at once.

'Do you mean denying loans for lack of guarantees, or perhaps demanding immediate repayment from persons who . . .'

'. . . who might take it the wrong way,' Montalbano said, finishing his sentence.

Caruana did not reply at once, but thought it over for a moment. Then he said:

'Well, three years ago, just after he arrived, Mr Lopresti refused to grant five million euros of credit to Li Puma, the builder.'

Salvatore Li Puma, as was well known, belonged to the Sinagra crime family. And word had it that he was involved in wholesale drug-trafficking.

'And did Li Puma then threaten Mr Lopresti?'

Caruana gave a little laugh.

'Of course not. He came back a week later and got what he wanted.'

'What happened in the meantime?'

'General management phoned Lopresti and ordered him to open that credit line. Or at least that's what Lopresti told me confidentially. And he added that he'd also received another phone call from the Honourable Saccomanni, currently Undersecretary of Justice, who lobbied heavily in Li Puma's favour.'

Great! Saccomanni! Someone triply bound to the Sinagras who instead of being in jail was in the government.

'So Li Puma had no more reason to want revenge?'

'Of course not. Lopresti had been domesticated, so what reason would there be to kill him?' the chief cashier said bitterly. 'He might prove more useful alive, don't you think?'

'Listen, isn't it possible that other people of the same ilk as Li Puma may have taken advantage of Lopresti's domestication, as you call it?'

'It's possible. But in order to find out I would have to audit all the work the late manager did during his tenure here. And a lot of papers are no longer in this office. An inspector from general management came yesterday and took them away to Palermo with him. It would take divine intervention at this point for us to consult them.'

'Right,' said Montalbano, discouraged.

NINE

When he came out of the bank there was another fifteen minutes to go before he could head for Enzo's for lunch at the usual hour. But that day, too, it wasn't on the cards.

Not only was he not the least bit hungry, but he felt a kind of distress in his stomach that bordered on a troublesome nausea. Certainly an effect of the headache that hadn't left him for an instant. And so he decided to go home and rest.

Once there, he felt around behind his head and immediately groaned in pain.

Right at the base of the skull a lump as big as a walnut had sprouted, so sensitive that he couldn't even touch it lightly with his fingers.

He took off all his clothes, turned on the tap in the washbasin, and put the back of his head under the cold running water. He stayed that way for about ten minutes, and when he'd finished, it seemed to him – but it was only an impression – that the pain had diminished.

'Now I'm going to go and lie down for an hour or so,' he said to himself, unplugging the phone.

*

When he woke it was five-thirty. He'd slept for four straight hours. The moment he opened his eyes, he could tell that the headache was gone. He carefully touched the back of his head: the swelling was already three-quarters reduced. He got up, washed, dressed, plugged the phone back in, and called the station.

'Ahh, Chief, Chief! I'd a jest about given up 'ope o' 'earin' yer verse, Chief!'

'Did you try to reach me?'

'Oh yessir, Chief! I tried rilly 'ard!'

'Any news?'

'Nah, Chief.'

'Then why were you trying to reach me?'

'No reason, jess to know where ya was.'

'Listen, Cat, I'm not coming back in today. I'll see you in the morning.'

'Mine if I ax where yer goin'?'

'Not at all: I'm going to see a fortune-teller.'

*

Stuck to the door of apartment number one on the ground floor of building number two on Via Saverio Cucurullo was a yellow piece of paper with a photograph of the clairvoyant fortune-teller from at least thirty years before. Under the photograph were the words:

115

TINA FACCA
Fortune-teller and clairvoyant
Your past, present and future
and everything else you want to know
No tricks, no gimmicks!
Reasonable prices

When Signorina Tina came and opened the door, the inspector did a double-take.

The Tower of Pisa that had soared above her head when he first met her was gone, or rather, it had changed into a more complex construction that looked vaguely like Cologne Cathedral. Clearly in honour of the inspector's visit, the woman had dolled herself up big-time: eyes lined in black, lips blood-red with lipstick, a good half a ton of foundation on her face. On top of this, she'd given herself a sly little mole at the left-hand corner of her bottom lip, a tiny black point of the kind that in the days of King Umberto I used to be called a *tirabaci*, or 'kiss magnet'. She was wearing a purple dress so snug that, to keep from exploding, it must have had its seams reinforced with the materials used for cables in regattas. Tina Facca had also dumped a good half-pint of barber's perfume on herself.

'Captain, what a sight for sore eyes! I knew you were a man of your word! Come in, come in, and make yourself at home!'

She led him into the small sitting room where she received her clients, and pointed him to an armchair.

'Would you like a cup of coffee?'

'Sure, why not?'

While Tina was bustling about in the kitchen, Montalbano got up and started looking at the framed photographs hanging on the walls.

They featured men as well as women, smiling customers who in their dedications attested to the benefits they'd received from Signorina Tina Facca's clairvoyance. One in particular caught the inspector's eye: it showed a toothless man of about eighty without a hair on his head with the expression of one who knows he's less than ten miles from the grave. The dedication said:

> To Tina Facca the Seer
> who saved me from an unhappy love

'Come, Captain, come!' the fortune-teller suddenly called, all excited.

Montalbano raced into the kitchen.

'That stinking son of a bitch is about to arrive! I recognize the sound of the bastard's car! Over here, by the window!'

As she was saying this, Signorina Tina went and stood in front of the window, covering it entirely with her mass, which, even without the addition of Cologne Cathedral, stood at least five foot eleven.

'You're going to have to move over a little,' said the inspector.

'Nah, I wanna see too!'

She grabbed Montalbano by one arm, pulled him on top of her, practically shoved his head between her tits, and then held him pressed face-forward against the window with her whole body.

Immediately Montalbano, half suffocating, felt his nose begin to itch. It was that nauseating perfume. And he sneezed, just as a brown car was passing by the window.

'Did you get a look at his face, Captain?'

'No, unfortunately I sneezed just as—'

'He'll be back in five minutes, and you can get a better look at him.'

But what did the fortune-teller have in mind? Did she mean to keep him pressed between her tits until the car returned? He was scared. He couldn't breathe. He said the first thing he could think of.

'Think the coffee's ready yet?'

'You're right!'

Momentarily liberated, Montalbano discovered that there was a very small window in the kitchen, a kind of loophole, which gave onto the street. He took up position in front of it and did not abandon his post even when Tina served him his coffee.

'He's coming back, he's coming back! Come with me, Captain!'

Montalbano quickly jammed his head inside the narrow window, at the risk of getting stuck in it. A bit disappointed, Signorina Tina ran over to her window. The brown car passed by again, and the inspector was able to see the driver's face clearly. A man of about fifty with a 'nonymous face, as Catarella would say.

'This time I got a good look at him. I thank you so much for—'

'What? Are you leaving? But we still have to go and see Filippo Nicotera! The good man is expecting us!' said Signorina Tina.

And who the hell was he? Then the inspector remembered: he was the saintly Christian who'd mended Signorina Tina's pipe, the one from whose bedroom window one could observe the tail end of the mysterious journeys of the truck and brown car.

'Oh, all right,' said Montalbano, resigned.

The fortune-teller disappeared and then returned wearing a kind of mantilla that hung from the central spire of Cologne Cathedral and fell back down onto her shoulders.

They went out, heading for building number six.

The street was rather narrow, and in order to get through, the truck had to perform acrobatics, because the buildings facing one another along the street were not lined up on a straight axis, but were all either a bit forward or a bit set back with respect to the others.

Mr Filippo Nicotera lived on the third floor, and there was no lift. The fortune-teller knocked on his door, which then came open. All by itself, or so it seemed at first to the inspector.

If he'd been three inches shorter, Mr Nicotera would have been a midget, but that difference wasn't enough to make him look any different from a midget. He was about fifty years old, skinny as a rake, pale, and without a hair on his face or head. An albino earthworm.

'Inspector, what an honour! Please come in!'

'He's a captain,' the fortune-teller corrected him.

'Would you like some coffee?' asked the saintly man, not acknowledging the fortune-teller's correction.

'Signorina Tina just made me a cup. But I would like you to tell me at once . . . because afterwards I have to . . .'

'Please come with me.'

Mr Nicotera's bedroom, aside from a brand-new, probably steel-reinforced double bed that could hold at least three people, also had a balcony at the French windows. 'I always keep it closed; otherwise the stink from the dump comes into the house,' Nicotera explained. 'But you can still see perfectly well.'

Montalbano approached. Signorina Tina as well, pulling up beside him. Luckily there was enough room for everyone.

The view was excellent. One could see the last portion of the street, which ended in a paved open space with its own street lamp, as well as a wall about six feet high and, beyond this, the dump, which stretched as far as the eye could see. It had everything: cars, refrigerators, oil drums spilling liquids of every imaginable colour, scattered rubbish, animal carcasses, a boat, something that Montalbano ardently hoped was a mannequin, and even an aeroplane wing.

Mr Nicotera wedged himself in between the

fortune-teller and the inspector and began to describe what he saw from that observation post.

'So, every night, when the truck driver arrives with his truck, he stops near the street lamp, gets out, picks up a stepladder and a package, and goes over to the wall, right there – see, Inspector, where you can read the words, pardon my Italian, "you can all just take it up the arse"? He plants the ladder just under the *RS* in *ARSE*, takes the package, climbs up, leans over, drops the package down on the other side, gets the ladder – aahhh – goes back to his truck, and leaves. Aaahhh.'

But why was Mr Nicotera using only his right hand to point and groaning every few seconds?

Montalbano took a few steps back and looked. The saint's left hand was passionately stroking Signorina Tina's posterior dome, while the fortune-teller, looking blissful, gave him free rein.

Better wrap things up fast before they degenerated.

'And when he comes by car, as he did just now?'

'Recovering the package is more complicated, Inspector.'

'He's a captain,' said Tina.

'Knock it off!' the saintly man burst out. 'Where are you getting this captain crap? He's an inspector!'

The fortune-teller did not react, but began looking at Montalbano with suspicion.

'So he arrives in his car,' Mr Nicotera resumed, 'he stops near the street lamp, gets out, takes an extendable ladder from the luggage rack, goes over to the wall, puts the ladder in its usual place, climbs up, aaahh, straddles the wall, grabs the ladder, transfers it over to the other side of the wall, climbs down, disappears, then reappears with the package, puts the ladder back on this side, aaahhh, puts the package and ladder back on the luggage rack, and drives away. And there you have it, aahhh.'

'Aahhh!' said the fortune-teller, echoing him.

Montalbano thought he'd better hurry up before the irreparable happened.

'Were you able to read the licence-plate number of the—'

'Of the truck, no, because it's too dark at night and the street lamp doesn't give off much light. But I got the car's number. Here, I wrote it down on this piece of paper.'

He handed it to Montalbano, who put it in his pocket.

'As for the truck, however . . .' Mr Nicotera resumed.

'Speak.'

'From here I can see inside the empty body. I've looked through binoculars. I could be wrong, but in my opinion, it's used to transport salt. It must be a truck from the Cristallo mine.'

Montalbano thanked him, declined an invitation to stay for dinner, promised them a quick investigation, raced out of the apartment, reached his car out of breath, and drove off.

On the way home it occurred to him that at that moment the earthworm and Cologne Cathedral were rolling around in that bed, bought specifically to bear the weight of the fortune-telling clairvoyant. First he felt like laughing, remembering a story by Philip Roth, but then the horror of the imagined scene blinded him, the car swerved, and he missed crashing into a car coming the other way by a fraction of an inch . . .

*

A wolflike hunger had come over him.

He opened the fridge: mullet in vinegar and onions, and caponata.

He felt at peace with the universe.

After laying the little table on the veranda, he sat down and began to eat. The air was cool and bright and added sparkle to the flavours. He had a feast. As he was clearing the table, the telephone rang. Since the meal had put him in a good mood, he went and answered.

It was the Author, calling from Rome. He immediately regretted picking up the receiver.

'Hello, Salvo, have you got a little time for me?'

'How much is "a little"?'

'Not more than ten minutes.'

'OK. Go ahead.'

'I can't go on this way. I need you to try and give me a hand.'

'In what sense?'

'The way you've always done. Riccardino's story, the one you're involved in—'

'Who told you?' Montalbano interrupted him resentfully.

The Author heaved a deep sigh.

'Good God, Salvo, are we still at that point? Do you really not understand, or do you do it on purpose?'

'I want to know who informed you.'

'Salvo, it's totally the other way around. It's me who informs you, and I don't know why you insist on thinking that it's you who inform me. This story about Riccardino, I'm writing it as you live it. It's as simple as that.'

'So I would be the puppet, and you the puppet master?'

'Cut the crap! So now you're going to resort to clichés with me? Have you forgotten how many times you forced me to follow, independently, of your own initiative, a completely different course from the one I was planning to write? For example, wasn't it you who chose the ending to *The Patience of the Spider*? I'd thought of ending it one way, but you forced me to use a different solution. And I even know why.'

'Oh, yeah?'

'Yeah. In the final section you made me insert some interior monologues into the story, which would have been impossible, for example, to stage. Which you knew perfectly well. In other words, you wanted to screw the television character, denying him the possibility of enhancing certain nuances. Isn't that true?'

'So you called me to tell me about this great discovery of yours? That I wanted to differentiate myself from the guy on TV?'

'It's not just that, Salvo. I do understand you, in a way, to the point that at the start of this story I faithfully presented your dislike of the TV Montalbano and the unease he caused you, whereas I could easily have left it unmentioned. But I have to warn you that you're heading down the wrong path.'

'Explain what you mean.'

'Comparing yourself with him, or, worse yet, challenging him, is a bad idea.'

'Why?'

'Because you are who you are, and he is who he is.'

'Easy for you to say, who live off the both of us! Of course it's in your interest to keep us separate and different!'

'Salvo, I'm just trying to tell you that this constant comparison is muddling your thoughts. And, as a result, you're damaging my story as well. Your investigations are not what they used to be. You're too often uncertain, vague, contradictory, and even scatter-brained. You keep invoking the problem of imminent old age, but I know perfectly well that it's just an excuse for covering your increasing indecision. Can't you see that you're presently unwilling, in this Riccardino story, to set the investigation on a specific, well-defined path? I offer you a lead, and you start joking around, and as a result I find myself in a pickle. As a writer, I mean. This can't go on, Salvo. It's imperative that your investigation—'

'Your ten minutes are up,' said Montalbano. And he hung up.

*

After thrashing about in bed for an hour, he got up, sat at the table, and wrote himself a letter, which was his way of taking notes.

Dear Salvo,

I'm writing this letter to myself not because of the phone call from the Author, but just to keep well in mind a number of leads I need to develop.

Incident at the Lopresti home

When I introduced myself at the gate of the residential complex, I had a tiff with the security guard and insulted him. He was an idiot, but I wasn't any less of one. I acted more like a mafioso than a policeman.

He gave me some misinformation, directing me to a street different from the one the Lopresti home is on. I wasted some time trying to find the house. When I finally tracked it down, I found the gate and front door both unlocked, seeming to indicate that someone was at home. But in fact Signora Else was not there, no one was. The working hypothesis is this: the guard gives me false information; I head off; he takes the bicycle that's parked right next to his booth, arrives at the house before I do, opens it with the keys that Else has left with him, and then lies in wait. I go in and, like an idiot, step right into the ambush. While I'm unconscious, he takes out my wallet and sees that I'm a policeman. And so he phones the station. The question is: who was the guard expecting instead of me when I arrived?

Let us not forget that the wife of Riccardino, who was shot dead, lives in that house. Is the widow also in danger?

Another oddity: when I asked the guard where the signora was, he replied that she'd gone to Palermo to pick up her father, who was arriving from Germany for the funeral. Except that the guard was about to call Else's father by his name, when he stopped in the nick of time and corrected himself.

He'd started to say: 'Wo . . .'

We need to find out everything there is to know about that guard.

The business of the truck

The business of the mysterious truck should not be part of this letter concerning the murder of Riccardino. But there was something Mr Nicotera said that deserves further exploration, which was that the truck must belong to the Cristallo mine. The same mine where the three friends of the late Riccardino work.

Don't forget to give Fazio the scrap of paper with the licence-plate number of the truck driver's car so that he can retrace it to its owner.

Because one never knows.

Sincerely, Salvo

PS for the Author: I don't think this letter will be as hard to stage as an interior monologue. I suggest that the scriptwriter integrate these considerations of mine into a dialogue with Fazio.

S.

TEN

'Welcome back, Chief, Chief!'

'Thanks, Cat. Is Fazio in?'

'Nah, Chief. 'E informed me t' inform yiz 'at 'iss mornin' 'e got a call from 'ome, an' after talkin' to the folks a' 'ome—'

'Wait a second, Cat. What "home" are you talking about? You mean he got a call from his parents?'

'Nah, Chief, 'twas some people from a funereal 'ome 'at called, but I dunno if 'is parents got nuttin' a do wit' it, bu' anyways, Fazio said 'e was goin' to the funeral an' aftawoids 'e'll be back 'ere.'

The inspector went into his office, sat down, took out of his pocket the scrap of paper the saintly man had given him, phoned a friend from Montelusa who worked at the bureau of motor vehicles, read him the licence number, and was told someone would call him back as soon as possible.

And indeed, within half an hour, his friend rang back.

The miracles of kapewters, as Catarella called them.

The car belonged to Saverio Milioto, residing in Vigàta at number 12, Via della Stazione.

Since he didn't have anything to do while waiting for Fazio, he went out, got into the car, and headed for Via della Stazione. Number twelve was a two-storey building. On the ground floor, beside a small front door, was a wide metal rolling shutter to a rather large garage, raised. Inside there wasn't a soul to be seen, only the brown car he'd seen drive by twice the day before, as well as a van, a small truck, and another car, this one dark green.

He approached the front door. There were no names beside the intercom. He rang the buzzer.

'Who is it?' asked a woman's voice.

'This is Cesare Battisti, signora.'

If the chief of the Flying Squad could call himself Enrico Toti, why couldn't he himself be Cesare Battisti?

'And what do you want?'

'I want to talk to Mr Milioto.'

'The father or the son?'

'Saverio.'

'Saverio's not here, he's working at the mine.'

'Could I speak to his son then?'

'Gnazio? Gnazio's out with the other van, making a delivery. Do you need something delivered?'

'Yes.'

'Gnazio'll be back in about two hours. Ya wan' me to give ya the phone number of the garage?'

'No, thank you, signora, there's no need. I'll pass by again later, after Gnazio gets back.'

So the trip hadn't been a total loss. Saverio Milioto, aside from driving a truck for the Cristallo mine, had set up a small delivery business that his son, Gnazio, looked after.

This was pretty good coin, all things considered. And helping to increase the capital holdings was also, no doubt, that mysterious parcel that Saverio would hide at night in the dump and then retrieve the following day.

*

'I just got back,' said Fazio, walking into the inspector's office.

'Have a seat. What did the undertakers want from you?'

'They called me because they wanted to know how they should proceed.'

'Concerning what?'

'Concerning something that happened. Before Mr Trallino – that's the man at the undertakers – went to the morgue in Montelusa to pick up Lopresti's body and put it in its coffin, a young man he didn't know brought him a letter addressed to him and a tiny little package.'

'How tiny?'

'The same size as a jeweller's box for a ring.'

'Was the name of the jeweller on the box?'

'No, Chief, there was no writing at all.'

'Go on.'

'In the letter, which was anonymous, the writer begged Mr Trallino to put the little package inside the coffin, and so Trallino called us to find out what he should do, since the request clearly wasn't being made by the wife of the deceased or anyone else from his family.'

'And so what did you say to him?'

'Well, Chief, the first thing I did was ask him to give me the letter. It had been written on a computer, and there was no signature. I've got it right here.'

He pulled an envelope out of his jacket pocket and handed it to the inspector, who opened it and spent a long time studying the letter, which said exactly what Fazio had just told him. There seemed no way to trace it back to the sender.

'Give me the package,' he said.

Fazio blushed slightly.

'I haven't got it.'

'So where is it?'

'Inside the coffin. I told Trallino myself that he could go ahead and bury it with the dead, that it wasn't a problem.'

Montalbano glared at him, feeling a bit vexed. 'Congratulations on your brilliant initiative. But did you at least open it before granting permission?'

'Yes, sir, I did. That's why I said it was OK.'

'What was inside?'

Fazio blushed more deeply this time. 'Some hair, Chief.'

'Hair?'

'Yeah.'

'What kind of hair? Blond, black, red? Boar bristle?'

'Human hair, Chief. Or, more precisely, female hair. Pubic hair.'

Montalbano blew up.

'Do you realize what you've done? We could have sent those strands of hair to the Forensics lab and, by testing the . . . you know, the stuff . . . what the hell is it called . . . ?'

'It's called DNA, Chief.'

'Tell me the truth: did you know you were doing something you shouldn't do? Did you even think it over?'

'I thought it over plenty, Chief. Long and hard. But I still decided that it was worth it.'

'Jesus Christ! Worth what?'

'Chief, we can just as easily retrace that hair to its — let's say its owner — on our own, without the help of Forensics. Whose do *you* think it is? It belongs to the late Lopresti's mistress, of course. And we already have an idea of who that might be. Right?'

'Yes, but with the help of Forensics—'

'Chief, and how were we going to get our hands on another pubic hair of Lopresti's mistress? Would we just politely ask her to drop her drawers?'

'Fazio, you're talking nonsense because you know perfectly well you made a mistake. There would have been no need whatsoever to ask the signora to drop her drawers: a hair from her head, a cigarette butt, a glass she'd drunk from would have been plenty . . .'

Fazio took a deep breath.

'You want to know the real truth, Chief?'

'I'll tell you what the real truth is. You felt sorry for her. You thought that for her to do what she'd done, they must have been very passionately in love. You dived right into a tear-jerker of a movie. And you didn't think it was right to say no to the unknown woman's request.'

'Would you have acted any differently?'

No, he would not have acted any differently. But then he asked a question that made him feel strangely ashamed.

'And what . . . colour . . .'

'Black, Chief.'

'And did you go to the funeral?'

'Of course I went. Everyone was there.'

'What do you mean, "everyone"? Give me a few examples.'

'Half the town came out for it: people from the Banca Regionale of Montelusa, of Palermo and other branches, all the members of the sporting club, the bishop's secretary, who gave a speech on Lopresti in the bishop's name . . .'

'Listen, how did the German widow act towards the wives of his three friends?'

'She acted like they weren't even there, Chief. Worse, actually. Her father, who came down from Germany, was holding her on one side, with her sister on her other side, and both of them, as soon as they saw the three friends approach with their wives, huddled together to form a barrier. The others realized there was nothing doing, and so they left without expressing their condolences.'

'So, a complete estrangement.'

'Yes, total.'

'And how did Riccardino's presumed mistress behave?'

'Adele Liotta? She was mournful and upset, breaking into tears a few times, but . . . how shall I put it? She suffered with dignity . . . No tragic scenes or shows of desperation.'

Montalbano sat and contemplated Fazio's words for a moment.

'So you're saying she didn't act like a lover who'd tragically lost the man she loved so passionately that she would want to put some of her—'

'Right, Chief. That's exactly right. And she also seemed too busy consoling her sister.'

Montalbano hesitated. 'What sister?'

'Chief, did you look at the outline I gave you? If not, you won't understand any of this. Adele's sister is called Maria, and she's married to Alfonso Licausi. Maria, for her part, was in a state of real desperation. She tried to control herself, poor thing, but couldn't. At one point she even fainted, but then immediately came to and didn't want to be escorted out of the church.'

Montalbano sat there thinking for a moment. 'Maybe she's just more emotional than her sister.'

'Right,' Fazio said drily. Too drily.

'What is it?' asked the inspector. 'You were fixated on Riccardino and Adele being lovers, so what's got into you now? Has Maria Licausi's behaviour turned your head? Then explain to me why Riccardino, moments before he was killed, rang Adele, not Maria, who, among other things, was at San Vito Lo Capo.'

'I have no explanation for that, Chief. But there is one thing I'm sure about.'

'And what's that?'

'That Adele is a natural blonde, whereas Maria's hair is black as coal.'

A heavy, thoughtful silence fell. Finally the inspector broke it.

'I need some information on two people.'

'Whatever you say, Chief.'

'The first is Saverio Milioto, a truck driver for the Cristallo mine. He lives at number 12, Via della Stazione, where he also has a small garage with two vans and a small truck, which he uses for transport and deliveries with the help of his son Gnazio.'

'Does that have anything to do with the Lopresti murder?'

'I don't think so. He's the driver who broke the pipe of Signorina—'

'Chief, are you trying to waste my time?'

'Fazio, just do as I say and don't argue. The second person is that security guard who bashed me in the head and who . . .'

Fazio chuckled.

'Did you want to bash me in the head too?'

'What are you saying, Chief?' asked Fazio. Then he added: 'He was at the funeral.'

'Who was?'

'The security guard.'

'Well, of course. He knew Riccardino, who lived—'

Fazio wagged his finger, to say no.

'He didn't just know him. They were related.'

'Related? Who were?'

'Riccardo Lopresti and the guard. They were brothers-in-law.'

Montalbano leapt out of his chair. 'What are you saying?!'

'Chief, when the security guard, who wasn't a security guard at the time, got back from Germany, where he'd been living, he brought his girlfriend, Erika, back with him. A few months later they got married, and Erika's sister Else, and her father Wolfgang, came down for the wedding. Lopresti met Else by chance on the beach and fell in love with her. They got married shortly afterwards. And that's the story.'

And that was why the guard called Else's father by name! Because he was his father-in-law.

'But how did you find these things out?'

'The security guard's behaviour with you seemed suspicious to me, and so I decided to inform myself. His name is Ettore Trupia, and it was the late Lopresti himself who got him the job as security guard.'

'What else did you find out about this Trupia?'

'He's a violent man, Chief. After getting back from Germany he found a job as a shipping agent, but one day he had a squabble with his employer and sent the guy to the hospital. Naturally, he was sacked. A few months later, he got a stint working at the fish market. But they ended up sending him home too after less than three years, because he kept getting into fights with everyone. So he went a long time without a job, until the late Lopresti found him a post as security guard. Is that enough information for you?'

'No. But tell me why the guard's behaviour seemed suspicious to you.'

'He told us that when you showed up at the gate, you acted like a bully and threatened him, and you wanted to enter at all costs . . . Is that true?'

'Absolutely.'

'And why did you act that way?'

'Because he started acting like a wise guy first, and then . . . Anyway, go on.'

'So this Trupia got suspicious, followed you on his bike, and when he saw you sneaking into the house, he sprang into action. At this point, though, I wondered: what need was there to go through all that song and dance? Why not pull out his gun, bar your entry even before raising the gate, and call the police?'

'Were those his exact words, that he saw me "sneak into the house"?'

'Yes.'

'He set me up, Fazio.'

And he told him about the fake directions the guard had given him and the fact that the Lopresti home had been unlocked so that he could go inside, thinking that Signora Else was in the house.

'But why did he do that?' asked Fazio.

'That, my friend, is the question. There are two possible explanations. The first, and simplest, is that Trupia, feeling offended because I was rude to him at the gate, set up a scenario that would allow him to get his revenge by bashing me in the head without having to pay the consequences.

Which he succeeded in doing. He acted like a good security guard. But he failed to take one thing into account.'

'And what's that?'

'That you guys were going to pummel the shit out of
him.'

'You got to understand, Chief. When we got there and
saw you sprawled out on the floor and Trupia told us he
put you there, we just spontaneously—'

'OK, but let's mention this episode as little as possible.
I don't like it. To continue. The second possible explanation
is something you lent credence to yourself, when you told
me that Riccardino and Trupia were brothers-in-law. In
other words, it's possible that Else is afraid that the affair,
or whatever it was, didn't end with Riccardino's murder
but could have further consequences. Which might involve
her directly. Was Else part of the circumstances that led
to her husband's death? Or does she merely know too
much and therefore feels threatened? Whatever the case,
she tells Trupia – in other words, her sister's husband –
that he should beware of people coming around asking
about her or coming to see her. Did she tell him why she
was afraid? We don't know. And so the security guard, not
knowing who I was, thought I was one of those people
Else was so afraid of. Make sense?'

'Makes sense. But at this point it seems more important
than ever for you to talk to Else.'

'I plan to pay her a visit tomorrow morning.'

*

Every meal is an adventure, and the success of every meal is a matter of chance. The slightest thing — an odd smell, a flavour too strong, a fly attempting to land on the plate, a neighbouring patron talking too loud — is enough to hopelessly shatter the harmony of a good meal.

That day at Enzo's everything was perfect.

And Montalbano left the trattoria raising hymns of thanks to the gods who protect good meals. He didn't know who these gods were, but they must certainly exist.

*

Heading for the jetty to take his customary stroll, he stopped for a moment to look at a truck from the Cristallo mine that was unloading salt into an enclosure paved with cement. The salt was forming a small white mountain. Also within the enclosure was a large sort of warehouse in which the salt was apparently packaged. Above the entrance to the warehouse was a sign that said Siculsal — 'Sicilian Salt'.

Walking ever so slowly, one foot up and the other foot down, he came at last to the lighthouse and sat on his customary flat rock.

According to what Fazio told him, it appeared that Riccardino's mistress was not Adele, but her sister, Maria. But then why had Riccardino phoned Adele? Maybe she served as a liaison for her sister.

Wait a second, Montalbà.

Adele and Maria were Gaspare Bonanno's sisters. Bonanno was married to Ida Liotta. And Ida was in turn Mario's sister.

As intertwined and interlinked as they all were, the men with the women and vice versa, they might all have been aware of the affair between Riccardino and Maria. All of them? Including Alfonso Licausi, who would be, so to speak, the cuckold of the arrangement? No, that could be ruled out. Completely ruled out? Maybe not, considering Alfonso's self-control when at the station. There was clearly some kind of rift between him and the other musketeers. Could it be that this rift was occasioned by Maria herself, who'd managed to gain the complicity of all the others? And why was Else the German so ill-disposed towards the group? Had she found out about her husband's relationship with Maria? And how long had the affair been going on?

Wait another second, Montalbà.

Are you so sure you're only dealing with a case of hanky-panky? Could it really be, yet again, that all this hoopla was only over a bedroom drama, as often happened on their accursed island?

Wait still another second, Montalbà.

Why then was Else afraid that something might happen to her? Why did she ask her security guard brother-in-law to protect her? If all it involved was an extramarital affair, the killer could only be Alfonso Licausi, the bishop's nephew. And that was perhaps why the bishop was worried. But it had been proved that Licausi was not at the scene of the crime. By the time he arrived, the deed had already been done. He could, of course, have hired an assassin. Else, too, could have hired an assassin, to avenge herself for her husband's cheating. But what need was there for

Else to pay an assassin when she had her brother-in-law, what's-his-name, Trupia, within reach? So there were now two names of possible suspects: Licausi and Trupia. But this was all still within the sphere of cuckoldry. And Montalbano's instinct wasn't picking up much of a scent of cuckoldry.

He got up from the flat rock feeling more confused than ever, and started heading back.

When he passed the Siculsal yard again, another truck had just finished unloading more salt. The driver was Milioto, and the inspector could see him talking intensely to someone in the cabin. It was Licausi. Montalbano continued on his way. The two men never noticed him.

ELEVEN

He hadn't even got through the front door of the police station when Catarella, all worked up and sweaty from the excitement, assailed him.

'Ahh, Chief, Chief! Hizzoner the C'mishner called twice! 'E was lookin' f'yiz to talk t'yiz poissonally in poisson! An' when ya wasn't in e'en the seccun' time neither, I tink 'e was considerately pissed off!'

'But doesn't the man ever go out for lunch? Like every other human being? And if he has no appetite, what makes him think that nobody else has any?'

The inspector had only been thinking aloud, but Catarella took his comment as a question directed to him.

'Chief, I dunno nuttin' 'bout the c'mishner's ap'tite, poissonally.'

'What did he want?'

'Chief, wit' me 'e din't dame a tell me wha' 'e wannit a tell yiz poissonally in poisson. Know wha' I mean? 'E's the c'mishner, an' I'm jess nuttin' mixed wit' zilch.'

'Cat, let me get settled in my office, and then put him on the line.'

He noticed a yellow envelope on his desk, one of those that used to be called 'business' envelopes. The address on it (to Inspector Salvo Montalbano, Chief Inspector Vigàta Police) was written all in caps with a ballpoint pen. There was no return address. Stamp postmarked Montelusa. It smelled like an anonymous letter from a mile away.

'Ya all nice 'n' sittled now, Chief?'

'Yes, Cat.'

'So, ya wan' me to put Hizzoner the C'mishner tru?'

'Yes, put him through.'

'So, Montalbano, did your little friend call you too?'

He knew immediately from the commissioner's tone, which was supposed to be sardonic, who his boss was referring to as his 'little friend'. Whenever he wanted to be witty, Commissioner Bonetti-Alderighi became simply unbearable. And so Montalbano decided to waste a little time playing with his head.

'Unfortunately, sir, he stopped calling me about two years ago,' he said, punctuating his statement with a melancholy sigh.

'What are you saying, Montalbano? Are you raving again? Two years! But just a few days ago you—'

'No, sir, I haven't heard from him for two years. And what a fine little friend he was. I met him in a sleazy theatre. He was smoking a little cigar and had a glint in his eye . . .' In truth, Sandro Penna's poem didn't call his conquest a 'little friend' but an *amoretto*, but what the hell did the good commissioner know about poets and poetry anyway?

There was no reaction at the other end of the line.

Montalbano could hear the commissioner panting rather heavily, like someone who has almost drowned and just been pulled out of the water. Then his breathing grew normal again, and he calmed down.

'You misunderstood me, Montalbano. I wasn't referring to some little friend of yours I certainly want to know nothing about, but to Bishop Partanna.'

Now I've got you, my dear commissioner! I wanted you to say that name!

Montalbano then dressed his voice up in a tone somewhere between indignant and offended.

'Mr Commissioner, do you know why I didn't understand, and indeed couldn't understand? Because never, not even in my innermost secret thoughts, have I dared consider Bishop Partanna my "little friend"! Not in a million years! His Excellency, for me, inhabits such a lofty sphere that to call him a "little friend" would actually be blasphemy!'

And what's your next move now, you moron?

Indeed, the commissioner, upon hearing that declaration of deeply devout ecclesiastical respect, was scared. He was probably saying to himself: Want to bet that Montalbano and the bishop, who clearly has many powerful connections in Rome, are indeed hand in glove? Maybe the price for being sarcastic would be a sudden transfer somewhere without running water, electricity, gas, or telephone . . .

'But, Montalbano, I, too, have nothing but profound, devout admiration . . . for a person who . . . I was just joking . . . perhaps a little too disrespectfully, I admit, but—'

'All right,' the inspector said curtly, cutting him off and feeling not only in command but also sufficiently vindicated concerning their prior encounter. 'And now tell me why His Excellency phoned you.'

'He wanted to know how the investigation was coming along. And he asked me whether it was possible to speed things up.'

'Speed things up! Easier said than done! Mr Commissioner, do you remember what Walter Lippmann, the famous American criminologist, once wrote?'

Who was this Lippmann whose name had just popped into his head? Ah, yes, a political journalist.

'Actually, right offhand . . .'

The inspector decided to improvise, savouring every moment.

'He says that every investigation has its own rhythm, its own pace, which cannot be slowed down or sped up.'

'Interesting. His Excellency, in conclusion, also said something else, which I—'

'Well, if you would tell me . . .'

'He said, and I repeat verbatim, that a hole, as long as it remains a hole, can be covered up, but if it turns into a chasm everything becomes more complicated. I didn't understand a thing. What do you think?'

'Me neither, Mr Commissioner.'

Whereas in fact he understood perfectly what the bishop's words meant.

Since the prelate's nephew and his bosom buddies were involved, he wanted the case closed as soon as possible, before it could turn into a scandal. Which meant that Bishop Partanna knew, or intuited, far more about the whole affair than he let on.

'Well, do let me know when you begin to make progress.'

'Of course, Mr Commissioner.'

*

He opened the letter. He hadn't been mistaken. The words were spelled with vowels and consonants cut out of magazines. Classic.

Montalbano,
What are you waiting for to arrest Alfonso Licausi?
Riccardo Lopresti was his wife's lover, and Licausi took revenge. Or have you come to an agreement with Bishop Partanna to keep him out of prison?
A citizen

The citizen certainly must have taken a long time cutting and pasting! There were even two question marks.

The inspector rang Fazio, who, when he appeared, was handed the letter.

'We got the solution in the post.'

Fazio read it and looked pleased.

'This confirms what I said about the behaviour of the

two sisters at the funeral,' he said. 'We were making a big mistake. Riccardo Lopresti's mistress was not . . .'

Fazio trailed off, as Montalbano had raised his hand. 'You see, Fazio, at the funeral you got an impression. There's a precise fact that runs counter to this impression, however, and a fact is very different from an impression.'

'And what's that?'

'The fact that Riccardino's last phone call, the one left in his mobile phone's memory, was to Adele Liotta. And therefore, logic would dictate that the cuckold doing the shooting should be Mario Liotta.'

'But, Chief, you yourself, when we were talking about it, said—'

'OK, so I made a different hypothesis. But at the time I hadn't yet received this anonymous letter.'

'What do you mean? That letter, though anonymous, only confirms—'

'Yes, it certainly does confirm. A little too conveniently, and at just the right time.'

Fazio narrowed his eyes to little slits. 'So you think it's all a sham?'

'I can't say for certain. But that's a possibility. Somebody's trying to guide our suspicions onto Licausi. Who is, however, indeed at the top of our list of suspects. But the opposite is also true.'

'Meaning?'

'Meaning that it's not a sham, as you call it. Either someone knows for certain that it was Licausi and wrote to us to tell us, or else the same person wants to save the real killer and is handing us Licausi on a silver platter in exchange.'

Fazio made a sort of whining sound with his mouth closed.

'What's wrong?'

'Can I speak, Chief?'

'Of course.'

'Do you mind telling me what's up with all this shilly-shallying on your part? First you say something's white, then a minute later you say it's black. And then still later you say it's grey! Are you really at such a loss about everything, or are you just trying to make me lose my mind?'

'I have no desire to drive you crazy. You need to help me try to think clearly. What can you tell me about Saverio Milioto?'

'What time is it, Chief?'

'Not yet four o'clock. Why, don't you have a watch?'

'Yeah, I've got a watch. But it was already after one o'clock when you asked me to look into Milioto. And then I went to eat, like all other human beings. What did you do, fast? Suddenly didn't feel hungry?'

Almost the exact same words Montalbano had used for the ball-busting commissioner. He felt ashamed. So he, too, was a ball-buster. Like all superiors.

'I'm sorry, Fazio, I apologize.'

*

The first and only time he'd questioned the three musketeers as witnesses, his strategy had been to act like a cross between an idiot and an airhead, which had in fact yielded a result. Which was that there had to be something which, at that moment, had made Alfonso Licausi turn defensive towards his buddies.

And he'd also resorted to the old tactic of talking to one of the witnesses alone, selected at random, and asking him meaningless questions, so that the other two, if they had something to hide, would begin to suspect him, and he them. Therefore, to get the full effect, he had to re-perform the scene with Mario Liotta.

To avoid involving Catarella, who was liable to end up calling Crystal Palace Football Club instead of the Cristallo mine, he looked the number up himself in the phone book.

'Hello? Cristallo Mine? This is Inspector Montalbano of the Vigàta Police.'

'What can I do for you, Inspector?'

'Who am I speaking to?'

'The switchboard operator. Would you like to speak to someone?'

'No, there's no need. Could you simply inform Mr Liotta that there's something urgent I'd like to talk to him about in person, at my office? For heaven's sake, please don't forget, because it's really important.'

'Not to worry, Inspector.'

'What time does Mr Liotta get off work?'

'At five-thirty.'

'Tell him I'll be waiting for him at six p.m. sharp.'

'I'll let him know.'

'Oh, and I would ask you please not to mention this phone call to anyone but Mr Liotta.'

'I'll be as silent as the grave, Inspector.'

It was crucial to play up the drama.

If he spoke directly to Liotta over the phone, the chance was that he would say nothing about it to anyone. Whereas everyone had to know about it, and everyone had to wonder what the reason was. The switchboard operator, after being exhorted to remain silent, was sure to blab about the phone call even to people who lived ten miles underground. And everyone would wonder what kind of mischief Liotta the surveyor had been up to.

Montalbano enjoyed playacting. Like all true cops. Being a good thespian was perhaps indispensable to any detective worth his salt. But you had to be very skilled.

The fun ended when the telephone rang and Catarella spoke.

'Chief, th'author-perfesser, the one 'at lives in Rome, is onna line an' 'e wants a talk t'yiz poissonally in poisson.'

What to do? Tell him to fuck himself? But the Author, who was more stubborn than a Calabrian, would never let up; he was liable to call him at home in the middle of the night.

'OK, put him on.'

'Montalbà, you haven't been straight with me,' the Author began.

His voice sounded more gravelly than usual. How many cigarettes had he smoked since their last conversation, over a hundred?

'Why do you say that?'

'Montalbà, you were sincere a few minutes ago when you told Fazio you had no desire to drive him crazy. But my question is: do you want to drive *me* crazy? Or are you, better yet, acting in such a way that everyone else — my readers, not the reviewers, who in any case don't even read my books — will think that I'm no longer in my right mind? That I've gone completely dotty? That wouldn't be so far-fetched, you know, since I'll be eighty in a few months.'

'My sincere congratulations, and many happy returns. Listen, I'm in my office and have stuff to do. I have no idea why the hell you're so fixated on the idea that I want people to believe that you can't think any more because of your age. Could you please be a little clearer?'

'I'll be as clear as you want. You're making me write a shitty novel about the story of Riccardino. It's a pile of crap that doesn't hold together.'

'Do you really mean that?'

'I really mean it. You are putting far too many contradictory elements into play and keeping them all on the same level, so that the reader gets lost in the confusion. This mystery is a big hotchpotch that reads like it was written by a beginner.'

'Are you accusing me of doing it on purpose? And what if I told you that that is exactly the way things are, and I can do nothing about it?'

'No, that's not quite the way things are. It's you who's making them be that way.'

'But for what reason would I want to muck up my own investigation?'

'Oh, you're such an innocent little lamb, Montalbà! You started already quite a while ago with the story of the two women and the man who got killed with his thing hanging out. And there you made some mistakes. I didn't realize it at the time, but some readers did. And they brought it to my attention. I already understood your intention at the time. You don't give a fuck about the logic of the investigations nor the rules you should follow. I'll say it straight out: you merely want to expose me, Montalbà. You want to scorch the earth all around me. You want my novels about you to be unreadable.'

'If that's the way you feel, can I make you an offer?'

'Let's hear it.'

'Why don't you just forget all about me, and just go and write another of those historical novels you seem to be so proud of? First you tell everyone and their dog that they're the only works of yours that matter, and then, just like that, you turn around and drop your drawers with me? You claim that I've become a burden for you. So why keep shouldering that burden?'

'Montalbà, first of all, it's not that easy for me to write a historical novel. And, secondly, I don't feel like writing one.'

'But doesn't it ever occur to you that I'm not making these mistakes on purpose to ruin your reputation? That I really do feel tired and confused?'

'Don't get all upset if I don't answer right away. We

won't have been cut off, so don't freak out the way you always do. Just give me a little time.'

'All right.'

The Author was silent for a spell. Then he spoke again.

He sounded a little worried.

'Should I really believe what you said?' he asked.

'Believe it. I'm absolutely sincere. And if you don't believe me, you can go and take it you-know-where.' Another brief silence.

'Montalbà, I've come to the conclusion that I can't trust you. And you know why? Because just now you were gloating about how good an actor you are. And so I can't help but feel you're acting with me too.'

'Well, to show you how sincere I am, I propose we make an agreement.'

'OK, let's hear it.'

'Contrary to what you think, I'm carrying on this investigation as best I can. But let's do this: if I get stuck, if I find I can't go forward or back, then I'll let you know, and you can step in. And offer me a way out. You've gained a bit of experience about detective work through me, haven't you? What do you say?'

'I'm game,' said the Author.

※

'Hello, Inspector Montalbano? This is Father Bartolino, I don't know if you remember me.'

'Of course I remember you.' And he said nothing more.

Because if you let a priest know you're at his disposal, you're screwed. If you give him an inch, he'll take a mile, a hundred miles, a thousand miles.

'His Excellency was asking if you could find another fifteen minutes . . .'

Another visit to the bishop's office? To be followed by the same fuck-you mockery from Bonetti-Alderighi? Steer clear.

'To be honest, the last few days . . . to go and see him now, for me . . . I'm terribly sorry, but . . .'

'I think you're misunderstanding me, Inspector. It was something else His Excellency wanted from you.'

You see? How can one ever guess correctly what a priest has up his sleeve?

'All right, then, what is it?'

'Well, you see, we publish a modest weekly – not modest, of course, in its contents – which is called *The Diocese*. Have you ever seen it at news-stands?'

'Yes.'

A great big lie. He'd never seen it in his life. So why had he lied? Who knew?

Maybe just to make Father Bartolino a little happy and remain in his good graces.

'Well, His Excellency is well aware, and very appreciative, of your reserve with regard to the press and television. He has often noted that you do not allow yourself to make unfounded assertions, but carefully weigh the few words that you are obliged to say.'

'Thank you.'

Where were Father Bartolino and the bishop going with this?

'Well, His Excellency would like it if you could momentarily set aside your natural reticence and agree to do an interview for our little weekly.'

'An interview on what?'

'On that horrendous crime, of course. If you accept, you will receive a fax this very evening with all the questions, in writing, that our journalist has—'

'What is this journalist's name?'

'There are no bylines for articles in *The Diocese*. Everyone's anonymous.'

Montalbano remained silent.

'If you accept,' Father Bartolino continued, 'you should send us your answers, also by fax, no later than tomorrow afternoon. The weekly will come out in three days, and His Excellency has reserved a whole page for the interview.'

'All right, then, I accept,' said the inspector, breaking into a cold sweat.

He'd understood everything. The anonymous journalist didn't exist; surely it was His Excellency the bishop who'd formulated and drafted the questions poissonally in poisson.

He wanted Montalbano to set down in writing how he viewed the murder of Riccardino. In writing, because *verba volant, scripta manent*. How had Father Bartolino put it? That he, Montalbano, carefully weighed the few words he said.

Which, translated, meant:

'Be careful what you say, Montalbano!'

Because the bishop was liable to nail him to the cross like Jesus himself, over the wrong word . . .

TWELVE

At a quarter to six, Montalbano got up to talk to Catarella.

When he opened the door of his office, he found Catarella directly in front of him, right arm raised in a kind of Roman salute.

'I's about to knack, Chief.'

'I realize that. What is it, comrade?'

'A fax jess come in. An' on top it sez i'ss a rilly rilly oigent fax.'

Catarella handed it to him. It was the text Father Bartolino had promised to send 'this very evening'. How fast they moved at the Montelusa bishop's office! He handed the fax back to Catarella without even looking at it.

'Chief, i'ss rilly rilly oigent!'

'I don't give a fuck. Listen, there's something I want you to do. In five minutes a man by the name of Liotta will arrive. Bring him into my office, then wait about ten minutes and come back, but do your usual thing: crash the door into the wall when you come in, then tell me that an extremely urgent fax has arrived.'

Catarella looked at him with saucer eyes.

'But, Chief, I jess said the same ting a minnit ago!'

'Doesn't matter, Cat. I want you to repeat it when you crash the door open. Understand?'

'Poifeckly, Chief. Bu' are ya sure ya wanna great big crash? Iss not like, aftawoids, y'er gonna get, pardon my Frinch, y'er gonna get all pissed off an' all . . .'

'Don't worry if I get pissed off. Now go and get me Galluzzo at once.'

Catarella turned his back, disappeared, and reappeared. 'Galluzzo'll be 'ere straightaways an' immediackly. Bu' 'ere was som'n I wannit a say t'yiz, Chief.'

'Say it.'

'Fer 'bout the lass fitteen minnits 'ere's been a van from the TellyVigàta channel onna pavement ousside. I ast 'em wha' they was doin' 'ere, an' 'ey said 'ey was waitin' fer Mr Liotta, the guy ya summonsed. Whaddo I do, Chief, chasten 'em away?'

The mine's switchboard operator certainly hadn't wasted any time selling the news to the TV people! Which worked out just fine for the inspector.

'No, leave them alone.'

Catarella went out, Galluzzo came in.

'Listen, a person I called in for questioning will be arriving at six. I want you, at exactly six-twenty, to come in and say you absolutely need me for something. Got that?'

'Got it.'

*

As soon as he had Liotta in front of him, Montalbano
decided to change, in part, the strategy he'd devised. Because
while Liotta had indeed been in a state of turmoil when
the inspector questioned him at the station right after the
killing, he was nevertheless able to react and think ration-
ally, whereas now he didn't seem like the same man. He'd
lost a few pounds, his skin tone was verging on yellow,
and his hands trembled a little.

Would he be able to answer questions sensibly?

Montalbano decided that it would be best to take advantage of the deteriorated state Liotta was in, even if this
made him feel a little disgusted with himself.

He filled his lungs with air and began his attack openly.

'Mr Liotta, as I'm sure you'll remember, on the morning
of the murder, the late Riccardino, seeing that Licausi was
late, called him on his mobile phone. He dialled the wrong
number, but was convinced he'd spoken to him and then
told the rest of you that Licausi was on his way. Those
were his last words, because, a moment later, the killer
shot him dead. What I want to know from you is how
much time passed between the end of Riccardino's statement and the gunshot. If you're able to tell me, of course.'

Liotta coughed and cleared his throat, then took out a
handkerchief and mopped his brow. It visibly cost him
some effort to begin speaking, but as the words began to
come out of his mouth, he seemed to gain confidence.
And Montalbano realized that the man's brain was still
functioning, despite appearances.

'The first time we spoke, Inspector, I was too confused,

too disoriented. But I still can't get that scene out of my head. I even dream about it at night. Do you believe me?'

'Of course I do.'

'And because I've been thinking it over and over, I now have a very clear, sharp image of it before my eyes. And I can say with certainty that the shot was fired immediately Riccardino had finished talking; I would even say as soon as he'd said the last syllable, since both Gaspare and I were still facing him and therefore didn't see the killer as he was shooting him. And Riccardino didn't see it coming, because he was talking to us and looking at us.'

'Now I need to ask a very important question, and I would like you please to think carefully before answering.'

Liotta ran his tongue over his lips. And swallowed with some effort. He looked extremely tired.

'Could I have some water?'

At the top of a completely empty metal filing cabinet there was sometimes a bottle of mineral water and two glasses, sometimes not. This time there was.

Montalbano stood up, filled a glass, and gave it to Liotta, who took it and was about to bring it to his mouth when all at once a great crashing noise shook the room with a boom not unlike a bomb blast.

A few things occurred simultaneously. Liotta gave a start, the glass fell from his hand, crashed to the floor, shattering, he tried to stand up, his legs gave out, and he fell to his knees in the puddle of spilled water. Meanwhile, framed by the jamb of the half-unhinged door, white with chalk and plaster chips, Catarella stood in triumph.

'Ya gat a fax, Chief!' he shouted.

Along with Catarella, Liotta, still on his knees, also started yelling, as a shard of glass had torn through his trousers and lodged itself in his left leg, which was bleeding.

'Ya gat a fax, Chief!' Catarella repeated, just to be sure.

Montalbano exploded. It's true he'd been seeking a certain psychological effect with the door crashing open, but this was too much of a good thing. He kicked the desk so hard that it hurt, then cursed.

'Get the hell out of here!' he yelled at Catarella.

But, instead of leaving, he stepped into the room, went up to the inspector, then spoke to him conspiratorially in a soft voice.

'Chief, lemme know so's I can ack accoidinly: are ya rilly pissed off, or jess pretennin'?'

Montalbano seized him by the shoulders, turned him around on his feet, and pushed him out of the door and straight into a collision with Gallo and Galluzzo, who'd come running.

'What happened? What's going on?' they asked.

'Galluzzo, please give this man a hand; he's hurt himself. Then bring him back here. Gallo, get someone to clean this up. I'm going to smoke a cigarette.'

He left in a rage. Seeing him appear, Catarella crouched behind his desk.

Once outside the door, Montalbano set fire to a cigarette. And he realized that from inside the TeleVigàta van a cameraman was filming him. He let him film away. After finishing his cigarette, he went back inside. Opening the door to his office, he saw Liotta sitting again opposite the desk. There was a scent of spirits in the air. Apparently Galluzzo had disinfected and dressed Liotta's cut.

'Do you feel up to continuing?'

'Yes.'

'Moments ago you stated that the scene of the murder has remained clearly imprinted in your memory. Good. The last time you told me that Riccardino, after the phone call, was almost in the middle of the street, and you and your friend were on the pavement. Correct?'

'Yes.'

'Do you remember Riccardino's exact posture?'

'I'm sorry, but in what sense?'

'For example, what was he doing with his hands as he was talking to you?'

Liotta remained silent for a moment. Then he asked:

'May I stand up?'

'Of course.'

He stood up, moved away from the chair, and covered his eyes with one hand.

He was muttering something to himself. Then he stopped, put one hand in his pocket, pulled out his mobile phone, and froze.

'He was just like this, stock-still.'

Liotta kept his right arm extended along his side, the mobile phone still in his hand. His left arm was slightly bent and open outwards, towards those he was speaking to.

'Were the three of you all in a line?'

'Not exactly. Riccardino was a bit further up the street from us and was turned three-quarters as he spoke to us. Can I sit down again?'

'Yes. So therefore you couldn't see Riccardino's hand holding the mobile phone?'

'No. But is that important?'

'Very important.'

'Why?'

'Because as he was speaking to you, Riccardino had time to dial another number. We know this from his mobile phone's memory. It was a number he knew well, well enough to dial it without looking at the keypad.'

Liotta looked at him, wide-eyed and surprised. 'Are you sure about that, Inspector?'

'Absolutely certain. I repeat: it's in the memory.'

'But he didn't have the time to talk, that much I know.'

'I think you're right. But, you see, Riccardino didn't necessarily want to talk.'

'Then why would he dial the number?'

'I don't know. The ring might have been a prearranged signal, a silent greeting. People do that sometimes. Between friends . . . between lovers . . .'

Liotta opened his mouth and then closed it. He was sweating profusely.

'Don't you have any idea of who Riccardino might have been sending that signal to? Someone with whom he was on intimate terms?'

'Why . . . why do you say that Riccardino must have been on intimate terms with the person to whom he . . . ?'

He trailed off, as if he suddenly hadn't the strength to go on, then mopped his brow with his handkerchief.

'Because of the time of day, Mr Liotta. You don't call someone at that hour if you're not on intimate terms with them. If the term "intimate" bothers you, I can find something else to use. I could say, "If he wasn't in a close relationship" or "If he wasn't on familiar terms" . . .'

'Why . . . why should that bother me?'

'That was my impression.'

There was a knock at the door. Galluzzo stuck his head inside. Perfect timing.

'What is it?' the inspector asked sharply.

'Sorry to bother you, Chief, but Fazio has arrested that person you mentioned . . . It might be a good moment . . .'

'Oh, really? Good. I'll be right with you. I'm afraid I'm going to have to absent myself for fifteen minutes or so, half an hour at the most. Do you need anything? Would you like a newspaper to read?'

Resigned, Liotta shook his head.

Montalbano stood up, reached the door, but then stopped without speaking. Liotta, who was keeping his head down, sensed his presence and looked up at him. Then, following the best detective-movie scripts, beginning with those featuring Columbo, he fired his last shot before leaving.

'You know whose number Riccardino dialled, don't you?'

He left the door half-open behind him and said to Galluzzo:

'Post a guard here. He mustn't leave the room. If he protests, call me.'

'And where are you going?'

'To Augello's office. After all, Mimì's not back yet, is he? Is the TeleVigàta newsman still around?'

'Yeah, Chief.'

In a drawer of Mimì Augello's desk he found an old issue of *La Settimana Enigmistica*, the puzzle magazine, where there were still some crossword puzzles, rebuses, and an investigative problem to be solved. It was the latter that ultimately stumped him, after he'd worked the other ones out in half an hour. No matter how much he studied and studied the figures illustrating the problem, no matter how much he read and reread the dialogue, he couldn't understand a damn thing. He started getting upset. Somebody knocked lightly at the door.

'Come in!'

Catarella appeared, still a bit spooked from what had happened.

He was holding the fax from the bishop's office in his hand. 'Chief, I's tinkin' . . .'

'Wait, I want you to tell me something first, I'm curious. When you knock on Augello's door, do you always knock that way?'

'Why? 'Ow'd I knack?'

'Delicately. Whereas when you knock on my door you practically demolish it.'

'Chief, the fack is, yer door makes my 'and slip.'

'What do you want?'

'I tought I'd bring yiz the fax, jess to 'elp yiz pass the time.'

'Thanks. That was a good idea. Wait just a second. Here, have a look at this. Think you can solve this investigative problem?'

He handed him the magazine. Catarella started reading, moving his lips soundlessly. It took him only one reading and one look at the drawings.

'Chief, the killer's most soitanly the guy wit' the beard an' glasses. Ya wanna know why?'

'No!' Montalbano shouted angrily.

Catarella vanished after putting the fax and the magazine on the desk. Montalbano picked up the latter and set his mind again to solving the investigative problem. After five minutes, he came to the conclusion, cursing the saints, that Catarella's answer was right. He put down *La Settimana Enigmistica* and picked up the fax, and at that moment there was a knock at the door. It was Fazio.

'Got news for me?'

'Yeah.'

'Sit down and tell me about it.'

'I've got something big, Chief. I'll start with the truck driver, Saverio Milioto. He's been working at the mine for the past ten years or so. But until three years ago, things weren't going so well for him.'

'The mine doesn't pay their drivers well?'

'They pay them, as far as that goes. But Milioto had, and still has, a gambling addiction. And he belongs to the category of those who always lose.'

'And what does he play?'

'Lansquenet, *sfilapippi*, the usual games of chance. There are at least four clandestine gambling dens in town; they run from the fanciest, which is luxurious and reserved for rich people, to the seediest, which is for the poor.'

'And where, proportionally speaking, do people play the most? Which kind of gambling den does Milioto frequent?'

'Can I answer that question in a minute?'

'All right, go on.'

'Then, three years ago, Milioto's situation changed.'

'How?'

'He started having a lot more money. He paid off the debts that were weighing him down and told everyone that the wheel of fortune had finally started turning in his direction. And as a gambler, he rose in rank. He went from the bottom gambling den to the second one from the top, the one for the rich.'

'And how were things going for him in reality?'

'I don't know how things were going, at first. Somebody was clearly giving him that money, but I was unable to find out who or why. Then he was granted a big loan by the Banca Regionale.'

'By Riccardo Lopresti?'

'Yes indeed. The loan enabled Milioto to buy himself an apartment with a garage, two vans, and a car. There was another car he already had.'

'But how is this possible? If I go into a bank and ask for a loan, if I can offer no guarantees, they'll just—'

'Chief, but Milioto had people guaranteeing for him . . .'

And so saying, Fazio, his eyes sparkling, took a deep breath, the better for the bomb to burst.

'Stop!' Montalbano ordered him. 'I understand everything! The people vouching for Milioto were Mario Liotta, Gaspare Bonanno, and Alfonso Licausi.'

Fazio released his breath in frustration. He grew limp. 'Bull's-eye, Chief,' he said. 'But every damn time, you manage to rob me of the pleasure of surprising you.'

'Are any of the three related to Milioto?'

'No.'

'Did you find any indications that they were friends with Milioto?'

'No.'

'Do you know whether they made any similarly generous gestures to other associates of the mine?'

'No, I didn't find anything.'

'Still, it's clear that there's something linking them together. But what?'

'That's just it, Chief.'

'And what can you tell me about Ettore Trupia, the security guard?'

'I didn't have time to look into him,' Fazio said resentfully.

'Well, just to keep the conversation going, who told you all these things about Milioto?'

'A man he works with, another truck driver from the Cristallo mine by the name of Milluso. Just three months ago, the same Banca Regionale denied him a loan for an amount that was peanuts compared to what they gave Milioto.'

'Are you sure that driver is telling the truth and not just envious?'

'I did some cross-checking. You can rest easy, Chief. I never entirely trust something only one person tells me. You still need me?'

Fazio was sulking. He felt offended by Montalbano's questioning the reliability of Milluso the truck driver's statements.

'No, thanks. Send me Galluzzo.'

It was now half-past eight in the evening.

'Gallù, how's Liotta behaving?'

'The guard said he's still sitting there, not even moving. Just now he asked to go to the toilet, and so he went and came back without saying a word.'

'Did you escort him?'

Galluzzo stared at him.

'Chief, the man's not under arrest!'

That was true. But, for whatever reason, the inspector was still unconvinced, even though it was perfectly normal for Liotta to feel the call of nature after a three-hour wait.

'Let's let him stew for another hour.'

After Galluzzo left, Montalbano crossed his arms on the desk, laid his head down on them, and started to doze. Every so often he would look at his watch. Time seemed to be standing still. And if it seemed that way for him, what about for Liotta?

Finally nine-thirty came. He got up, opened the door to his office, and went and sat down. Liotta was staring at the floor.

'I apologize for having kept you here all this time. Something unexpected came up.'

Only then did Liotta raise his head slowly and look at him.

'Why did you say I know the person whose number Riccardino dialled?'

'It's quite simple, Mr Liotta. Because you didn't ask me the one question you should have, the question any other person would naturally and logically have asked. Which was: who did Riccardino call?'

THIRTEEN

Liotta opened his mouth to say something in reply, and at that exact moment, loud and distorted, the first notes of the triumphal march of Verdi's *Aida* resounded in the room.

Montalbano recoiled, took a look around, then realized that it was the ringtone of a mobile phone, turned up to full volume. The one Liotta was now calmly extracting from the inside pocket of his jacket.

'Hello?' he said.

He listened for a moment, then said by way of conclusion: 'OK, I'll be waiting for you.'

He then turned his phone off, put it back in his pocket, and solemnly said:

'I'm not going to say another word until my lawyer gets here. He told me he's on his way.'

Montalbano cursed the saints in his head. He hadn't been convinced by the story of him needing to go to the toilet. But they couldn't very well have refused him. There was nothing to be done.

'You called him when you went to the loo, right?'

'Yes, but my lawyer's phone was turned off. And so I called him at home and explained everything to his wife.'

Now the phone on the desk started ringing.

'Ahh, Chief, ahh, Chief, Chief! 'Ere's procusitter Tommasaneo onna line an' 'e wants a speak t'yiz oigently in oigency an' poissonally in poisson an' from 'is verse 'e sounz jess like a rapid dog!'

He picked up the phone as a deluge of curses cascaded in his head.

'Montalbano? This is Tommaseo. What the fu . . . hell are you up to over there? I got a call just now from Mario Liotta's lawyer.'

'What did he want?'

'What do you mean, "What did he want?" Don't you know? Apparently you've detained his client without my authorization, and without even telling me! You don't even deign to keep me informed! You always leave me in the dark! Release him at once!'

'I promise I'll fill you in on everything tomorrow morning. As for releasing him, I can't, because—'

'What do you mean, you can't?! That's an order, Inspector!'

'If you would let me finish . . . I can't release him in that I never arrested him. I merely had him come in for an informal chat. If I didn't go to talk to him at his own workplace it was to avoid gossip and insinuations . . . out of respect for the gentleman's privacy, really. At any rate, as I said, tomorrow morning I'll send you a detailed report.'

He hung up.

And complimented himself for the phrase 'the gentleman's privacy'.

Then he stood up and turned to Liotta.

'It's getting late,' he said. 'I'm going home. Will you wait here for your lawyer?'

And he went out.

The moment he stepped out of the building, he was assailed by a violent floodlight treacherously aimed straight at his eyes. It was the TeleVigàta crew, the newsman and cameraman.

'Inspector Montalbano, do you have anything to say to us?'

'Yes. Good night to all.'

*

He'd been back at home in Marinella for barely half an hour but had already emptied the refrigerator to quell the wolflike hunger mauling his stomach. Generous helpings of *pasta e fasoli*, sweet-and-sour anchovies, and Ragusan *caciocavallo* cheese allowed him to set his hand calmly, without agitation or curses, to writing the report he'd promised Tommaseo. The key was to include certain typical details likely to stoke and arouse the prosecutor's imagination and set him down a road different from the one the inspector wanted to continue to travel alone.

At half-past midnight, however, he took a break to watch the late-night newscast of TeleVigàta. The anchorman gave a rather dramatic account of the situation as a sequence of images flashed on the video behind him: Liotta going into the police station, Montalbano outside the door smoking a cigarette, Liotta's lawyer going inside in turn, in the dark of night and on the run, saying 'no comment' to the newsman's questions, Montalbano again, wishing a good night to all, Liotta coming out limping and frowning darkly, while the lawyer at his side repeats 'no comment'. The anchorman stated that in connection with the investigation into the murder of the manager of the Vigàta branch of the Banca Regionale, Riccardo Lopresti, a close friend of his, Mario Liotta, a surveyor by profession, had been subjected to an exhausting interrogation for no less than five hours at the Vigàta commissariat. The interrogation must have become particularly fraught at certain moments, because shortly after it had started, even outside the building Inspector Montalbano could be heard shouting and hurling expletives, and a number of police officers were seen rushing about.

When he came out, as the viewing audience could see, Mario Liotta was quite visibly limping.

Could it be that Inspector Montalbano had used heavy-handed methods with him? Was it acceptable for such a thing to happen? TeleVigàta would investigate the matter.

Whatever the case, the newsman concluded, a decisive turning point in the investigation had perhaps been reached. Around town people were saying that the motive behind the murder might be one of passion, and the repeated 'no comments' of the lawyer only managed, all things considered, to confirm the vox populi.

That was exactly how he said it: vox populi.

Whatever the case, Montalbano reasoned, Liotta's lawyer, who from the TV images appeared to be the same age as the musketeers, had made a mistake. He should have answered the journalist in the following manner, and in this order: by attacking (1) the magistrature, which was made up of people sick in the head and genetically unlike the rest of humanity; (2) the police, who when they became fixated on an idea were capable of fabricating false evidence to support it; (3) the communists, because Mario Liotta was a practising, observant Catholic; (4) illegal immigrants from outside and inside Europe, who made the crime rates in our country soar; and, of course, (5) the terrorists, who were intent upon destroying by any means the Christian values of the West. Surely a good half of the viewers would come away thinking that Liotta had been the victim of an abuse of power by law enforcement. By instead naively saying 'no comment', the lawyer was authorizing everyone to think the worst of his client.

He resumed writing his report ad hoc and *ad personam*, just to keep with the Latin theme initiated by the TV anchorman. It took him an hour. He reread it. It turned out to be a small masterpiece of erotic literature that was certain to have Tommaseo licking his lips, as the prosecutor loved to wallow in these kinds of details.

He wrote that Liotta's wife, Adele, a woman with a big sexual appetite (*he'd made that up just then, but Tommaseo would be pleased*), was in all probability the mistress of Riccardo

Lopresti, the murder victim. It was impossible to keep their fleshly congress a secret, in that the woman was in the habit, while performing the act, of shouting and screaming the pleasure she felt. On one occasion the carabinieri had even come to the scene, thinking she was being strangled.

It was therefore logical to conjecture that the person ordering the hit might be the betrayed husband: that is, Mario Liotta. However, apparently a manoeuvre to muddy the waters had been put into play, shifting suspicion away from Liotta and onto Alfonso Licausi. This manoeuvre consisted of making it seem as if Lopresti's mistress was not Adele, but her sister Maria, who was in fact Licausi's wife, and equally endowed with a highly sensual female temperament (*have fun, Tommaseo!*).

At this point, throwing down his ace, Montalbano cut loose with a lyrical, moving description of the colour of the pubic hair mentioned by Fazio and undoubtedly belonging to Maria, who had jet-black hair, whereas Adele was blonde, detailing how it had been sent in a jeweller's box to the undertakers to be placed in Riccardo Lopresti's coffin, in perpetual memory of their volcanic couplings. In addition, he devoted a few lines to the difference between blonde and black pubic hair, the first being notoriously indicative of long, exhausting lascivious relations (*that's right, Tommaseo, lascivious*), while the latter was more a sign of angry, animalesque copulations.

So, to conclude, what was the good inspector asking of the most excellent magistrate Tommaseo? To put the implacable screws on Mario Liotta, to his shapely consort, Adele, and again to his even shapelier sister-in-law, Maria, in order to ascertain:

1. whether the supposedly repeated consummation of adulterous congress between the abovementioned woman and the deceased (when, obviously, the deceased still belonged to the ranks of the living) corresponded to the truth;
2. in the event of a proven negative to the above question, obtain necessary elucidations as to why Lopresti, an instant before being rendered deceased by a still unknown hand, dialled the telephone number of the Liotta home while knowing with absolute certainty that the call could only be taken by the aforesaid Mrs Adele Bonanno Liotta;
3. in the event of a verified affirmative, penetrate the defences of the abovementioned Adele (*'penetrate' was exactly the right verb for Tommaseo*) and ascertain whether her husband had eventually learned of her relationship with the deceased, and what his reaction had been.

And that was all, with all due deference.

It was almost two o'clock in the morning, and he still wasn't the least bit sleepy. He didn't feel like reading a novel, either. How about a late-night movie on TV? No. What, then? Maybe, he thought, this wouldn't be a bad time to answer Bishop Partanna's fax. Which no doubt would contain contorted, convoluted labyrinthine logic and in any case dangerous questions.

Was he sufficiently lucid to rise to the level of a bishop who carried, imprinted in his DNA, the memory of the Holy Inquisition?

He decided he was.

He looked for the fax in his pockets, on the table, in the car, but couldn't find it. Then he remembered that he'd left it on Mimì Augello's desk.

Then he had what he thought was a good idea. It took him half an hour to find, about the house, the things he needed, and then he went out, got in the car, and drove off.

＊

Seen from above, the little apartment blocks of Borgonovo, bordered on one side by total nothingness, or rather by a sort of miniature Sahara, and on the other by the vast rubbish dump, looked as if they'd taken fright and were huddling together for safety. At that hour of the night, he didn't expect to find any more hookers or drug addicts on the streets; at most he might run into a burglar or two coming from or going to a job. The foul stench of the dump began to make itself felt inside his nostrils already a good half-mile away.

He stopped the car at the start of the little street on which the fortune-teller lived, took his revolver and a large torch out of the glove compartment, put them both in his jacket pockets, quietly closed the car door, and wrapped a large kerchief around his mouth and nose, knotting it behind his head to hold it fast. The stink passed through just the same, though a bit attenuated. Then he took a small folding ladder out of the boot, loaded it onto his shoulders, and headed off.

He didn't see a living soul anywhere, except for two dogs and three cats.

Reaching the open area with the street lamp, he looked up and glanced at the building in which the saintly man lived. All the windows and French windows were closed, all the lights turned off. And so he planted the ladder under the RS of 'ARSE', which was the exact spot the saintly man had indicated to him. He climbed up, straddled the top of the wall, pulled the ladder up behind him, lowered it on the other side, climbed down, and turned on the torch.

And saw horror.

Rats the size of tabby cats, long-haired rats that could be mistaken for Pekingese dogs, rats with three-foot-long tails, rats with corkscrew tails like pigs, rats with tiger teeth, rats with elephant tusks, rats with wild beastly red eyes, hundreds of them, all around his feet not giving a fuck that he was watching them frozen in terror and disgust.

Casting the torch beam around him, he immediately spotted what he was looking for, luckily only a few centimetres away: a large parcel of heavy cardboard bound with tape. In addition it had a thin rope wound around it and tied in a bow.

Turning the beam towards the wall, Montalbano noticed that beside his ladder was a long stick with a sort of harpoon at the end. Apparently the truck driver used it to recover the package.

Summoning his courage, Montalbano carefully bent down to pick up the parcel, and at once the rats became menacing. First they began squeaking very excitedly, then two or three leapt at Montalbano's hand, teeth bared, ready to bite.

Bite? With their size and those teeth, the rats were liable to lop his fingers right off. The inspector wasted no time, and in any case there was no other solution. Digging his revolver out of his pocket, he fired in the rats' direction. One he hit squarely, and the others scurried away, but Montalbano was convinced they would return immediately. He approached the package and squatted to have a better look at it.

There was a sort of buckling in the wrapping on top, which the beam of the torch made more visible. Montalbano ran a finger over its contours.

And everything became clear to him.

There must have been a large jerry can inside the package, big enough to hold twenty-five litres at the very least. Plucking up courage, he removed the kerchief from his face and bent down almost far enough for his nose to touch the parcel. And he sniffed.

Diesel. No doubt about it.

He covered his nose and mouth again, began climbing back up the ladder, and as soon as his head was above the top of the wall, he froze.

The saintly man and clairvoyant fortune-teller, apparently troubled by the sound of a gunshot during their abominable amatory exercises, had gone to the French windows to see if they could see anything. The holy man was actually peering through a pair of binoculars like a sea captain.

What to do? Wait with saintly patience for the two lovers to get bored with the fact they couldn't see anything and return to the matter at hand? After barely thirty seconds, however, Montalbano heard some furious squeaks nearby and rapidly coming towards his feet. The rats were returning with evil intent, perhaps to avenge their slain comrade, unless of course they were already eating him.

Montalbano cocked his revolver again, raised his arm, and fired in the air.

The effect was immediate: the saintly man and the fortune-teller vanished from sight and turned off the bedroom light. But the inspector didn't fall into the trap. Surely those two were still watching, gazing out from the darkness. So he aimed at the street lamp and put it out with one shot.

With the help of the torch, which he turned on every few seconds, he reversed his previous manoeuvre, hoisted the ladder onto his shoulders, and ran to his car.

Only when he began driving away did he realize he'd damaged public property for nothing. With his face wrapped in the kerchief, there was no way in the world the saintly man and fortune-teller would ever have recognized him.

*

When he got home, he didn't feel like going into the house with his clothes on, and so outside the front door he undressed completely, left his clothing, underwear, and shoes outside, and then went in and got immediately into the shower, where he stayed for half an hour. Unsatisfied with this, he wiped his body down with cotton wool and surgical spirit, then showered again.

There was a knock at the door. Who could it be at this hour of the grey and dawning day? Surely someone from the station. But why hadn't they called him on the phone? Then he remembered that he'd unplugged it before getting down to writing the report for Tommaseo, and he'd never plugged it back in afterwards. Wrapping a towel around his loins, he went to open the door.

The first thing he saw was an enormous motorcycle, gleaming with chrome, the front wheel of which was pressing so hard against the door that when he opened it, the vehicle came partly inside.

The man driving it was wearing a motorcycling suit and full helmet. Montalbano was certain he was the same man who had killed Riccardino. He felt less afraid than amazed. What could he want from him? He certainly hadn't come to give himself up.

Before the inspector could ask him anything, the man spoke. His voice sounded muffled but clear.

'May I come in?'

Two things flashed through Montalbano's mind.

The first was that he was naked and unarmed, in front of a likely killer.

The second was that even if he managed to come out of this alive, with perhaps some serious injury, Livia would have crushed his balls for all of eternity with the question: 'How many times have I told you to install a peephole in your front door?'

'I was sent by Bishop Partanna,' the motorcyclist continued.

'Come on in,' said the inspector, standing aside.

The man entered, still straddling the motorcycle. When he reached the dining room table, he put one foot on the floor, and leaned on the table with his left hand.

'His Excellency wants to know if you've answered his fax.'

Not remotely expecting such a question, Montalbano stammered.

'Well, I still haven't managed to find the time to . . . But please reassure His Excellency that as soon as I—'

'I'm sorry, but time's up,' said the motorcyclist, sticking one hand inside his suit.

The revolver he extracted was enormous and shiny. Maybe it was made by the same factory that built the motorcycles. Taking aim at the inspector, the motorcyclist raised his hand from the table and removed his helmet.

Beneath it was a rat's head, furry and wet, and as large as a man's. Horrendous. He was laughing, was the motor-cycle rat, flashing teeth as sharp as razors.

Crying out in terror, Montalbano woke up.

And he realized that there was no point, after that nightmare, in staying in bed. Any chance of sleep had vanished. He got up, went into the kitchen, prepared his customary mugful of coffee, and went and shaved as it was brewing. It was six o'clock in the morning.

*

Sitting out on the veranda, he drank his first cup.

It was a clear but coolish day, without wind, and the sea looked as if it didn't have the strength to wake up. The surf lapped the shore slowly, lazily, splashing sleepily.

What could his dream have meant?

Clearly it was some kind of gross synthesis of two stories that had both frightened him, each in a different way.

The first was the business of the fax, which he hadn't been able, or hadn't wanted, even to read.

The second was the descent into the inferno of the dump and the attack of the rats. Apparently he hadn't been able to work it all out, as those who understood these things liked to put it.

But how could something so simple and inoffensive as a fax become part of a nightmare?

Might it be a distant memory of his Catholic education, according to which the fact of not taking into immediate consideration the request of a churchman with a bishop's rank could be seen as a lack of respect?

No, the reason had to be something much more serious. In the dream, he'd immediately understood that the motorcyclist was the man who had shot Riccardino.

OK. But the motorcyclist's intention in coming to his house was not to shoot him right away.

He wanted first to know whether he'd answered the fax. And if Montalbano had happened to say yes, he would have turned his bike around and driven away. But since he hadn't answered the question, the motorcyclist was about to kill him.

Which meant that the bishop's fax was in no way a journalistic matter, but a matter of life and death.

Right? Right.

And so? And so the first thing to do, the minute he got to the office, was to run and read the fax and try to understand it in some way.

But had he really needed to rack his brains so much to reach that conclusion?

A question popped treacherously into his head: how would the other Montalbano, the one on TV, have acted?

The bitter answer was that he, damn him, would certainly not have left the fax on Mimì's desk.

This ruined the inspector's day.

FOURTEEN

When he left home it wasn't even seven a.m., but as soon as he turned onto the road to Vigàta, he realized that the situation was hopeless.

Dozens and dozens of trucks, cars, even a car transporter, bumper to bumper and athwart one another. The traffic jam looked like a rope full of knots that it would take at least two hours to disentangle. All he could do was be patient and sit tight; at any rate, he had plenty of cigarettes in his pocket.

It was past nine by the time he finally got to the station, and he immediately raced into Mimì Augello's office.

His heart sank. The desktop was clean as a whistle. There wasn't a single sheet of paper on it. He opened the drawers to see if someone had put it in one of them, but only found Mimì's papers there. He looked on the floor, under the desk to see if it had fallen. The floor was polished and shining. He was scared to death.

'Catarella!'

It wasn't so much a yell as the roar of a wild animal.

He didn't have time to complete the last syllable before Catarella materialized with his eyes all a-goggle with worry.

'Yer orders, sah!'

'Did the cleaning ladies perchance come this morning?'

'Yessir, Chief. At seven-toity onna dat.'

'And did they come in here?'

'Assolutely, Chief.'

The cursed traffic jam! If there hadn't been one, he would have arrived in time.

'Do you know where they throw out the rubbish?'

'Inna street righ' behin' 'iss buildin', Chief. The street's called Via Tòccali, an' 'iss gat four bins.'

'Do you know at what time of day they're emptied?'

'Chief, the rubbige truck normally comes rounnabout six inna evenin'.'

Montalbano made a snap decision.

'Everyone present and available in the office must come with me!'

He ran out of the building in a rage, followed by Catarella and eight uniformed officers.

Racing out to the street behind the station, whose name was naturally Via Dògali, he stopped in front of the bins.

'There's a shop around here that sells washing-up gloves. Go and buy two pairs for each person. I'll pay for them myself. Then hurry back, close the street off if the cars driving past start to bother you, and empty out all these bins. We absolutely have to find a fax addressed to me with some questions from a journalist. Now get busy.'

Never in a million years would he, for any reason, ask

the bishop's office to send a copy of the fax. The churchmen might get offended.

He called Catarella aside.

'In a little while I'm going to interrogate someone. You absolutely have to find the fax, even if it takes all day. You can give it to me when I get back.'

✳

A sudden treacherous thought stabbed him in the back as he was getting into the car: with which woman would the other Montalbano, the one on TV, have started the questioning?

Surely with the wife of Mario Liotta.

All right, then, he would call on Riccardino's widow first.

But he'd forgotten her name.

Cursing the saints, he got out of the car, went into the office, and looked at his papers.

Her name was Else Hohler.

As he was heading out of the office, the phone rang.

'Hi. It's me.'

'No, listen. This isn't a good time. I was on my way out to—'

'I know, to go and talk to the widow. And I also know why you're starting with the German lady. You want to do the exact opposite of what the other Montalbano would do. Did you know that you're banal, boringly banal?'

'Me? Why?'

'Because this desire to challenge, to fight your double is

nothing new. The story's been told and retold. Novels have been written about it, beautiful ones, even masterpieces. Werfel, Jean Paul, Maupassant, Poe, and if you read Foucault's essay on Raymond Roussel, you'll find—'

'Stop right there. A good while ago, I obeyed the command of Baudrillard: Forget Foucault.'

'You put up a good fight, Inspector. But let's end it right here. I can't show off too much erudition, since I'm considered a genre writer. Or, more precisely, a commercial genre writer. To the point that my books are even sold in supermarkets. But to return to the subject at hand, I want to warn you: you should be careful. The kind of wrestling match you're engaged in always ends up with the double winning. And you're not in any condition to constitute an exception.'

'Are you so sure about that?'

'Just think. The other Montalbano, whenever he appears on TV, has millions and millions of people watching him and cheering for him, whereas you, whenever a new novel comes out, might get a maximum of five hundred thousand readers.'

'And that's how you, of all people, view this thing? So that's all that matters to you? Numbers, print runs, TV and radio? Then I guess those who write in the papers are right when they say that you're not even a genre writer, but a product of the mass media.'

'But don't you realize how many of those who accuse me of being a product of the mass media – which is utterly untrue: if anything, my success is the result of word

of mouth – would desperately love to be products of the
mass media themselves? Do you know the fable of the fox
and the grapes?'

'Listen, I don't have any more time to waste. What did
you want?'

'I wanted to tell you that I may have found a solution
to this case.'

'Oh, come on!'

'But, since you haven't got the time right now, I'll call
you at home this evening.'

*

No, come to think of it – he said to himself at the wheel
of his car – it wasn't only the desire to proceed differently
from the other Montalbano that had made him choose
the German woman for the first round of questioning.

He knew perfectly well that even when he thought he
was acting according to instinct or out of spite, there was
always, deep down – so far down that it almost never came
to the surface – a logical, rational motive. In this case his
brain was telling him that interrogating Adele Liotta would
be a waste of time and he would have nothing to show
for it. She would wildly deny ever having been Riccardino's
mistress. Whereas there was a great deal that might be
drawn out of his widow.

*

Inside the guard's booth stood Ettore Trupia, who, on
recognizing him, gave him a dirty look but said nothing.

He merely raised the barrier, which meant that his sister-in-law was at home.

The gate to her little garden was wide open. The front door of her house was not.

He rang the doorbell, and at once a thirtyish housekeeper in slippers came to the door, wiping her hands on her apron.

'I'm Inspector Montalbano, of Vigàta Police. I would like to speak to Mrs Lopresti.'

'Please come in.'

The maid led him into a sitting room so anonymous that it looked as if they had bought whole, and wholesale, the waiting room of a high-class clinic. Removing her apron, she sat down in an armchair.

'What can I do for you, Inspector?' Montalbano's eyes popped open.

So she was Else? . . . Riccardino's wife?

Here he'd been expecting some sort of blonde Valkyrie, while there before him sat a plain little woman, poorly dressed, with dishevelled pitch-black hair, looking like a girl born and raised in some godforsaken village in Tunisia. On top of that, she spoke Italian without the slightest German accent.

The woman realized what he was thinking.

'You imagined me different, didn't you?'

'Yes, I did,' admitted the inspector.

'My sister, who's married to Ettore, the security guard you met – I was told about what happened, by the way, he told me himself, I'm so sorry, it was all a terrible misunderstanding, I'd gone to pick up my father, who—'

'I know, signora.'

'Anyway, my sister, as I was saying, is tall and blonde with blue eyes. The way Sicilians think all German women are. My father, who came here for Riccardino's funeral but has already left to go back home, always used to tease my mother, saying that I wasn't really his daughter but the fruit of a fling of hers with some Turk. There are so many of them in Germany, you know, that . . .'

She just talked and talked . . . But the inspector had the impression that all her nervous chatter was her way of postponing the moment of serious discussion.

And so he decided on a frontal attack of sabre thrusts, giving her no quarter.

'Excuse me, signora, if I get straight to the point. Your late husband's three closest friends told me clearly, when in my office, that you were always against the fraternal bonds they shared, and that you'd done everything in your power to prevent him from frequenting with them. Is that true?'

'Yes.'

Calm, unruffled.

And with a sort of sigh of relief, as if that was not the difficult question, the serious discussion that might spell trouble for her.

'Could you tell me why?'

'Are you married?'

Whenever someone he was interrogating started asking him questions, Montalbano wouldn't answer with the standard police statement, 'I'll ask the questions around here.' It didn't really bother him, in fact. He knew perfectly well that certain questions could become implicit answers. And so he answered her question.

'No.'

'Were you ever married?'

'No.'

'Too bad. It might have helped you to understand a little better. You see, when Riccardino asked me to marry him, at the time I didn't understand Italian very well, and I thought he was asking whether I wanted to get married. In a general sense. So I said: "Of course." And then he kissed me and took me to his parents' place for dinner that same evening. And you know what? I never actually told Riccardino that our marriage originated in a misunderstanding.'

'Why, didn't you love him?'

'I'm sorry, Inspector, perhaps I haven't expressed myself clearly enough. I just could never have imagined it, and in the early days I simply couldn't believe it.'

'Believe what?'

'That Riccardino had married me. Sometimes I'd be in the middle of doing something, anything, and I would say to myself: You'll see, it's all just a dream, and now you're going to wake up . . .'

'Did it really seem so impossible to you?'

'Quite honestly, yes, Inspector. Riccardino was very handsome, elegant, athletic, and outgoing; he always had so many girls flocking around him, whereas I . . . When

I look in the mirror, I can see perfectly well what I look like.'

Montalbano felt a little sorry for the woman.

'No, come on, signora, your husband certainly must have found many good qualities in you, which—'

'No, Inspector. As far as his plans were concerned, my only quality of use to him was the fact that I wasn't pretty.'

Plans? So there was a specific design behind that marriage? What exactly did Riccardino expect to gain from it?

'I don't understand, signora.'

'Well, the person who got Riccardino the job at the bank, and set him on his career path, was Partanna, His Excellency the Bishop of Montelusa, who had always been very fond of those four lads, one of whom is, among other things, his nephew, and is—'

'I know. You mean Alfonso Licausi.'

'Well, the bishop was very insistent that Riccardino should take a wife. His three friends were already married. And so, feeling forced into marriage, he chose me because he was counting on my gratitude.'

'I don't really—'

'Inspector, as unattractive as I am, it would have been very hard for me to find a husband.'

'But was it so important for you to find a husband?'

'It is for most women. And it was extremely important for me in particular. You see, my father is a retired labourer; my parents weren't able to put me through school, and so I have a very low level of education. My only future was as a cleaning lady or, at best, a shop assistant in a department store.'

'I see.'

'And that's why I said that he was counting on my gratitude in marrying me.'

'But what did this gratitude consist of?'

'Not noticing, and not reacting. In essence, letting him do as he pleased.'

'Meaning?'

'Continuous infidelity.'

Shit! So who knew how many other women were involved? Which meant so many more husbands, boyfriends, brothers, and lovers, all potential killers!

'Were there really so many instances?'

'Yes, Inspector. Riccardino could have any woman he wanted, including the wives of his three friends.'

'Are you joking?'

'Absolutely not, why would I joke about such a thing? Riccardino was, as you Italians say, a mandrill. He started – though the affair predated our wedding – with Ida, Gaspare Bonanno's wife, then, after we got married, he carried on with Adele, Mario Liotta's wife, then revived things for a while with Ida, then ended up going to bed with Maria, Adele's sister and Alfonso Licausi's wife. I could—'

'Just a second,' said Montalbano. 'You're telling me that your late husband was first Adele's lover and then Maria's?'

'That's correct. The last lover he had in tow was in fact Maria. But now, be honest, you can maybe say I wasn't entirely right—'

'Of course you were! You were absolutely right!'
Montalbano seconded her somewhat hastily. He didn't give
a damn whether she was right or about what, but he didn't
want to waste time talking about it.

'But do you know whether their husbands knew?'

'*Schnuck schnuck*,' said the widow.

'Excuse me?' said Montalbano.

'*Schnuck schnuck*,' she repeated.

Then he realized that the woman was snickering in
German . . .

'Of course they knew! And how!' said Else, resuming
her odd laughter.

'And did they accept it?'

'*Schnuck schnuck*. Of course they accepted it!'

'Did they do so simply because they were all for one
and one for all?'

'I don't understand,' said the widow.

'I'm unable to imagine why the husbands would ever
tolerate . . . or allow your husband to . . .'

'You might be able to find the reasons by asking some
questions.'

'Asking who some questions? You?'

'Me, no. I wouldn't know what to say.'

'Tell me something. Do you know whether the three
friends were engaging in wife-swapping?'

'No, the others were faithful to their wives.'

'Listen, signora, an instant before he died, your husband
dialled the number of Mario's house, even though Mario
was with him. So, from what you're telling me, it may be

reasonable to think that perhaps he was sending a signal to Liotta's wife, his ex-mistress Adele. So my question is: why? Can you explain this to me, if, as you say, it's true that it was over between them, and that his present lover was Maria?'

Else didn't have to think twice before answering.

'It's possible the flame had been rekindled between Adele and Riccardino. It had already happened before with Ida.'

'Before you broke off relations with your husband's friends and their wives, did you all see one another often?'

'Of course.'

'Did you ever spend much time alone just among the women?'

'Naturally. Sometimes we would make plans to go shopping together, or to the movies, or we would play cards or get in our cars and go to Montelusa . . .'

'None of you has a job?'

'No, none of us.'

'Have you ever noticed any tension between Ida, Adele, and Maria?'

'What do you mean?'

'I'll try to explain. When your husband left Ida to go with Adele, didn't you notice some kind of tension between the two women? A certain cooling in their relationship?'

'No, there was no cooling. Now that I'm more aware of things, I remember that Ida not only remained friends with Adele as though nothing had happened, but she did nothing to try and win Riccardino back. I can say that with assurance.'

'So then why did your husband go back to Ida?'

'It was his own free choice. He always wanted to do whatever came into his head, and he could. He was, in effect, the only cock in the henhouse.'

'One more thing. Before the break occurred, did your families get together often?'

'At least once a week. That was the custom. Every Sunday we would get together for a big lunch.'

'Did you go out to eat?'

'No. We would take turns. Every Sunday one couple would cook lunch for the others and host the party.'

'And what would happen after lunch?'

'What happened after lunch? . . . Nothing. What was supposed to happen?'

'Did the men have some time alone amongst themselves?'

'Actually, yes.'

Then a tiny little correction, a half-step back:

'Normally we women would start clearing the table, putting things back in order, washing the dishes, and they would go into the living room to chat over coffee.'

'Did you ever manage to hear what they talked about?'

For the first time the woman appeared a little uneasy. 'Well . . . it's not as if I would stop and listen when I brought them the coffee . . . I'm not nosy . . . I think they talked about my husband's banking business, mostly . . . and what was happening at the mine . . . things like that . . . of no importance.'

'Did it ever happen that they asked you explicitly to

leave them alone so they could talk about confidential matters?'

'Once or twice, if I'm not mistaken.'

'So, as you can see, it wasn't always about subjects of no importance.'

The woman shrugged.

'What about after you broke off with them?' Montalbano continued. 'Did Riccardino keep going by himself to these lunches?'

'No. He stayed at home. But they adopted another routine. They started going on long walks that took all day.'

'Did any of the wives ever go along with them?'

'I really don't think so.'

'Do you know whether your husband had other mistresses besides his friends' wives?'

'I'd say no. I don't think there was anyone else, at least not in recent times.'

Well, thank God for that! thought the inspector.

If the catalogue of the beauties loved by Riccardino numbered only three women, then only three husbands could be suspects. Otherwise, Riccardino the Lionheart with his lance forever couched would have forced him to interrogate half the town.

'You see, Riccardino was a model citizen and a practising Catholic. He wanted to appear irreproachable in every respect; he was always afraid of being criticized or giving rise to gossip. This way it all remained within the family, so to speak.'

FIFTEEN

He thanked her, said goodbye, went out, got in his car, and drove off.

He felt satisfied. Starting with the widow had been the right move, as dictated by his instinct, which was still working well, and not by spite towards the TV Montalbano.

The widow, among other things, had not only drawn a detailed, previously unknown portrait of Riccardino, but she'd filled him in on the sometimes odd relationships between the musketeers. And he had reason to believe that she had told him at least one lie: when she said she'd never had any desire to hear what the four men were talking about when they were together without the women.

Signora Else knew perfectly well what the subject of those conversations was, and it was that very subject she was seeking to avoid and feared from the start that he might broach.

*

'Ahh, Chief, Chief! Ahh, Chief, Chief!'

'Calm down, Cat. What is it?'

'We foun' it, Chief!'

Montalbano breathed a sigh of relief.

'It took us most o' half the mornin', bu' inni en' we foun' the damn fax, Chief, we foun' it!'

'Well done, all of you. Give it to me.'

It was all soiled and wrinkled, but legible.

'OK, thank everyone for me. Who paid for the gloves?'

'I did, Chief.'

'How much did you spend?'

Catarella handed him the receipt, and Montalbano gave him the money he owed and went into his office.

He started reading immediately.

This week we begin a debate with the well-known police detective, Salvo Montalbano, in hopes of arousing the interest of a broad range of personalities inhabiting the province of Montelusa.

Ours is essentially a philosophical debate, and therefore bears no relation whatsoever to any local realities or ongoing situations, but should be read within a much more general frame of reference. We like to imagine it as a small contribution to an apparent new interest in philosophy currently reawakening in our country, to the point that several philosophical conventions have been recently held in a number of cities with considerable public participation.

And so we have formulated for Inspector Montalbano a number of questions concerning his profession and his relationship to justice, to what lies within and outside the bounds of the Law, to freedom, and to its privation.

FIRST QUESTION

Inspector Montalbano, considering that Socrates maintained that defining a thing or an event was already a step towards knowledge of the thing or event, how would you define murder, in an absolute sense? And, in a secondary respect, do you personally tend to treat all murder in the same manner, or do you think, just to cite one example, that murder dictated by passion might benefit from extenuating circumstances inapplicable to a murder motivated by self-interest?

SECOND QUESTION

John of Salisbury, a friend and auxiliary of Thomas Becket, about whom T. S. Eliot wrote the tragedy entitled *Murder in the Cathedral*, asserts that tyrannicide is legitimate. St Thomas, on the subject, writes that the man who kills the tyrant is praised, but does not add that he is praiseworthy. Would you, Inspector Montalbano, arrest a tyrant's killer?

THIRD QUESTION

Pascal writes that we succeed in knowing the truth not only through reason, but also with the heart. Pascal, however, by the word 'heart', is referring not to feelings, but to the inborn ability to recognize the obvious. Do you agree with Pascal?

FOURTH QUESTION

Pascal also says that often one ends up loving the hunt in itself more than the capture of the prey. Which do you love more?

He read and reread the sheet, feeling more and more lost at sea. Socrates? St Thomas? Pascal?

But hadn't Father Bartolino told him on the phone that the interview would be about the horrendous crime – his exact words – of Riccardino's murder? So why were they now so keen to point out that the interview was in no way connected to 'any local realities or ongoing situations'? Was His Excellency joking or something?

No, Partanna didn't seem like the joking type.

That was no interview, but a sort of written exam on moral philosophy, as it used to be called.

And an exam is still an exam.

This wasn't something to respond to right away.

He had to think long and hard about this. Choose the right words and put them in the proper order. When dealing with priests, you also had to be careful to cross your t's and dot your i's.

He still had a little time. Father Bartolino was expecting the answers by the end of the day.

He put the sheet in a drawer, to keep it from ending up in the bin again, and called Fazio.

'I just got back now, Chief.'

'Where were you?

'I was talking to the caretaker at the gym. Remember when I said I had the impression that she wanted to tell me something? I was right on the money.'

'And what did she tell you?'

'She said that sometimes the musketeers' wives also used to come to the gym, all of them except for Riccardo Lopresti's wife, who the caretaker said was so ugly that there was no point in her working out at the gym.'

'And that was all?'

'Just be a little patient, Chief. She told me something else, too.'

'Are you going to tell me or do I have to extract it with pliers?'

'She told me that three days before Lopresti died, she saw him making love to a woman.'

'Are we really sure they were making love? Or was it merely an embrace between friends?'

Hadn't Signora Else said that Riccardino took great care to avoid scandals? So why would he expose himself at the gym?

'Chief, the lady went into great detail. She said they were doing it right there, standing up, and in a hurry because they were in the women's changing room, which was momentarily empty. But someone could have come in at any moment, and therefore it was going to have to be . . .'

'A quickie, Fazio. That's the technical term. Did the caretaker manage to see who the woman was?'

'Of course, Chief. And it surprised me.'

Fazio artfully stopped there. He had a knack for suspense.

'How about we share this surprise, Fazio? What do you say?'

'The woman in question was Signora Ida, wife of Gaspare Bonanno and sister of Mario Liotta.'

Matre Maria santissima! Three days before dying he was doing it with Ida!

But wasn't he with Maria, according to his widow? Did he fall prey to a sudden compulsion? Or was Riccardino on some kind of sexual merry-go-round? Maybe once he'd made the full rounds of the three women, he started all over again. Or maybe it was like the game of the goose for him: he would wake up in the morning, throw the dice, and depending on the number that came up, he would go back one square, skip the one in front and advance, or simply move to the next box.

'I can see that you're confused, too, Chief.'

'Yes, Fazio, I'm confused, but for a different reason.' And he told him what he'd found out from Signora Else.

When he'd finished, Fazio, like a true policeman, commented: 'Chief, it's not possible for three husbands to let themselves be cuckolded by a fourth man without reacting, purely out of a spirit of friendship! I don't even think that sort of thing happens with Eskimos, who apparently will offer their wives to guests passing through.'

'So you've reached the same conclusion that I have. Which is that Liotta, Bonanno, and Licausi could never refuse Riccardino anything, not even their wives. They were dependent on him for everything, and in every respect.'

Silence fell. Then Fazio ventured a hypothesis.

'Think he blackmailed them?'

'No.'

'But then how did he manage—'

'Fazio, it's possible they were all engaged in some less-than-clean business dealings. And that whatever it was, Riccardino was the overseer. And Riccardino's enjoyment of their wives was some kind of "user's right" granted to him, some kind of payment to the protection racket he was at the top of.'

'But then why didn't the wives themselves ever rebel?'

'That is something we'll need to ask *them*, at the right moment.'

'So where do I start, Chief?'

'Start with the Cristallo mine. You need to find out exactly what kind of responsibilities our three musketeers have there. Then I want to know how the transportation of salt to Vigàta functions: how many drivers, how many trucks, how many runs per day.'

'All right.'

'Wait, there's something I discovered. Do you remember that truck driver for the mine, the one who also has two vans of his own for personal deliveries?'

'Saverio Milioto? Sure.'

'Well this Milioto, every week, from Monday through to Thursday, screws the mine out of almost twenty-five litres of diesel per day, apparently to keep his own personal vans running.'

'But that's a hundred litres a week, Chief!'

'So?'

'Seems like a lot. How could the mine staff not notice?'

'I was wondering the same thing. But the answer is: they couldn't. It's not possible. They would notice. Therefore he has someone covering for him. I want you to look into it.'

✻

After a medium-size helping of *purpiteddri a strascinasale*, he set to a seafood salad as if he'd been fasting for the past week. Then he polished off a dish of fried mullet. After which he indulged a whim for a thick slice of Ragusan *caciocavallo* cheese.

The owner of the trattoria, Enzo, expressed his gratitude.

'You know, Inspector, it's worth keeping this trattoria going just for the pleasure of seeing you eat.'

With certain people, eating heartily tends to fog their brains. For Montalbano, with rare exceptions, it had the opposite effect.

With his mind now clear, clean, and light, he reached the lighthouse at the end of the jetty, sat down on the usual flat rock, and began thinking about the fax.

And with a cooler head he immediately realized that

the fax was not in fact a moral philosophy test, as he'd thought at first. It must have another meaning.

At once something Bishop Partanna had said about Tiananmen came back to him.

Not to dwell on initial appearances, but to try to see what was not visible.

As he was contemplating this idea, his gaze fell on a small crab trying to clamber up the green slime covering the lower part of the rock beside him, the part that the sea, rising and falling, kept continually wet.

The little crab managed to climb not by proceeding straight upward, but by walking sideways, as was its nature.

The right path to take appeared to him in a flash. How do priests think, according to their nature? Sideways, like crabs.

They never head straight for their target, never move in a straight line. Sometimes they reason in zigzag fashion, other times by labyrinthine logic, still others in concentric circles.

They nevertheless always reach their target, though from the side, or on the backswing.

The little crab had shown him how to decipher the fax.

It was indeed a test; that much he'd gathered from the start. But a private test, not remotely an interview, to which the bishop was subjecting him poissonally in poisson. A written exam. Which meant that he couldn't later say, if needed, that his words had been misconstrued. He would remain nailed to those words like Christ to the cross.

Verba volant, scripta manent . . . And paper sings, in black and white . . .

He began to sweat.

That was why the fax had been in the nightmare with the motorcyclist! In essence, that fax was just like a gun pointed at him. Be careful what you write, Montalbano — it said — *ex ore tuo te judico*. From your mouth I will judge you.

And condemn you to death, if necessary.

And it was equally clear that Socrates, Pascal, St Thomas à Becket, John of Wherever the Fuck, had nothing whatsoever to do with the essence of the questions, but merely served to cover with philosophical chatter the weapon pointed straight at him.

Drenched in sweat, he got up and began walking back to the office.

Halfway up the jetty was the usual fisherman. He'd just caught a fish, which was struggling to free itself of the hook. But it was clear that it would never succeed. It was condemned. The fish felt like a brother to Montalbano.

*

'Cat, where'd you put my *napoletana*?'

'In my cubbid, Chief.'

'Make me some coffee and bring it to me, would you? And don't put any calls through, I don't care if they're from God in heaven.'

He waited for Catarella to bring him the coffee, then locked the door to his office and got down to work. He looked at the clock. It was almost four.

He began reading the questions, then rereading them, one, two, three, four times, weighing every syllable. Then he took a blank sheet of paper and wrote at the top: *Translation of the questions in simple terms*, and continued:

TRANSLATION OF THE FIRST QUESTION
Is there any chance that the murder of Riccardino could be considered a crime of passion? And, if so, couldn't the perpetrator of the crime benefit from some extenuating circumstances?

TRANSLATION OF THE SECOND QUESTION
Let's assume for a moment that the motive did not stem from passion, but that what triggered the crime was a kind of revolt against Riccardino's bullying and lording it over everyone. In this case, Inspector, how do you think you should proceed?

TRANSLATION OF THE THIRD QUESTION
Do you intend to carry the investigation forward using only cold reason? Can't you put a little heart into it as well?

TRANSLATION OF THE FOURTH QUESTION
Do you really need to capture your prey? Must you stuff him at all costs in your game bag? Can't you limit yourself to the pleasure of the hunt for its own sake?

After dispatching another *napoletana*'s worth of coffee for six, a pack and a half of cigarettes, an entire bottle of mineral water, and some ten crossed-out, corrected, ripped-up, and jettisoned sheets of paper, he considered himself satisfied with what he'd written.

It was now eight o'clock. He reread his text one last time.

ANSWER TO THE FIRST QUESTION

I consider murder above all a crime against reason. And I am therefore unable to conceive how one can grant extenuating circumstances to a certain kind of murder while denying them to a different kind. The sole distinctions I am able to make are between wilful murder, culpable murder (without malice aforethought), and manslaughter. I do realize that the Law entertains the possibility of granting extenuating circumstances, but I, luckily, am not a judge.

ANSWER TO THE SECOND QUESTION

To be honest, this is the first time in my life that I've heard mention of John of Salisbury, and therefore don't feel up to answering. As for St Thomas on tyrannicide, I believe I recall that things are not quite so simple. In reality Thomas makes a precise distinction, between the tyrant who seizes power due to the people's cowardice, indolence, and non-participation (today we would call it abstention) in the public weal, and the tyrant who imposes himself through force and bloodshed, destroying liberty and justice.

In the former case, says St Thomas, it is not legitimate to kill the tyrant, but in the latter it is. As an officer of the law,

I would of course arrest the tyrannicide without taking into consideration which of St Thomas's categories he belonged to, yet remaining ready to remove his handcuffs after his arrest or to institute a committee in his defence.

ANSWER TO THE THIRD QUESTION

All I have ever done over the course of my career is seek the truth by means of reason and the heart (intended in both the Pascalian and non-Pascalian senses). The problem in every one of my investigations has been that of maintaining a constant balance between these two elements in my pursuit of the truth, or in the quest to attain that minimum of truth necessary to convince me that I have at least caught a glimpse of the truth, or touched it in passing.

ANSWER TO THE FOURTH QUESTION

The answer to this question is contained, in part, in the previous answer. Searching for the truth means hunting for the truth.

And it is often so long, complex, intricate, and unnerving a hunt that sometimes the metaphorical sweat from this effort fogs one's vision and image of the prey, turning it into an almost indistinguishable shadow.

This hunt, however, is not driven by pleasure but by duty, instinct, chance, and naturally by necessity, and we are forced to carry it through to the end. Careful, though: it is a very particular form of hunting, because the hunter, once he catches the prey, does not keep it for himself, but turns it over to others, to the judges who will decide what to do with it.

Anyway, isn't it quite commonplace for hunters not to like to eat their prey?

＊

He summoned Catarella.

'Here, send this fax at once.'

He handed it to him. As soon as Catarella went out, he flicked his cigarette lighter, set fire to the sheet of paper on which he'd written his translation of the bishop's questions, and left it to burn in the ashtray.

SIXTEEN

As he was sitting on the veranda after finishing a large casserole of *pasta 'ncasciata* that Adelina had left for him in the oven, the telephone rang. Certain that it was Livia, he went and picked up. Only to hear the voice of the Author.

'My compliments, Montalbà, for the way you answered the bishop. He put some pretty convoluted questions to you, and you answered him with the same convolution.'

'What do you think Partanna will do next?'

'Nothing, in my opinion. He was testing your willingness to give the investigation a certain inflection. And you replied by saying maybe yes, maybe no.'

'But in plain words, what does he really want from me?'

'Partanna is asking you to submit a report on the investigation that would allow Prosecutor Tommaseo to request, from the courts, an allowance for extenuating circumstances.'

'And do you have any idea why Partanna is going through all this trouble?'

'Of course! His Excellency knows who the killer is.'

'And who is he?'

'His nephew Alfonso.'

'Licausi? And why would he kill Riccardino?'

'But, Montalbà, isn't this a case of infidelity? Some cuckolded husbands tend to react badly and immediately once they discover the infidelity, whereas other husbands are patient and put up with it. But the second category is a dangerous one indeed, because they swallow it down today, swallow it down tomorrow, swallow it down again the day after tomorrow, and then after a while they explode, lose their patience, and become worse than the more naturally violent cuckolds.'

'So then, in your opinion, Riccardino's bosom buddies were all cuckolds of the patient variety until the moment when Licausi lost patience?'

'Exactly.'

'And so they hired someone to restore their offended honour, so to speak, by killing Riccardino?'

'No.'

'What do you mean, no?'

'It was Alfonso himself who fired the gun. The patient cuckold who loses his patience does the deed himself, poissonally in poisson, as Catarella would say. He doesn't delegate the task to anyone. To save his honour, he must do it himself.'

'What the hell are you saying? Alfonso Licausi wasn't even there when the crime was committed.'

'Oh, he was there, all right.'

'Where?'

'On the motorcycle.'

'Oh, *matre santa*! Are you saying he was the motorcyclist?'

'That's correct.'

'But Liotta and Bonanno say that Alfonso Licausi arrived right after the killing! In your opinion, are they Licausi's accomplices or are they telling the truth?'

'They're telling the truth.'

'Then can you explain to me how Licausi managed to hide the motorcycle, riding suit and helmet so quickly, since he appeared on the scene just a few minutes after Riccardino was killed, all clean and normally dressed? Who is he, Mandrake the Magician?'

'Hahahahha . . .'

'What's that little laugh supposed to mean?'

'It means that you're slowing down, Montalbà. Licausi is certainly not Mandrake, but he did do something rather James Bond-like.'

'Explain.'

'Licausi had an accomplice.'

'Oh, yeah? Who?'

'Saverio Milioto, the truck driver. It's a diabolical plan, believe me. On top of everything else, a great many readers will love it if I'm able to write the episode a bit in the American style, like so many Italian authors do nowadays. Let me explain a little better. So Liotta, Bonanno, and Lopresti are in Via Rosolino Pilo. A motorcycle comes out from Via Nino Bixio, driven by Alfonso Licausi. Licausi stops, fires, kills Riccardino, speeds away, turns right onto Via Tukory, and . . .'

'. . . nearly runs himself over.'

'That's what he, Licausi, said. But that's not at all what really happened.'

'And what really happened?'

'The motorcyclist still turns right, then goes into Vicolo Marsala, which is a short dead-end street with no shops.'

'Look, this Vicolo Marsala is not where you say it is.'

'It doesn't matter. We'll put it there anyway.'

'But that's a line from the Marx Brothers!'

'I don't give a damn where the line is from. If I say the street exists, and that's where it is, there's nobody in the world who can prove me wrong. Not you, not the TV people. I invented Vigàta myself. And now, please, let me continue. Licausi drives onto Vicolo Marsala, and there Milioto's van is waiting for him with its back doors open and a mounting ramp ready. Licausi drives the motorbike straight up the ramp and into the van, hops off the bike, takes off his suit and helmet, under which he's wearing his regular clothes (remember Bond?), gets out of the van, turns the corner, and finds himself back in Via Rosolino Pio, ready to play his part. Meanwhile the van comes out of the blind alley and vanishes with the motorcycle, suit, and helmet inside. And it's bye-bye, birdie. What do you think?'

'I think it's stupid as shit! Among other things, it's a scene people have seen over and over again in the movies!'

'So what? No doubt Licausi himself remembered the scene, which gave him the idea.'

'On top of everything else, that model of motorcycle

is hard to drive, and I don't know if Licausi would be capable of executing the acrobatic manoeuvre of turning and speeding straight up the ramp . . .'

'But that's just a detail, Montalbà. It can be easily resolved. We arrange for Fazio to tell you that in his youth Licausi was a champion motocross cyclist, and it's all taken care of.'

'But there's another, bigger problem.'

'And what's that?'

'Your writing. You're not very good at writing American-style stuff. If you insert this story of the van with Licausi as the motorcyclist and killer, you'll have to rewrite the novel from the beginning, give it a completely different slant, and remove everything that's not related to the action: such as the memory of the Day of the Dead. And, now that I think about it, all that business with the bishop and the fake interview will seem totally out of place.'

'You're right, in part. But I want to bring this story to an end. Because there's another problem you have to consider. My age.'

'So what?'

'Come on, Montalbà. You spend half your day rehashing the fact that you feel old, whereas I actually am old. And I'm also a wee bit tired.'

'So what's that supposed to mean?'

'That I'm starting to get tired of writing. And I want to find a solution to this case right away.'

'But I'm the one who's supposed to find the solution, not you!'

'Well then, let me be the one to ask you this time: are you up to the task? Just give some thought to the solution I proposed. You'll see, I'll find a way to make it work. So how shall we leave things?'

'Let's talk again.'

*

No, the Author was wrong. Of that he was certain. The story of the van just didn't hold water; in fact it bordered on the ridiculous. Mr Fancy-Pants Author was offering him an off-the-wall conclusion, something pulled right out of a hat, because he felt tired, he said. But wasn't he, Montalbano, also tired? Wasn't he, too, at the end of his rope? Wasn't he also fed up with everything? And he certainly wasn't trying to cut corners on the case simply by settling on the first solution that came into his head. Writing a novel was one thing; sending an innocent man to jail was another thing entirely.

He couldn't very well go to bed now, all upset from his conversation with the Author. He needed to find a way to distract himself, otherwise he might never manage to get to sleep.

He went outside, stepped down from the veranda, walked to the water's edge, and went on a walk so long that by the time he returned home his legs were cramping.

*

Moments after Montalbano arrived at the station, Fazio came into his office.

'I found out what you wanted to know, Chief. Mind if I have a look at my notes in my pocket? Just to refresh my memory.'

'As long as you aren't going to give me their vital statistics and family histories.'

'Nah, Chief, don't worry.'

He dug a half sheet of paper out of his pocket, glanced at it, and set it down in front of him on the desk.

'So. Mario Liotta, surveyor by profession, is the sole assistant of the managing director of the mine, the engineer Stoltz.'

'German?'

'No, Chief, he's from Bolzano. His father's name was Alfred, and he was born in—'

'If you keep it up with that records-office stuff, I'll shoot you,' the inspector said, cool as a cucumber.

'Sorry, Chief. To continue: Alfonso Licausi, also a surveyor, is responsible for the day-to-day organization of the trucks transporting salt to Vigàta.'

'Give me a better idea of what he does.'

'The mine has six trucks and six drivers assigned to them, respectively. The salt is first refined in the mine itself, then transported, loose and in bulk, to the Vigàta plant, the one at the port.'

'I know where it is. Go on.'

'Other salt from other mines around the island is also brought to this plant, where the material is further cleaned, packaged, and then sent wherever it's supposed to go.'

'Stop right there. How many trips back and forth does

each truck make each day from the mine to the processing plant?'

'Well, that's just it, Chief. Deciding how many trips each truck should take each day is, in fact, Licausi's job.'

'And on what does he base his decisions?'

'It depends on the amount of salt extracted, refined, sifted, and so on . . .'

'Can you give me some kind of average?'

'Sure. The trucks get going at two o'clock in the afternoon and finish at eleven at night. But the schedule can vary, which is also something decided by Licausi.'

'Why should it vary?'

'Because you have to take into account that he might get a call from the processing plant saying that they're tied up with other salt from a different mine, and so the Cristallo mine has to postpone its delivery. Or they might call and say to come early.'

'That makes sense. And what's the daily average?'

'Five runs a day per truck.'

'Tell me something. Do you know how the packets of salt are then sent out of the processing plant?'

'Yes, some by train, some by boat, and also some by truck.'

'With the same mine's trucks?'

'No. They go out on HGVs from other companies.'

'And who takes them to the trains and boats?'

'The mine's trucks.'

'And tell me something else: these trucks, do they all stop working at eleven p.m., even if they started early?'

'Yes. It's considered overtime.'

'OK. Now tell me about Bonanno.'

'Gaspare Bonanno, accountant, handles all the books for the mine.'

'Therefore also the diesel fuel accounts.'

'Of course.'

'And to whom do Bonanno and Licausi have to report the results of their labours, to the managing director?'

'No, to Liotta. Stoltz, who's involved mostly with excavation and extraction, delegates all the administrative chores to Liotta.'

'So, from what I gather, our truck driver, Saverio Milioto, steals a hundred litres of fuel per week . . .'

'He gets away with it because Gaspare Bonanno closes one eye,' said Fazio.

'And when Bonanno shows Liotta the balance sheets—'

'He closes both eyes,' Fazio concluded.

'So there's only one question: how are they allowed to do this?'

'Apparently nobody says no to them. Anyway, we also ascertained that they were the ones who vouched for Milioto at the bank.'

'Right. They can't say no to Milioto when he steals the diesel, and they couldn't say no to Riccardino when he wanted to fuck their wives. They'd made a crown of rats.'

'A what?'

'It's something I saw when I was a little kid and could never forget, that's how much of an impression it made on me. My grandfather had decided to demolish the bread oven, which was a kind of little room attached to their country cottage, and so he called in two stonemasons to do the job. They got going with their pickaxes and had knocked down about half a wall when ten or so rather large rats came running out of a hole. There was a nest inside, with six rats with very long tails intertwined, forming a sort of crown. Their tails were so tightly wound together that the rats couldn't move, because each of them was trying to flee in a different direction. They were able to move an inch or two, but could go no farther. A disgusting sight. A sort of animal with six heads and twenty-four legs. And they were big. Apparently the other rats brought them food. The masons killed them with their pickaxes. And there you have it: I think the four musketeers held one another back with their intertwined tails, just like the rats. But then one of them decided to break the crown, killing Riccardino.'

'So, how are we going to proceed, Chief?'

'OK, I'll tell you.'

And he told him.

*

At eleven o'clock that evening, before heading off for Borgonovo, Montalbano and Fazio procured a couple of white medical face masks, some heavy work gloves, and a small ladder.

They took the inspector's car and arrived at the first buildings of Borgonovo at exactly half-past eleven. Before getting out of the car, they put on the masks and gloves and the inspector took his revolver and torch out of the glove compartment. Fazio was already armed. Then they got out, and Fazio took the ladder out of the boot and hoisted it onto his shoulder.

As soon as they turned onto the fortune-teller's street, the first half of which was in total darkness, since the two street lamps hanging from walls had been shattered with stones, they heard a kind of constant groaning coming from inside a front door dangling from its hinges. They immediately thought someone was hurt. Montalbano lit his torch. A man and a woman lay fucking on the ground, amid shit piles, piss puddles, soiled paper, and empty cans of beer and Coca-Cola.

'What the fuck do you want?' the man reacted, springing to his feet, naked.

Where did he get that eight-inch knife gleaming in his hand?

'We beg your pardon. Don't mind us, it was an honest mistake,' the inspector said in a drawing-room tone, turning the torch off.

Another ten feet away was a young man on the ground, back against the wall, who'd just finished shooting up, needle and strap still hanging from his arm. He was gone.

'If we leave him here,' said Fazio, 'the truck will run him over when it passes.'

He bent down, lifted him to his feet, grabbed him under the armpits, and stuck him inside another building entrance. Then came the part of the street illuminated by a hanging street lamp miraculously still intact. There was nobody about.

They reached the cul de sac with the open space, and consulted each other with their eyes. Fazio then broke into a run and ducked into a hollow in the wall of the rubbish dump where the light didn't reach. Montalbano for his part took up position with his back against the front door of the building in which the saintly man lived, which was locked.

They didn't have to wait long.

The truck soon arrived and stopped close to the wall. The driver got out, holding a sort of stepladder in his hands, set it down right under the 'RS' in 'ARSE', went back into the truck's cab, got his parcel, climbed up the stepladder, hoisted the package with both hands over his head, and at that exact moment Montalbano, who'd come up behind the truck, called out:

'Milioto!'

The man turned into a statue. He looked like a telamon.

Then he got hold of himself and was about to throw the parcel to the other side of the wall but was unable, because by now Fazio had his revolver pointed at his stomach.

Then something funny happened.

Milioto, frightened by the man threatening him with a gun and looking, moreover, like some kind of masked outlaw, could no longer bear the weight of his package and therefore opened his hands, letting the jerry can, with twenty-five litres of diesel inside, fall directly onto his head, knocking him first off the stepladder and then to his knees, like a bull in the arena.

And, just like in an arena, there was a burst of applause and shouts.

'Bravo, Captain!'

'Bravo, Inspector!'

Montalbano, in shock, turned to look.

Up on a balcony above them were the holy man with his binoculars and the clairvoyant fortune-teller, clapping, and when they realized the inspector was looking at them, they raised their arms in a gesture of celebration.

All that was missing was for them to start shouting, '*Olé!*'

But how had the fortune-teller managed to recognize him behind his mask?

What a question! Wasn't Mrs Tina Facca a clairvoyant?

Fazio, meanwhile, had brought the truck driver to his feet with a kick in the ribs.

'Ya don' have to kill me, for Chrissakes!' said Milioto, who, still dazed from the blow to the head, hadn't heard what the fortune-teller and the saint had said.

The truck driver was still thinking they were muggers or enforcers sent to make him pay for some mistake.

'If you talk, I won't shoot,' Fazio reassured him.

'What've you got in the package?' Montalbano asked.

'A jerry can of diesel.'

'So why do you pack it up like that?'

'So you can't tell it's a jerry can.'

'Did you steal it?'

'Yes.'

'From where?'

'From the Cristallo mine.'

'All right, take the package and come with us.'

'What about the truck?'

'Leave it here.'

'Are you kidding me? It belongs to the mine.'

'Just lock it up and come with us,' Fazio cut in, giving him a light tap on the forehead with the barrel of his gun.

Silently, Milioto obeyed, locked the truck, and picked up the package.

Not until they reached Montalbano's car did he venture to ask:

'Can you at least tell me who you are?'

'Police,' said Fazio.

And for the entire journey to the station, Milioto never once opened his mouth again.

SEVENTEEN

There was nobody at the station, just an on-duty officer half asleep at the switchboard. So much the better. This time there was no need to publicize the event.

As Montalbano had instructed him when they agreed on their plan, Fazio took Milioto into Mimì Augello's office.

'What should I do, Chief, cuff him?'

'Yes,' said Montalbano.

There was no real need to handcuff Milioto. Trying to escape or use force was the last thing on his mind, but handcuffs always have a strong effect on the morale of someone who's not a habitual crook.

Fazio began the interrogation in the inspector's presence.

'Do you confirm that your name is Saverio Milioto, born in Vigàta on—'

'Before answering I want to know who the bastard is that ratted on me,' the truck driver said, interrupting him.

Fazio, feeling denied the pleasure of reciting all of

Milioto's personal particulars from the start, leapt up from his chair as if bitten by a tarantula.

'Answer my question or I'll bust your ass!'

Montalbano intervened.

'Let's try and understand each other, Milioto. You answer our questions without imposing conditions. OK? But in any case, to satisfy your curiosity, I'll tell you straight out: nobody ratted on you. Someone who lives on the street where you drive by every night in your truck got tired of all the noise you were making and reported you. And so we got interested in all your comings and goings.'

Then, turning to Fazio:

'I'm leaving now. You continue and then come and tell me what he said. You can put it on the record afterwards.'

He went into his office and looked a number up in the phone book, wrote it down on a piece of paper, then dawdled about for almost an hour.

He looked at an old report, tried to fix a broken rubber stamp, tidied up his desk a little.

Then Fazio appeared, looking satisfied.

'I put him in a holding cell.'

'Did he talk?'

'He spilled all the beans.'

'All what beans?'

'All the stuff that was going on, down to the finest details: how he got the jerry can, how he was able to screw them out of a hundred litres of diesel a week.'

Montalbano interrupted him.

'And why did he talk, in your opinion?'

'Come on, Chief, how could he deny anything? We caught him in the act!'

'That can't be the only reason. Milioto isn't the brainiest guy on earth, but in my opinion he had instructions.'

'Such as?'

'Such as: if they catch you, tell them everything about how you steal the diesel, but get this straight: the idea of stealing the diesel was all yours, you worked it out all by yourself without anybody's help. And so Milioto goes ahead and gives you everything in fine detail so he can draw a line around the incident. I'm not sure I'm being clear. He tells us he's a thief, he explains the whys and wherefores of his act, he describes all the details, and we come away feeling satisfied and dig no further. Since there's been a breach in the hull, he tries to seal off the watertight compartment so it doesn't flood the whole ship.'

'And so that way we won't ask him how he managed to steal all that fuel without anyone at the mine finding out?'

'Precisely.'

'In short, he wants to keep his little friends out of this.'

'Absolutely. Did he give you a lot of details?'

'Yeah.'

'Can you see I'm right? What did he say?'

'I'll sum it up for you. The whole thing's been going on for two years. After each trip, he stops for a spell on a certain country road, where there's a dry well that he's covered up with an iron lid that remains shut and padlocked. And that's where he keeps his jerry can. He pours out some fuel and then leaves.'

'Good God, how complicated! Why not just keep the can in his truck? There's nothing terribly unusual about there being a jerry can of diesel inside a truck.'

'Chief, the mine has inspectors who do checks on the trucks, sometimes stopping them for inspection during salt deliveries. He says these inspectors are pretty meticulous.'

'Go on.'

'On his last trip, Milioto finishes filling the jerry can, packs it up again, unloads the salt at the processing plant, drives to Borgonovo, drops the package into the dump, and then goes back home.'

'But why doesn't he just bring the package directly home with him in the evening to avoid having to go and pick it up the next day?'

'Because every truck driver, when he gets off work in the evening, drives home in the truck he's used for the last trip. And he returns the truck to the mine when he drives to work the next day. More than once the mine has sent someone out at night to inspect the parked trucks and check their fuel consumption and mileage.'

'But that mine is worse than a concentration camp! So why do they check on trucks when they're out of service?'

'Because in the past some drivers have used the mine's trucks for their own personal affairs.'

'And who ordered these night-time inspections?'

'Licausi.'

'Who naturally would have already told Milioto how to dodge these checks, both in the daytime and at night. But there's something that doesn't make sense to me: how did Milioto manage to retrieve the parcel from the dump at seven p.m. if he was still on duty at the mine at that hour?'

'I was wondering the same thing. So I asked Milioto, who replied that there's about a forty-five-minute pause in deliveries between six-thirty and seven-thirty because that's when the shift changes at the processing plant. So he uses that time to get his parcel. What should we do now, Chief? Go on to part two of the script?'

'OK. But now stay and listen to my phone call.'

He took the piece of paper on which he'd written the phone number, then dialled it. The recipient's phone rang for a long time, but was finally answered by someone with a voice hoarse from sleep.

'Hello?'

'It this the Licausi home?'

'Yes. What happened?'

'Where?'

'At the mine, what happened?'

'I don't know; I'm not calling from the mine!'

'You're not?'

'No.'

'So who is this talking?'

'Montalbano.'

'So it's you, Inspector? For a second I thought . . . surely you understand . . . it's past three in the morning . . . I thought maybe something had happened at the mine . . . some accident . . . I don't know . . . Well, I'm glad to hear. What can I do for you?'

'There's something fairly important I wanted to tell you, which is why I took the liberty of—'

'Don't worry about that, just tell me,' insisted Licausi, sounding a little irritated.

'We've made an arrest.'

The news took his breath away, to the point that even Fazio, who was sitting beside the phone, could hear the sucking sound Licausi made with his lips.

He's going to have a heart attack, thought the inspector.

'An arrest?'

'Yes.'

'Wh . . . who . . . did you . . .'

'That's just it, you see.'

'No . . . I don't see.'

'I see perfectly well why you don't see. But you could, easily, see. Know what I mean?'

'Wha . . . what?'

'Maybe the best solution is for you to come here, at once, to the police station.'

He hung up.

'Fazio, how much do you want to bet that I know what Licausi is doing right now?'

'Nothing. Because I know too.'

'So what's he doing?'

'He's calling Liotta and Bonanno.'

'He sure is. Three families will be up waiting for Santa tonight. Now go and get Milioto, take him into Augello's office, and start writing the transcript of his admissions. Meanwhile, Licausi will be blazing in here in about ten minutes. Wake up the officer on duty and let him know he's on his way.'

*

Instead of ten minutes, it took Licausi twenty-five to appear.

He was dishevelled and not wearing a tie.

He'd probably decided, after weighing his options, to ring his lawyer, thought Montalbano.

Licausi seemed less nervous than when they'd spoken on the phone.

It was clear that he'd learned from the phone calls he'd made that the arrest didn't involve either Liotta or Bonanno, and so he'd calmed down a little.

But he still felt uneasy, and one could see that he was impatient to find out what this arrest had to do with him.

'Inspector, I would like you to explain—'

'Just give me a little time, Mr Licausi. If I asked you to come down here at this hour of the night, it's out of consideration for you and His Excellency Bishop Partanna. Is that clear?'

'Thank you. But, in all honesty, I don't—'

'I want to avoid doing a repeat, you know.'

'I'm sorry, but . . . a repeat of what?'

'Of when I was careless enough to summon Mr Liotta here through the mine's switchboard operator. The man apparently passed the information on to others, even though I enjoined him in every possible manner not to tell anyone, and then what happened, happened: TV, newspapers, lawyers . . . Oh, no! I said to myself. Just like that: Oh, no! In honour of the profound respect in which I hold His Excellency Bishop Partanna, I have to avoid all manner of publicity and sensation that might damage . . . Well, anyway, that's why I summoned you here in the middle of the night, so that nobody, and I mean nobody, would ever find out.'

'And I thank you for that, but I would like to know—'

'I'll tell you straightaway. Oh, but wait, I'm sorry, but I just thought of something. Just a minute, I'll be right back.'

He got up, went out, closed the door behind him, and went into Fazio's office to smoke a cigarette.

'Stew in your own juices a little,' he said to himself, thinking of Licausi.

*

Ten minutes later, he returned.

'I'm sorry, Mr Licausi. So, you were saying?'

'Actually it was you who were doing the talking.'

'And what was I saying?'

'That you were going to tell me the reason why—'

'Ah, yes. We have arrested, purely by chance, a man driving a truck belonging to the Cristallo mine.'

Licausi's face immediately lost colour.

'What did he do?'

'We found him in possession of a large jerry can full of diesel stolen from the mine.'

'Ah!'

But why aren't you asking what his name is, you son of a bitch? Maybe you already know? the inspector asked himself. Then he continued.

'And you know the most shocking thing? He was regularly stealing a hundred litres of diesel per week.'

'Re . . . really? But who is it?'

So now you ask the question you should have asked before, idiot? But now it's too late!

'That's just it, Mr Licausi. He's got no ID on him, no driver's licence, and refuses to give us his personal details. I therefore took the liberty of disturbing you in the hope you might lend us a hand.'

'In what way can I . . . ?'

'Easy. It'll take just a few seconds, and then you can go home in peace. Please come with me.'

Speechless and worried, Licausi stood up and followed him into the corridor.

Outside the door to Augello's office, Montalbano, one hand on the door handle, said in a soft voice to Licausi:

'We think we've identified him as Saverio Milioto. You need only answer my question.'

Without giving him time to react, he opened the door à la Catarella.

The crash made Fazio and Milioto, who were sitting facing each other on either side of the desk, give a start and turn towards the door.

Milioto's eyes locked with those of Licausi, who by now was as pale as a corpse.

'Is it him?' Montalbano asked.

'Yes,' Licausi said under his breath.

'Louder, please. Is it Milioto?'

'Yes.'

Montalbano closed the door.

'What now?' asked the man.

'Now you can go, Mr Licausi. I apologize again for the disturbance, and if you happen to see your uncle, please give him my solemn regards.'

'Yes, but . . .'

'What is it?'

'But what's going to happen, now . . . to Milioto?'

'He'll appear before the prosecutor this morning. I believe he'll then be set free to await trial. And what will you do?'

'Me?!'

'Yes, aren't all the truck drivers for the mine under your command?'

'In a certain sense, yes. I'll report everything to Liotta immediately.'

*

'What now?' Fazio also asked fifteen minutes later, after putting Milioto back in his holding cell.

'Now we wait,' said Montalbano. 'Milioto is the weak link in the chain. And do you know why he's the weak link in the chain? Because he's too hungry, too greedy, too addicted to gambling. Without question he did Liotta, Bonanno, and Licausi a huge favour. They no doubt also paid him, aside from vouching for him at the bank. But

Milioto still wasn't satisfied. He claimed to have a free hand to steal diesel; the theft was authorized. But now I'm quite certain he's convinced that Licausi's thrown him under the bus. And he'll make some false move that'll help us to understand what kind of chain it is that got him and the other musketeers shackled together.'

The inspector paused for a moment, then resumed.

'And have you seen the state Licausi is in? He's scared to death. I'm convinced that there's something really big at the bottom of all this.'

'Listen, if you don't need me any more, I'm going home to bed,' said Fazio, yawning.

'OK. I'll stay here a little while longer. I still have to write the report for the prosecutor, which I'll leave on your desk. After you've had your three hours of sleep, I want you to come back here, pick up Milioto, and take him to the prosecutor in Montelusa. They'll put him on a fast track and set him free right away, since on top of everything else he has a clean record. As of that moment, we absolutely must not let him out of our sight, not even for a second. Oh, and I'll also leave an authorization request to tap Milioto's two phones, the home line and the truck rental line. Good night.'

'Good morning, rather,' Fazio corrected him, since it was already four-thirty.

*

He'd just come out of the shower when the phone rang. Instinctively, he looked at his watch: almost six o'clock. So who could it be, at the crack of dawn?

He picked up the receiver.

'My compliments!' the Author said straight off the bat.

'Tell me something, I'm curious,' said Montalbano.

'I'm at your service.'

'How is it that you never appeared in any of your other novels, but you decided to come and break my balls every five minutes in this one?'

'I'm doing it against my better judgement and only out of generosity, because I want to help you. Never before had you seemed so bewildered and anguished as at the start of this story. So I repeat: my compliments.'

'You already complimented me last time.'

'No, these compliments are today's catch. Because with your arrest of Milioto and the trap you set up for him, making him think that Licausi threw him under the bus, you've brought to light the shady connections between the two.'

'What an earth-shattering discovery!'

'Earth-shattering or no, it simply means you accepted my offer. The two are accomplices in Riccardino's murder.'

'So now you're going to pull out again that ridiculous idea of the van with the ramp that Licausi drives straight up like Evel Knievel? But can't you see how fucking stupid that is?'

'I'm sorry, Montalbano, but then why did you arrest Milioto and link him inextricably with Licausi?'

'But do you read what you write?'

'Of course!'

'Then I guess your memory's starting to fade with age.

A short while ago I explained to Fazio, as you were putting it down on paper, that Milioto is the weak link in a chain that binds him to Licausi, Bonanno, and Liotta. Have you forgotten? I don't give a fuck about Licausi the individual; I want to get the whole group, understand?'

'Ah, I do understand now. So you think that the killing of Riccardino was an act of revenge on the part of the group, to make him pay for cuckolding them? In your opinion, were the three musketeers all in on the plan?'

'No.'

'Shit! Then I really don't understand you.'

'Well, I understand myself. Now let me go, so I can get a couple of hours of sleep.'

'Wait, one last thing. If you absolutely refuse to accept the Licausi–Milioto solution, I've thought of another one that doesn't seem bad at all to me.'

'Can you tell me next time?'

'What, you mean you're not curious?'

'No.'

*

He barely managed to get an hour and a half of sleep, because when he was right at the edge of a deep, deep chasm of dense black sleep into which he was blissfully about to plummet, the ringing of the invention of the damn Mr Bell, or the damn Mr Meucci – it was anybody's guess who really was the first to come up with the idea – startled him awake.

He got out of bed, cursing the saints. It was Livia.

'Salvo, I apologize for calling at this hour before going to the office.'

'Not at all! Tell me, what is it?'

'We can't go to Johannesburg after all.'

As the bells started chiming joyously in his head, he asked in an artificially disappointed tone of voice:

'Oh, no, really? And to think I was already enjoying a foretaste—'

'I'm sorry to let you down, my darling. But those idiots at the agency screwed things up, and it couldn't be fixed. But I found the right remedy. We'll be going to another amazing place.'

'Oh, yeah?' asked Montalbano, feeling his heart already starting to skip some beats. 'Where?'

'Rio de Janeiro. I can already see us together at Copacabana . . .'

And thus began a not entirely happy day.

EIGHTEEN

So Montalbano was awaiting a false move?

Well, the false moved arrived right on time, just after Milioto's arrest. As the inspector had foreseen, the truck driver was released on bail after the first hearing.

Then the blow arrived as well.

But it was preceded by a few phone calls, some of which made direct mention of Milioto, and others of which chose to skirt around the same subject.

*

'Inspector Montalbano? Good morning, this is Liotta.'

'Good morning.'

'I wanted to let you know that this morning, after my friend Licausi told me our truck driver had been arrested, I immediately informed our managing director, Stoltz the engineer, of the arrest, and he in turn called in our head of personnel, Bonamico, to talk to him about it. We all decided together to suspend Milioto without pay, while awaiting the final verdict. I just wanted to let you know, so that—'

'And that's all? There's nothing else?'

'What else should there be?'

'I'm sorry, Mr Liotta, but are you aware that this business of stealing a hundred litres of diesel per week had been going on for two years?'

'Yes, that's what I was told.'

'By whom?'

The man hesitated.

'Well . . . by Licausi, I think.'

'You're right to say, "I think," because I certainly didn't tell Mr Licausi how long it had been going on.'

'You didn't?'

'No. But never mind, for the moment, who it was that told you. I'll ask you another question which I'm sure you'll be able to answer with assurance: how many weeks are there in a year?'

Liotta did not answer right away. Then he made up his mind.

'Fifty-two, Inspector. And I also realize what you're getting at.'

'And what am I getting at?'

'You're asking me, how is it possible, given the massive amount of diesel purloined, that not one of us at the mine ever noticed.'

'Good guess.'

'Stoltz and I asked ourselves the same question, and we found the answer. It's because the final tallies of the fuel used for transport are always done at the end of the year, on December the thirty-first.'

'Who does the bookkeeping?'

'Gaspare Bonanno. But, you see, Gaspare was unable to do last year's balance sheets because he was ill. Crisafulli the ragioniere did them instead, and he didn't have a lot of experience at it, so he didn't notice the excess consumption. This year's accounting hasn't been done yet; there's still over a month to go. I'm certain that Gaspare Bonanno would have noticed this time round.'

'But then he might be ill again this year too.'

'I'm sorry, what did you say?'

'Never mind. Have a good day.'

The fucking bastards. How had they managed to foresee all this and cover their arses?

Bonanno who calls in sick, another guy who doesn't know a damn thing about bookkeeping brought in to replace him . . .

And surely by 31 December they were bound to come up with a few other brilliant plans . . .

*

'Chief? Fazio here.'

'Where are you calling from?'

'From Montelusa Central Police headquarters. There's something important I wanted to tell you. Barely an hour after Milioto got home, he'd already made three phone calls.'

'To Liotta, Bonanno, and Licausi.'

'Nope.'

'To who, then?'

'All to the same person.'

'Enough with the sibylline utterances! Who did he call?'

'Salvatore Li Puma!'

That name left Montalbano stunned, slack-jawed. 'Li Puma the builder?!'

Then he was silent for a few moments.

'Inspector, what's happening? Are you there?'

'Just give me a minute to recover. What did they say to each other?'

'They didn't say anything. Milioto tried to reach Li Puma on the construction company's phone, and the secretary, after making him wait a bit, told him the first two times that Li Puma wasn't in, and then the third time said that Li Puma had called to tell them he was leaving for Palermo and would be away for two or three days.'

'He clearly doesn't want to talk to him.'

'Clearly. But the last time he called, Milioto told the secretary that it was an urgent matter, and that he wouldn't call back, but that when Li Puma returned, he would go in person to talk to him.'

There was the false move!

And if someone like Li Puma was involved in this affair, it meant that the boat was carrying some heavy cargo.

'Don't let him out of your sight. I mean it.'

'I put Manzella and Vadalà on his tail. They're really good.'

*

'Inspector Montalbano? This is Father Bartolino, His Excellency Bishop Partanna's secretary. Good morning.'

'Good morning. Everything all right with the fax I sent with my answers?'

'Yes, quite all right. His Excellency read it and reread it, you know. He was very, very appreciative. He said that you, aside from being a cultured man, are also able – though I didn't quite understand what he meant – to see who is inside the tank. Unfortunately, however . . .'

'However?'

'The interview will not be published. The editor in chief of our weekly, who had invited many distinguished men of our province to participate in this series of interviews, got only one other acceptance besides yours. And so this wonderful initiative unfortunately will go no further. His Excellency expresses his deepest, sincerest regrets, and asks you to forgive him.'

'For heaven's sake, say no more! Please give His Excellency my most reverential regards.'

'I certainly will.'

QED: quod erat demonstrandum . . .

It was all confirmation that His Excellency, using St Thomas à Becket and Pascal for cover, wanted simply to know where Montalbano stood on the case.

*

'Chief, ahhh! Chief, Chief!'

'What is it, Cat?'

''Ere's some guy phonin' onna phone 'at says 'e gatta

sack o' money an' 'at 'is justice is annarable an' 'iss sack is atta minitstree in Rome, an' 'e needs a talk t'yiz rilly oigently an' poissonally in poisson! Whattya say, Chief, shou' I put 'im on?'

This was no doubt the Honourable Saccomanni, current Undersecretary at the Ministry of Justice, who'd managed three times to dodge convictions for collusion with the Mafia, each time thanks to the statute of limitations.

'Put him on.'

'My dear, dear Inspector Montalbano! How nice to be talking to you! We met only once, in Montelusa, at Central Police headquarters, for a celebration. Do you remember?'

'No.'

'Ah, but I do remember, perfectly in fact, and I also recall having had a highly favourable impression of you on that occasion. At any rate, the fame surrounding you—'

'Thank you, your honour. What can I do for you?'

'As you certainly know, Montelusa is my electoral base. And I am therefore constantly informed in great detail by my constituents of everything that happens in the province.'

'And what have they informed you of in great detail this time?'

'Well . . . of something that may be of no consequence, or which, alternatively, could have dire consequences, depending on how the matter is presented to the public.'

'And what is this something?'

'The arrest of that truck driver for the Cristallo mine, what's his name, Gilloto, Migliocco . . .'

'Milioto, your honour.'

'Yes, that's it.'

'But why should the arrest of a diesel-thief have dire consequences, as you seem to fear?'

'As long as the arrest involves the actions of a disloyal employee, and as long as the matter remains limited to that episode, there are no objections. On the contrary.'

'And so?'

'And so, this episode, which is quite negligible in and of itself, or at least of only very limited, relative importance, could become a serious problem if the salt mine is involved.'

'I don't see how the salt deposits would mind if they were involved.'

'What are you saying? I wasn't referring to the salt, Montalbano!'

Clearly the honourable undersecretary was wondering whether Montalbano was really as stupid as he seemed or merely pulling his leg.

'Then what were you referring to?'

'To the mine in and of itself, Montalbano!'

'Do you mean the Platonic idea of mine?'

It was hopeless. Try as he might to control himself, whenever faced with the pomposity, arrogance, disdain, false cordiality, and rhetoric of a politician of this man's ilk, who acted only out of self-interest while pretending to serve the common good, Montalbano could never resist the urge to resort to mockery, derision, and provocation.

Undersecretary Arturo Saccomanni lost his cool and changed his tone.

'Listen, Montalbano, I'll speak very clearly, so that even an idiot can understand me.'

An idiot like you, he meant.

'The salt mine – and by "the salt mine" I mean the administrative offices, the employees, and the managers who are part of them – must not in any way be subjected to unjustified suspicions. That mine is one of the greatest economic resources of our province. If rumours, suspicions, and malicious gossip begin to circulate, it could sully the good reputation of our mine, which could in turn cause severe damage—'

'To the province's economy. Yes, I understand, your honour.'

'Ah, I'm so glad you finally understand. And I'm counting entirely on your *savwahr fair*.'

He said it just like that: *savwahr fair*.

All of which meant, translated into Italian from the unlikely French of Undersecretary Saccomanni:

Careful, Montalbà! Tread lightly. Liotta, Licausi, and Bonanno must, at all costs, be kept out of the case of the stolen diesel.

*

'I don't like it, Montalbano.'

'What don't you like?'

'The turn the investigation is taking,' the Author said in an irritated tone.

'And what can I do about that?'

'Wasn't it you who arrested Milioto?'

'You know perfectly well that I arrested him purely by chance, because the clairvoyant fortune-teller—'

'No, my friend. You're not being straight with me.'

'Meaning?'

'Meaning that you didn't decide to arrest him until you found out the driver's name was Milioto. If his name had been, I don't know, Gasparotto or something, you wouldn't have given a flying fuck about the stolen diesel.'

'Could you be a little clearer?'

'You're a hunting dog, Montalbà, and you've still got a good nose. You jumped at Milioto because Fazio told you Riccardino Lopresti had awarded him a loan guaranteed by Liotta, Bonanno, and Licausi. You simply did the maths. You picked up a scent – that is, a probable connection between those five people. And you're following that scent with acumen and intelligence – in your own way, of course. The only problem is that that's a path I don't want to go down.'

'You're not the only one. Bishop Partanna doesn't want to either, nor does the Honourable Saccomanni . . .'

'I don't like it for other reasons. Once upon a time I would have been all for it. No longer.'

'Then let me repeat: what can I do about it?'

'You can do a great deal, and you know it.'

'For example?'

'Montalbà, the other day I offered you a solution that you found downright ridiculous.'

'Well, I apologize. That was maybe a little excessive on my part.'

'I had to make a big effort not to feel offended; nobody has ever called anything I've written ridiculous.

But then, taking into consideration that we've been working together for so many years with mutual love and respect, I let it slide and thought of another solution.'

'Let's hear it.'

'On one condition: you must promise you will consider my offer with due attention and not dismiss it out of hand.'

'All right, I promise.' There was silence. 'So, are you going to tell me?'

'Over the phone? No, no . . . I'll send you a fax.'

'You've already written it? You've already written the ending?! The ending of my case? How dare you!'

'Stop getting so upset, Montalbà, and just think for a second. I wrote it for the sake of convenience, because it's one thing to work things out on a well-studied page, weighing each word, and it's something else entirely to say things aloud, because sometimes, when they come out, they're not the right words. And anyway, when you really come down to it, I'm just making an offer.'

'Right, but in the meantime you've already cooked up the ending.'

'Montalbà, on my word of honour. Yes, I've cooked it up, but I haven't brought it to the table yet. We'll decide together whether to use it or not. I don't understand why you're getting so pissed off.'

'OK, send me the fax.'

✳

'Montalbano?'

'What can I do for you, Mr Commissioner?'

'I wanted to inform you that just a few minutes ago I got off the phone after a long conversation with Bishop Partanna.'

'What did he say?'

'Don't you know? Are you no longer in communication with His Excellency?'

'No.'

'Your beautiful friendship is over?'

'There never was one, Mr Commissioner.'

'Whatever the case, His Excellency told me that he's very displeased with the way you're conducting the investigation.'

'Excuse me for being so bold, but does His Excellency Bishop Partanna work for the Ministry of Justice?'

'Skip the irony, Montalbano. You know as well as I that in our country, the priests are in on everything. In the present instance, however, the bishop has a precise motive: his nephew Alfonso. And he revealed something to me that you took great care not to tell us.'

'Namely?'

'Namely that the murder victim, Riccardo Lopresti, was sleeping with the wives of his three friends. You knew that, didn't you?'

'Yes.'

'Montalbano, for all these years that I've been the head of Montelusa Police, I've tried hard to understand your methods. But I've never succeeded.'

'Mr Commissioner, I can easily explain that my methods—'

'Be quiet and listen to me. This time, however, you seem to me to be acting in a truly abnormal, lunatic fashion. You have a perfect motive staring you in the face. Lopresti's killer can only have been one of the three husbands. You, however, instead of taking your investigation in that direction, would rather go and arrest a petty diesel thief.'

'Pardon me, Mr Commissioner, but if in following your suggestion I happen to discover that the killer is Alfonso Licausi, His Excellency Bishop Partanna's nephew, how, in your opinion, will the bishop react? Don't you think there's a danger he'll turn to his highly placed Roman friends, while you and I are left to take it up the—'

'Don't be so vulgar, Montalbano. I am sure that His Excellency would know how to face the situation with dignity, without reacting indecorously. But that's not the point.'

'Then what is the point?'

'The point is that His Excellency is absolutely certain that his nephew was neither the material executor of the crime, nor its instigator.'

'And how does he manage to be so certain?'

'Montalbano, His Excellency has given me to understand that he is bound to the secrecy of the confessional.'

'Ah, so he's Licausi's confessor?'

'Not just Licausi's, but also Liotta's, Bonanno's, and Lopresti's.'

'So one can safely say that His Excellency Bishop Partanna is in possession of the facts?'

'Don't be silly, Montalbano! Even if he is, it's as if he wasn't!'

'The secrecy of the confessional?'

'Precisely. His only concern is for the health of his sister, Licausi's mother, who has suffered a great deal knowing that her son is suspected of a horrible crime. His Excellency maintains that you shouldn't be dilly-dallying – those were his exact words, "dilly-dallying" – by arresting two-bit petty thieves.'

'Well, his crime wasn't so petty. Do you know how much diesel he—'

'I know, I know . . . Listen, Montalbano, we have to find a way out of this predicament.'

'All right, tomorrow I'll arrest either Bonanno or Liotta, keeping Licausi out of it.'

'And how will you decide?'

'I'll flip a coin. Heads, I arrest—'

'Montalbano, for the love of God! I'm giving you two days, understand? Two days!'

'And what if I can't manage in two days?'

'Then the case will be turned over to Inspector Toti again. Goodbye.'

'All the best, Mr Commissioner.'

✣

'Chief! *Matre santa*, Chief!'

'What is it, Fazio? Has something happened?'

'Milioto was just shot. Right in front of Manzella!'

'Did they kill him?'

'Yeah.'

And there it was. The blow.

But it wasn't what the inspector had been expecting. Because, more than a blow, this was a bomb, a cannon blast.

NINETEEN

FAX 0922 885***
Attn: Inspector Salvo Montalbano
From: the Author

Dear Salvo,
After faithfully transcribing your story up to the
killing of Milioto, I was forced either to add a sort
of preamble to the fax I'd already drawn up, or to
revise the fax itself, reducing it to a sort of
cinematic pre-production outline entirely open,
therefore, to changes, variants, substitutions . . .
    Here is my preamble:
    Knowing you as I do, I know how you
stubbornly intend to proceed on this case. At any
rate, you've already skilfully brought the characters
of greatest interest to you into the fray: Li Puma
the mafioso; the honourable Undersecretary Arturo
Saccomanni, a politician in the Mafia's back pocket;
and a bishop who is ambiguous to say the least

(concerning this latter character, I will admit quite frankly that I harbour a variety of fears perhaps best summed up in the ancient saying, 'Joke with the lowly but not with the holy,' even if His Excellency Bishop Partanna is certainly not holy).

In short, you're trotting out the usual puppets of your customary puppet theatre. That is, the one where the forever stale and oft-reheated relationship between the Mafia and the political class takes centre stage, concerning which my readers are beginning to show quite justifiable signs of weariness. Do you realize how many of them keep asking me for 'a good mystery story' pure and simple – that is, one in which neither politics nor the Mafia plays any part? And so I ask you: are you so sure that they'll even let you bring such an investigation to its logical conclusion? I'll give you a practical example, which might help you to understand what I'm trying to say. Until about three years ago, in dealing with someone like the Honourable Arturo Saccomanni, a man long in bed with the Mafia, who got him elected (I have no problem saying that), you, as a police inspector, and head of a commissariat, could carry out, with the requisite difficulties of investigating a sitting member of parliament, any kind of investigation you wanted, with the usual sort of foreseeable caveats.

But things are no longer the way they were then;

they've changed radically. How? Easy: Saccomanni, a former Christian Democrat who hopped aboard the wagon of the majority at the opportune moment, was not only re-elected in a landslide, but has become, under this government, no less than Undersecretary at the Ministry of Justice. In other words, he has and exercises power.

Of course he had power before, too, but it was limited — regional, one might say. Now, however, if Saccomanni so desires, he could have you liquidated not with a *lupara* (as he might wish deep inside), but with a tailor-made law which he would have confirmed by votes from his party comrades and other MPs from other ~~affiliated~~ parties ('affiliated' is not the right word, and so I struck it out; I'll replace it with 'allied'). A law, for example, stating that, considering the long-term, stressful activity in which they're engaged, all senior police detectives over the age of fifty-four must immediately retire. Or else they'll allow you to scrape by, busying yourself with livestock poaching, shoplifting, brawls, and petty theft, but inexorably undermining you every time you happen to get your hands on a more important case.

I could be wrong, but I have eighty years of experience under my belt. And I think that my ending can <u>make the best of both worlds</u>.

Read it without preconceptions, and give it careful consideration.

And don't make any mental smirks or sneers while reading it.

For Christ's sake, in the end I'm not asking you to move the action to the Middle Ages, amidst Gregorian chants, illustrated manuscripts, crypts, and the rest, even though you're hardly a police detective any more, but more a cloistered monk with the vocation of, who knows, a captain of justice!

Let me know what you think.

A.

OUTLINE OF A POSSIBLE ENDING

§   Milioto is lying on the ground in a pool of blood, having been shot square in the back with two bullets outside the front door of his residence.

Montalbano arrives as the victim's son is taking his distraught mother back into their apartment. Fazio calls Officer Manzella over and has him fill Montalbano in. Still rather upset, Manzella tells him what happened. He'd been tailing Milioto's car since morning, when the suspect went to Li Puma's construction company's head-quarters. Apparently, however, Milioto didn't find who he was looking for, since he re-emerged almost at once, got back in his car, and drove to the Cristallo mine. He came out again carrying a small suitcase in his hand. He got back home around eleven, parked his car in the garage (the one in which he keeps his vans), and came back out to enter the building through the front door.

In fact there is no communication between the garage and the apartment building. At that moment, a powerful motorcycle driven by a fully helmeted man drove up at wildly high speed and fired two shots into Milioto. Manzella saw the victim fall to the ground and began to pursue the perpetrator. After a while the motorcyclist was forced to slow down, and the policeman was able to fire some shots at him. He is certain that one hit him in the shoulder. But the killer managed to get away just the same. The motorcycle's licence plate was covered with a piece of cardboard. The small suitcase contained only some personal effects that Milioto kept at the mine.

§ As the Forensics lab personnel, the medical examiner, and the public prosecutor arrive from Montelusa and get down to work, Montalbano goes to visit Li Puma's company.

There the secretary confirms to him that Milioto came looking for Mr Li Puma, and had also phoned asking for him, but unfortunately the company's director had been forced to prolong his stay in Palermo.

'Did you inform Mr Li Puma that Milioto wanted to talk to him?'

'Of course.'

'When?'

'The first time he called, and all the other times as well.'

'Did Milioto say anything today when he learned that Li Puma wasn't back yet?'

'Yes,' said the secretary, blushing.

'Tell me exactly what he said.'

'I'm too embarrassed.'

'Don't be silly.'

'His words were as follows: "If you talk to him, tell him that I won't be the only one taking it up the arse." '

§   Now Montalbano runs straight to the Vigàta branch of the Banca Regionale. The new manager hasn't yet arrived from Palermo; his duties are still being fulfilled by the chief cashier, whom we've already met, Sergio Caruana.

The conversation between Montalbano and Caruana takes place in the manager's office. The door has been locked.

'If I remember correctly, during our earlier encounter, you said that three years ago Lopresti had refused a big loan to Li Puma the builder, but that after a couple of phone calls, one from general management and one from the Honourable Saccomanni, Lopresti had to give in. Is that correct?'

'Yes, precisely.'

'The last time we spoke, you used an unusual verb, do you remember? You said that Lopresti had been "domesticated".'

'Of course I remember.'

'Why did you use that verb?'

'It just came to me by itself. Maybe because of the way Lopresti acted whenever Li Puma came into the bank after that.'

'And how did he act?'

'The first time he treated him quite rudely. But after granting him the loan, he behaved rather obsequiously, like an underling eager to serve and please.'

'And did Li Puma come to the bank many times?'

'Quite a few. Now that I think about it, he even came by four days before Lopresti was killed.'

'Did he come solely for banking reasons?'

'I couldn't really say. Every time he came they would lock themselves in the manager's office, and so I don't know what they talked about. But I do believe . . .'

The chief cashier trails off, hesitant to complete the sentence. He realizes that he's about to say something important.

'I believe they'd become friends.'

'What makes you say that?'

'I ran into them one evening at a restaurant in Mondello, where they were dining together. Lopresti was with his wife, Li Puma with his girlfriend. Have you ever seen her?'

'No.'

'A gorgeous Russian girl who's about forty years younger than him.'

'Did they notice that you were there too?'

'I don't think so.'

'Might it not have been a normal work-related dinner?'

'No, it really wasn't. They were drinking too much to

talk about work. Anyway, you could see they were on very familiar terms with one another.'

'Listen, to return to the phone calls from general management and the Honourable Saccomanni, you said you weren't present when they were made, but that Lopresti told you about them.'

'Yes.'

'Don't you think it's strange that Lopresti granted such a massive loan to Li Puma after just two phone calls? I'll be more precise: how is it that there were no written guarantees? Some kind of, I don't know, formal authorization or letter of endorsement from general management for granting the loan . . . Because, in short, if somehow that loan money got lost, Lopresti had a great deal at stake, maybe even his whole career.'

'You're right. It is rather strange, in fact.'

'Now think hard before answering: is it possible that those phone calls actually never happened, but were made up by Lopresti to justify that unusual loan in your eyes and in those of the other branch employees?'

'I suppose it's possible.'

'A final question, this one on a personal level: why have you told me all this?'

'Haven't you ever met an honest person before, Inspector?'

§ Montalbano talks to Fazio. It's clear that Li Puma gave the order to kill Milioto, who had not only made the mistake of trying to contact him, but had also gone to his office to threaten him.

The timing works out. As soon as he's informed by the secretary of Milioto's visit, Li Puma, from Palermo, phones the killer in Vigàta. When Milioto goes to the mine, the killer has all the time in the world to get organized and go to his home and wait for him.

'In your opinion, Chief,' asks Fazio, 'is Milioto's killer the same man who killed Riccardino?'

'I don't know. That fact that a motorcycle was used in both cases does not automatically establish a connection between the two killings.'

'And what are you going to do now, Chief?'

'I'm going to go and talk to Riccardino's widow. Apparently she knew Li Puma. I'm under the impression that Else Lopresti only sang me half the Mass; I want to hear the whole thing.'

§ The gate barring the entrance to the residential community is closed. Ettore Trupia is in his booth. He sees Montalbano pull up and presses the button to raise the bar. But it won't open, because the power is out. Trupia is forced to come out of his booth and raise the bar by hand. He's surly and in uniform, his big pistol at his side. Curiously, he's unable to open the gate. Montalbano gets out of his car to lend him a hand and notices that Trupia is sweaty, agitated, and extremely nervous. Then he sees something strange: Trupia isn't using his right hand, but is keeping the arm motionless at his side. At last the gate is opened; Montalbano gets back in his car and pulls up in front of the Lopresti house.

Signora Else, normally quite passive, is waiting for him in the doorway.

'Ettore informed me you were coming.'

Without letting her see, Montalbano takes his pistol from the glove compartment and sticks it into his waist-band.

§   'Signora, what sort of relationship do you have with Salvatore Li Puma, the builder?'

It's the simplest of questions, but direct, and thus Else, who apparently was expecting an entirely different sort of question, blanches and stammers her reply.

'I . . . I don't actually know him, but I've heard his name . . . He was a client of my husband's, at the bank.'

'So you don't know him personally?'

'No.'

'You are either lying, or have a very short memory.'

Montalbano is almost brutal. By this point he feels he is on the right track and doesn't want to waste any more time.

'You were seen having dinner with your husband, at Mondello, in the company of Li Puma and his Russian girlfriend.'

'I was?!'

'Yes. We have a reliable witness.'

'He's mistaken.'

'Why do you want to deny the obvious, signora? There's nothing wrong with having dinner with Li Puma.'

'I've never been to dinner with him.'

Montalbano begins to sense that her absurdly adamant denial must be hiding something big. And so he becomes even harsher.

'You must come with me at once to the police station.'

'Why?'

'To face the witness who saw you that evening with Li Puma.'

At this point the widow breaks down in tears, heaving with sobs, in an outburst at once desperate and liberating.

'I can't take it any more! I can't take it any more!'

And then Montalbano fires the question point blank:

'Signora, was it you who had your husband killed?'

'No! I loved him! Despite his continual betrayals, I loved him! I wanted to keep him with me for eternity!'

'Was it you who sent that little box to the under-takers . . . ?'

'Yes. So that part of me would go with him to the grave!'

'Then let me ask you a precise question: do you know who had your husband killed?'

'Yes.'

'It was Salvatore Li Puma, wasn't it?'

'Yes.'

The woman, by this point, has completely broken down. She can't help but answer, without resistance, all of Montalbano's questions.

'How can you be so sure?'

'Li Puma himself told me. We used to socialize with them, but always out of town. Riccardino didn't want there to be any gossip. A couple of weeks before Riccardino was killed, Li Puma paid me a visit here when I was alone. He said he was absolutely certain that Riccardino was sleeping with Irina, his girlfriend. He told me to warn my husband that the affair must end at once, or he would have to face the consequences. I repeated everything to Riccardino, but he just laughed. And what happened, happened.'

'Do you know why your husband and Li Puma saw each other?'

'Because Li Puma supplied the whole gang with free cocaine: Riccardino, Mario, Gaspare, Alfonso, and their respective consorts. They couldn't live without the drug any more.'

'How did he get it to them?'

'Through the truck driver who was killed, Milioto. He would bring it to the mine, and one of his friends would pick it up there—'

'Wait a minute, signora. How did you know that Milioto was killed? The crime only occurred a few hours ago, and the news hasn't yet been broadcast.'

The widow says nothing, but only weeps convulsively. Montalbano springs into action. He has realized that the time is right. He is almost violent.

'Do you know who shot your husband?'

No answer. Montalbano grabs her by the shoulders and shakes her.

'Is it the same person who killed Milioto?'

'Yes,' says a voice behind Montalbano.

Standing in the doorway to the sitting room is Ettore Trupia. He's holding his big revolver in his left hand. Now it is clearly visible that his right sleeve is drenched in blood. One of the shots Manzella fired hit its target. Montalbano is not surprised. On the contrary, there is a hint of a smile on his lips.

'I was expecting you,' he says to Trupia. 'I realized you'd been injured when you opened the gate, and then I did the maths. May I turn around?'

'No.'

But Montalbano's hand has already reached the butt of his pistol, which he grabs, and he fires the gun over his shoulder without aiming. Trupia fires a return shot and runs away. Montalbano gives chase.

But as he's going out of the door he hears a cry of pain and stops. Signora Else has been accidentally shot by Trupia. The inspector has a moment of hesitation, then goes to help the woman and realizes that her wound is not serious.

'Call an ambulance,' he says.

And he resumes his pursuit. And here a scene practically out of a Western unfolds. The two men exchange gunfire, using tree trunks as cover.

Montalbano hurdles over two or three fences as in an obstacle race, firing his weapon with icy calm. He closes in on Trupia, who is terrified and firing mechanically. But then the man's revolver goes *click*. He's run out of bullets. Montalbano draws near.

'Open your mouth.'

The man obeys. Montalbano sticks the barrel in his mouth and pulls the trigger. The inspector's gun also goes *click*.

As Trupia falls to the ground, fainting, Montalbano says:

'I, unlike you, keep track of how many shots I've fired.'

§   There is one last meeting between Montalbano and the bishop. The latter confides to him, naturally through tortuous language, that he was convinced that it was his nephew Alfonso Licausi who had murdered Riccardino, because of his love affair with Maria. And that this was why he had intervened and turned to Montalbano: to ask him to do his duty, but with compassion and understanding.

Send me your observations by fax. That way we can discuss things on paper, and not simply over the phone.

I impatiently await your response.

A.

FAX 06 9944****
for: the Author
from: Salvo Montalbano

I have read and reread your outline, not because I was looking for anything to change, but because I couldn't believe my eyes. How can you possibly propose such hogwash? The story doesn't hold up;

it's full of inconsistencies and even drifts at moments into ridiculousness. And you can keep for yourself the scene where I ask Signora Else whether the pubic hair to be placed in the coffin is her own! Go on! You sent me an ending that does not make the best of both worlds, as you put it, but only of one world: yours.

The Honourable Saccomanni practically disappears, the mafioso Li Puma commits murder because he's cuckolded, and all the bishop ever had in his heart was concern for the fate of his favourite nephew (who, among other things, as you yourself wrote, is a fucked-up cokehead and an accomplice of Milioto's).

I can understand how, at your age, you don't want any more hassles, headaches, or flak. But there's a limit beyond which I'm unwilling to go. To say nothing of the Western scene! With me hurdling fences like the actor in the old Olio Cuore commercial (or was it Olio Sasso?). And speaking of actors: the Western scene is much more fitting for the TV character than for me. What is going on? Are you starting to confuse me with him? And then you come to me with that bullshit about the double?

My dear Author, I believe that this story has broadened the rift that has existed between us already for some time and has made each new collaboration between us increasingly difficult.

I'm not sure what happened. I don't think it's only our mutual weariness, but in any event I believe it would be extremely hard, at this point, to glue the broken pieces back together again.

And then I ask myself (and you): Is it still worth it?

Salvo

TWENTY

'I want to tell you straight out, Prosecutor Tommaseo,'
Montalbano began, 'that I've reached the conclusion, and
conviction, that the murder of Riccardo Lopresti has
brought to light a criminal organization, you could almost
call it a gang, whose purpose is . . .'

The prosecutor looked at the inspector as if completely
stunned, and raised a hand for him to stop.

It was ten-thirty in the evening. Montalbano had
adamantly insisted on the urgency of the meeting, forcing
the magistrate to receive him at his home during off
hours in Montelusa, and it was clear that Tommaseo,
who was not married, had been in such a hurry to tidy
up his study in anticipation of Montalbano's arrival that
he hadn't done a good job of it – that is, he hadn't very
well managed to hide, behind whole years of bound
volumes of the *Official Gazette*, the *Laws and Decrees*, and
The Scales of Justice, less sober periodicals such as *Playboy*,
Penthouse, and *Oui*. For a moment Montalbano was
distracted by the sight of a female posterior only partly

covered by a dense tome entitled *Crimes Against Common Notions of Decency*.

'I'm sorry, Inspector, but I just don't understand what you're saying. Following your advice, I'd decided to interrogate the two women you indicated to me in as thorough a fashion as possible, going deep, deep into their secrets, and they . . .'

He trailed off. The memory of the interrogation of the two women, going deep, deep into their secrets, seemed to have brought a twinkle to his eye, and he licked his lips, swallowed, and a little band of sweat appeared under his nose. Whenever Tommaseo questioned a good-looking young woman, he revelled in it as much as if he had her in his bed.

'. . . and they had no trouble at all admitting to their adulterous relations with Lopresti. On my own initiative I also called in Signora Ida, Gaspare Bonanno's wife, and she also admitted to having sexual relations with Lopresti, who apparently never let an opportunity slip, the lucky dog. And you – who I'm sure had the chance to meet them over the course of the investigation – you will surely agree—'

'No, I never had a chance to meet them,' Montalbano cut in.

'Oh, really? If you'd had the chance, not necessarily to interrogate them, but just to meet those three splendid young ladies – Ida, Maria, and Adele – if you'd even so much as caught a glimpse of them, you certainly wouldn't be here talking to me about criminal organizations and gangs . . .'

'What, then, would I be talking to you about?'

'Inspector, this whole affair is utterly simple. Those three ladies betrayed their respective husbands with Lopresti. And so one of the three men, or maybe all three in cahoots – but that's yet to be determined – decided to have Lopresti killed. It's so obvious!'

And now how was the inspector ever going to knock him off his cuckoldry murder hobbyhorse? On top of everything else, it was he himself who had sent him down this path. Maybe it was time to stroke his feathers a little.

'Well, sir, given your profound knowledge of the feminine mind . . .'

In reality Prosecutor Tommaseo dedicated his quest for knowledge to several somewhat more tangible feminine attributes. But Montalbano's statement had an effect on him.

'Well, in all modesty . . .' the prosecutor said, smiling and pleased.

'Anyway, given this knowledge, haven't you ever wondered why these three women, who had all been with Lopresti and were each in turn abandoned by him and then taken back depending on the momentary whims of their lover, why they never reacted in any way to being messed around by him, why they always remained friends, why they never quarrelled among themselves? Don't you find that behaviour a bit unusual?'

'Well, yes,' said Tommaseo. 'And I pointed that out to them.'

He gulped several times, trying to swallow all the spittle that had accumulated in his mouth.

'Each one in her own way,' he continued, 'the ladies gave me to understand that Lopresti was a . . . highly . . . ahem . . . *well*-endowed man . . . *Super*-endowed, know what I mean? And insatiable! A veritable sexual gymnast!'

He heaved a long, disconsolate sigh. Envy? Unpleasant comparisons? Feelings of inferiority? Self-commiseration? Then he resumed.

'And they also told me that they considered every encounter with Lopresti as a sort of . . . gratification. A break from the routine of married life. And they were keen to point out that it wasn't a question of love, it wasn't a relationship involving the heart – it was just sex, pure and simple. Like a sporting exercise.'

'Did you ask them whether their husbands knew about these gymnastic workouts?'

'They all said the same thing: no. Or if they knew, they pretended not to. And this, in my opinion, lasted until one of the husbands found out, or else got tired of pretending not to notice. Oh, and I almost forgot: all three women denied being the one who sent the pubic hair in the jewel box. You're going to have to dig a little deeper into that,' he said, eyes flashing.

Montalbano, whose balls were by this point in a dangerous spin, went on the attack.

'Mr Prosecutor, all this cuckoldry stuff is irrelevant. But everyone is doing everything humanly possible to make us think that we're looking at the revenge of a jealous husband.

I even think the business of the pubic hair is a clever red herring.'

'I beg your pardon, Montalbano. I've learned on my own that even His Excellency Bishop Partanna, who actually has a nephew mixed up in this – Alfonso Licausi – is leaning towards the hypothesis of an honour killing.'

'The bishop is perfectly well aware that the matter is much bigger than that and is just trying to limit the damage! He doesn't want a more clamorous scandal to break out, that's all. He knows, moreover, that it could not have been his nephew who killed Lopresti. Therefore it costs him nothing to nudge us in the direction of a crime of passion. But things are not, believe me, the way they're trying to make them look to us. Among other things, I arrived at the scene right after the murder, and I can assure you the three men's shock was genuine. Later, at the station, there was, at a certain moment, some unease among the three, owing to something I didn't grasp but which I can now explain: they were worried that the murder of Lopresti might lead to the discovery of the shady stuff they were involved in. As could still happen.'

'So you've changed your mind. Your report first encouraged exploring the revenge lead. But now you're telling me it's not a case of a cuckold's revenge,' Tommaseo said with a note of disappointment. 'But are you so sure?'

'No, I'm not. But I can only get real assurance with your help.'

'Then tell me what you have in mind.'

'As you know, a man named Milioto was killed. He drove trucks for the Cristallo mine, and—'

'He stole diesel, I know. Go on.'

'Well, here's the point: he could never have done that without accomplices inside the mine's administrative offices. And the names of these accomplices are Licausi, Bonanno, and Liotta.'

Prosecutor Tommaseo started laughing, eyes squeezed shut:

'Hee hee hee! And did they divvy up the proceeds? Come on, Montalbano! Do you really think they needed those pennies?' he asked, still laughing.

'No, they divvied up other proceeds, which I'll tell you about in a minute. May I continue? A few years ago, Milioto was granted a loan by Lopresti's bank. He got it because Licausi, Bonanno, and Liotta underwrote it, vouching for him. That was the only time they did such a thing, mind you; never before or after did they do anything similar for other truck drivers or clerks from the mine. They did not, in short, have any vocation for charity. If they did it, it was because they had no choice.'

'And what do you mean by that?'

'By that I mean that there was some sort of inexplicable bond tying the three mine employees to Milioto. It's undeniable. And when Milioto started stealing the diesel, they pretended not to notice. On top of that, I'm convinced they cooked the books. So the question I asked myself was this: what was keeping the four men bound together? They weren't friends with Milioto and did not socialize together. Maybe the truck driver was in a position to blackmail them? But then he gets killed after being suspended from his job.'

'And what's that got to do with anything?'

'A lot, sir. Because Milioto – and this I found out from questioning the secretary – had gone to the offices of a builder suspected of Mafia ties and drug-trafficking, a certain Salvatore Li Puma, after trying several times without success to reach him by phone. And, not finding him in this time, either, he says in exasperation to the secretary to tell Li Puma that he doesn't want to be the only one to have to pay. And two hours later he's killed. Which means that there's yet another unexplained link between Milioto and Li Puma.'

'And so?'

'And so I remember something the chief cashier of the Banca Regionale, Sergio Caruana, said to me. Which is that as soon as Lopresti was appointed branch manager, Li Puma came in and asked for a loan in the millions. Which he was refused, the first time around. But Lopresti was then "domesticated", to use Caruana's term, by two phone calls: one from the bank's general management office in Palermo, and the other from the parliamentarian Arturo Saccomanni.'

Prosecutor Tommaseo gave the slightest of starts in his chair and his eyes goggled.

'Saccomanni, the current Undersecretary at Justice?'

'Yes.'

Tommaseo pulled a handkerchief out of his pocket and

used it to mop his brow, which had suddenly become sweaty.

'Following those two phone calls, which are impossible to verify, and with nothing written on paper, Lopresti granted the massive loan. I think some kind of pact was made between the two that day.'

'What kind of pact?'

'You see, sir, the problem for a man like Li Puma, who, as they'll surely confirm for you at the commissioner's office, is suspected of being a major narcotics importer, is that he must always find new, different arrangements for transporting and delivering large quantities of merchandise. Li Puma has known for a while about the strong bonds of friendship between Lopresti and the three administrators at the mine. So he goes to the bank to Lopresti to ask for a big loan. I think he probably needed the money to buy more drugs. When Lopresti turns him down, Li Puma has his friends intervene: somebody from the general management of the bank, and the Honourable Saccomanni. Lopresti afterwards is forced to receive Li Puma, who then makes him a deal. Lopresti thinks about it, and finally accepts.'

'But what was this deal, Montalbano?'

'Li Puma offers Lopresti the chance to become part of the drug ring, telling him there are huge profits to be made. But he adds that it is imperative that Bonanno, Licausi, and Liotta also be part of it.'

'Why?'

'Because the mine and the salt transport are at the very

heart of Li Puma's plan. Maybe you'll get a better idea if I explain how the thing worked. In one way or another the merchandise – camouflaged in a variety of ways and moved in quantities of at least half a kilo at a time – is brought to one of our three friends at the mine. I believe they established some kind of rotation so as not to arouse suspicion. Licausi, while performing his daily inspection of the trucks, puts the drugs in Milioto's truck. I've examined the flatbed: in one corner, there's a sort of square whose edges are just barely a bit more raised, but then it vanishes under a plank of the bed itself. And that's where they put the drugs. Afterwards, it all gets literally buried, submerged, under the loose salt. So Milioto comes to Vigàta, to the Siculsal establishment, in his truck, dumps his load, grabs the coke and turns it over to someone working in the warehouse at the packing plant. The man then packages it as if it's salt, and marks the packet in some way to tell it apart, before it is mixed with the others and sent off. Brilliant, don't you think?'

'It would be brilliant if you could prove it,' Tommaseo said doubtfully.

'If you want, it could be proved,' Montalbano retorted.

'How? I suppose we could have Forensics examine the little square in the flatbed to see whether—'

'I've already looked at it myself. It's been carefully cleaned. But there must be a way. Let's put a tap on all their phones. You'll see, those taps—'

The start Tommaseo gave this time nearly made him fall out of his chair.

'Stop, Montalbano, stop right there! For the love of God! What on earth are you saying? What is going through your head? Don't you read the newspapers? Don't you watch TV? Don't you know that the Prime Minister in person is presently drafting a law that limits, severely, our ability to tap people's phones? And you come to me to ask me to do just that? With Saccomanni right in the middle of this? No, Montalbano, it's entirely out of the question.'

'But you granted me authorization to tap Milioto's phones just the other day!'

'The other day was the other day. The Prime Minister hadn't yet—'

'But then you're blocking my investigation!'

'I'm sorry, but I won't be granting any more phone taps. Find another way.'

'Well, I suppose we could try and investigate the financial assets of Licausi, Bonanno, Liotta, and Lopresti.'

'But what's the motivation, Montalbano? Don't you realize that you have nothing in hand? Not a thing! No concrete clue whatsoever! No proof! Only suspicions, suppositions, hypotheses that don't have so much as a spider's web supporting them! Let's try to be serious about this!'

'If we could search the Siculsal warehouse, we might—'

'At this point in time, if there's any truth to what you've been saying, they will have already got rid of all the evidence. We would be making a lot of commotion for nothing. And, anyway, I'm not a gambler, you know. I have no intention of blindly jeopardizing my career. Because, in a case like this, you're gambling your career if you make a false move. Meanwhile, I have noticed, you know, that you still haven't told me why Lopresti was killed and by whom!'

'It's possible Lopresti had become a dead weight. Once the mechanism had been set in motion, he became a useless cog. But I'm not sure he realized this himself. He may have increased his demands on Li Puma, just as he'd already done with his accomplices, whom he forced to become consenting cuckolds. And the wives, by going to bed with Lopresti, mixed business with pleasure. Until Li Puma grew weary of the whole setup and gave Milioto, or someone else, the order to bump him off. Then Milioto was killed in turn because he knew too much and, after being arrested and losing his job, also lost control and started threatening to compromise Li Puma, Bonanno, Licausi, and Liotta.'

'More conjectures, Montalbano!'

'Look, sir. When I first went to interrogate Lopresti's widow, I walked into a sort of ambush set up by her brother-in-law, who's the security guard for the residential complex and hadn't recognized me. They were clearly on the alert. They were worried that Li Puma wanted to eliminate the widow, who obviously knew about everything.'

'But those are also nothing but speculations! It's not idle chatter I need, but a solid foundation, however small, on the basis of which I can take action.'

'But that's absurd, sir! You're asking me for evidence without giving me the opportunity to gather it!'

'Montalbano, I play by the rules. It's not up to me. And therefore I have no choice but to say no, without reservation, to all of your requests.'

He stood up. Montalbano did likewise. They had nothing more to say to each other.

'You're very attached to your arse, aren't you, Mr Prosecutor? Need to cover it well, eh?'

The prosecutor looked at him, and instead of getting angry, he merely said coldly:

'You don't know how to lose.'

'You're wrong. I do know how. But when it happens, it pisses me off.'

*

As he was slipping the key into his front door, he could already hear the phone ringing.

At that hour of the night, it could only be Livia. He ran inside. He needed to hear her voice, at least, whereas . . .

'Montalbano? This is the commissioner. I apologize for calling you at home, and at such an ungodly hour, but . . .'

'It's quite all right, Mr Commissioner. What can I do for you?'

'I wanted to tell you that I just now got a rather alarmed, and alarming, phone call from Prosecutor Tommaseo. And when he had finished talking, I must say I shared his concerns.'

'What concerns?'

'I think, my dear Montalbano, that you're perhaps getting too tired, too weary. And so I've decided to turn the investigation back over to Inspector Toti. I'd already told you that anyway, I believe.'

'Yes, you had.'

'I will add, Montalbano – and I don't know whether you'll like this or not – but a short while ago I called Inspector Toti and told him to follow the directions contained in the fax I had sent to him.'

'What fax are you talking about?'

'The one the Author had already sent to you, of course! He sent me a copy.'

'The Author did?! To you?!'

'Yes, to me. Why are you so surprised? Have you forgotten that I'm one of his characters too?'

*

He never went near the bed, but remained seated on the bench on the veranda, watching the colour of the sea change as the light of the new day began to approach. Every so often he needed to spit.

His mouth tasted of rancid butter and rotten fish.

Maybe it's the taste of defeat, he thought.

Though the night was cold, he didn't feel cold. The blood coursing in his veins was too hot.

At a certain point he felt a fever coming on, but he didn't worry. That change was not due to anything directly concerning his body, but was born instead of everything that was going through his mind and bringing him to the only possible conclusion to be reached.

He thought of Livia, of Fazio, of Mimì Augello, of Catarella, and got a lump in his throat. And so he allowed himself the luxury of a tear.

The last time he'd cried had been upon learning of someone's death. And this, too, all things considered, was a kind of death.

He dried his eyes with one hand and, moving it ever so slowly from left to right, tried with the same hand to erase the landscape as if it were a scene drawn on a blackboard.

And he saw, to his shock, that he'd succeeded: to his left, the horizon line looked torn, broken up, now but a jagged edge of peaks, like those of a sheet badly ripped out of a notebook.

The fishing trawler out at sea was now only half-visible: the ship's bows had gone, and as it sailed on, passing the jagged edge, it dissolved and vanished.

He continued slowly erasing.

He wanted to take that landscape with him. He couldn't allow anyone else to enjoy it.

And in this way, little by little, the beach, the sea, the sky also disappeared.

In the end, all there was before him was a blank page. And he understood what there remained for him to do.

✻

This is the Author's answering machine. I'm not at home. Please leave a message and your telephone number after the beep. You will be called back.

Montalbano here. Seeing that our decades-long collaboration has gone to the dogs and deteriorated to the point that you have given another character, the commissioner of police, the power to prevent me from solving the case in my own way, I have made a decision. If you are replacing me in my own investigations, then it means that I myself am becoming a dead weight.

And so I'm leaving. Of my own spontaneous free will. I will not give you the satisfaction of getting rid of me in one way or another. I will disappear on my own. I've discovered that it's easy. And so, starting right now, I'm beginning to erase myself. It won't take long. I'm already starting no longer to exist . . . I can feel myself qui . . . ckly los . . . ing wei . . . ght an . . . d vo . . . lume . . . Wo . . . rds . . . are star . . . ting . . . to fai . . . l me . . .

I don't know . . . if I . . .

can . . . st . . . ll . . . sp . . . k

goo . . . by . . .

I am no

I a

I

Author's Note

This is the final novel with Inspector Montalbano as its protagonist. I first started writing it in July 2004 and finished it in August 2005. I will not write any more in the series. I regret this, but at eighty years of age, one cannot avoid the fact that many, too many things must come to an end.

Naturally, the story is entirely invented out of whole cloth, and no character can be traced back to any living, real-life person. The same goes for the situations, the names of banks and companies, and the surnames of characters.

The context, on the other hand, is all too real, unfortunately.

I thank Emilio Borsellino, who gave me the idea for the story of the truck, which I naturally turned into something entirely different.

This novel is dedicated to Elvira Sellerio, a true 'friend of the heart'.

A. C. (2005)

＊

That's what I wrote almost twelve years ago.

Then, in November 2016, after turning ninety-one and feeling surprised at still being alive and still wanting to keep writing, I thought it might be a good idea to 'adjust' the story of *Riccardino*.

I've lost my eyesight and therefore had no choice but to ask my friend Valentina to read it to me aloud. As I was listening I became surprised at my own words. I no longer remembered the story, which I found good and unfortunately still relevant.

And in fact I changed nothing in the plot. But I did find it necessary to bring the language up to date. It has evolved so much over the years, thanks in part to the loyalty of the readers who have followed and understood me and therefore made it possible for me to work in this vein.

As should be clear, the title of this book is an anomaly with respect to all the others in the series, and indeed *Riccardino* had been simply a working title for me, something I'd promised myself to change when it came time to publish the book. Now that we're here, however, I prefer keeping it as the definitive title, because in the meantime I've grown rather fond of it.

The novel remains dedicated, with more affection than ever, to my 'friend of the heart'.

A. C. (2016)

Notes

NB: The present novel is peppered with far more literary and cultural references than was the norm in all the other episodes in this series. As this was clearly a conscious choice on the author's part, I will not spoil his fun by pointing out and explaining the less obvious allusions, but leave enterprising readers to suss them out on their own. I shall limit myself to elucidating only those references that might elude the English-speaking reader because they take for granted a general familiarity on the part of the Italian audience.

6 Inzolia and Verdicchio . . . 'table wines' . . . 'wild beasts' . . . Lupo and Leone . . . 'chicken coop' . . . Gallo and Galluzzo: Inzolia is a mostly Sicilian white wine, while Verdicchio is a white wine from the region of Le Marche. In Italian *lupo* and *leone* mean 'wolf' and 'lion', respectively, and *gallo* and *galluzzo* mean 'cock' and 'cockerel', respectively.

8 If they turned out to be soldiers in civvies, he could bow out at once and pass the case to the carabinieri: The carabinieri, Italy's national police force, are a branch of the army, like the gendarmes in France and the Guardia Civil in Spain.

12 'We were all born in 1972': The action in this novel should be considered to occur around 2003–2004, around the time, that is, in which the author wrote it. This is why Riccardino's three friends are all said to be around thirty years of age.

38 these young and able functionaries from Lombardy, Piedmont, Veneto, and Friuli: These are the four northernmost regions of Italy (aside from the half-Tyrolean Alto Adige region), and therefore the furthest removed, in terms of both geography and mentality, from the island of Sicily.

60 'How about the carabinieri?' / 'You know what they're like, Chief! Even if they're working with the Pope, they're never going to come and tell *us*!': The national police force of carabinieri and the local police forces under the jurisdiction, like Montalbano's, of the provincial *questura* (commissioner's office) are in constant competition with each other.

71 the sweets of the dead: In celebration of the Day of the Dead (All Souls' Day in the English-speaking world), Sicilian pastry shops and homemakers traditionally bake sweets in various shapes and forms reminiscent of the dead (bones, skeletons, etc.).

71 He sat there thinking of a time when the dead used to leave presents on the morning of the second of November: Such was the custom in Sicily until after the Second World War. See also note to page 74.

74 *carcagnette, tetù:* *Carcagnette* are Sicilian pastries, *tetù* are pralines.

74 The following year, the presents appeared under the Christmas tree instead. Maybe the dead could no longer find their way home: Before the end of the Second World War, Italians were generally not in the custom of exchanging presents on Christmas Eve/Christmas Day, but on the feast of the Epiphany in Central and Northern Italy, and on the Day of the Dead in Sicily and the deep south. (Nor did they know the figure of Santa Claus, who comes out of a German tradition.) 'Then,' Camilleri wrote in 1997, 'when the American soldiers came they also brought the Christmas tree, and slowly, with each passing year, the dead began to forget the way home, where their children, and their children's children, were waiting for them happy and breathlessly awake. It was a shame.' Andrea Camilleri, 'Il giorno che i morti persero la strada di casa' ('The Day When the Dead Could No Longer Find Their Way Home'), *Il Messaggero*, Rome, 2 November 1997 (my translation).

77 the Author's smoke-shredded voice: Camilleri was a notoriously heavy smoker until the end of his days.

86 Minister of the Interior: In Italy, the Minister of the Interior is more or less the equivalent of the Attorney

General in the United States and the Home Secretary in the United Kingdom; in other words, the nation's 'top cop'.

86 *Sàvuta 'u trunzu e va 'n culu all'ortulanu:* Send the shears flying and they'll always find their way up the gardener's arse. A Sicilian saying that basically means that those at the bottom of the totem pole always get blamed when things go wrong.

129 **This is Cesare Battisti:** It is unclear whether Camilleri is referring here to Cesare Battisti (1875–1916), the Italian nationalist who was a native of Austrian-held Italian territories in the north of Italy and fought for their independence before his capture and execution by the Austrians; or to Cesare Battisti (born 1954), the far-left militant who escaped prison in 1981 after his conviction in 1979 for armed insurrection and spent the subsequent decades abroad, often dodging extradition requests, until he was finally arrested in Brazil in 2019 and sent back to Italy, where he is currently serving a life sentence. In all likelihood Camilleri is tipping his hat to both men, the patriot as well as the revolutionary, especially since the latter Battisti, in his long years in exile in France, had become a successful writer of political mysteries based on some of the intrigues he had personally experienced, and is believed by many to have been wrongly charged in association with the violent crimes for which he was eventually punished.

**157 right arm raised in a kind of Roman salute. . . .
'What is it, comrade?':** What is known in English as the
'Fascist salute' (right arm extended and slightly raised, palm
down) is called the *saluto romano* in Italy, an ancient Roman
gesture of greeting found in sculptures and frescoes from
antiquity, but not fully understood in the modern age.
After its touting by nationalist poet Gabriele D'Annunzio,
it was adopted by Mussolini's Fascist party and later by
the German Nazis. The Italian Fascists also took on the
habit of calling one another *camerata* (here translated as
'comrade'), to distinguish themselves from socialist and
communist militants, who called one another *compagno* (also
normally translated as 'comrade').

195 mandrill: Indeed, in Italy an oversexed man is sometimes referred to as a *mandrillo*.

209 *napoletana*: The traditional espresso pot of the
Neapolitans, which must be turned upside down when the
water starts boiling, to let it filter through the coffee
grounds.

240 Mr Meucci: Antonio Santi Giuseppe Meucci (1808–
1889) is credited by some as having invented the first
telephone. He is also mentioned in this capacity in Francis
Ford Coppola's *The Godfather: Part III*.

241 But those idiots at the agency screwed things up:
This book was written in 2005, when people still often
resorted to travel agencies for plane tickets and hotel
reservations, instead of doing it all online themselves.

258 he could have you liquidated not with a *lupara* (as he might wish deep inside): The *lupara* ('wolf gun'), basically a sawn-off shotgun, used to be the weapon of choice of the Mafia. In recent times the Mob generally resorts to more modern means . . .

259 a captain of justice: The office of *capitano di giustizia* was instituted in medieval Sicily under Norman rule. The captain was chosen by the feudal lord to exercise police and sometimes juridical powers and was the chief law enforcement official in the area under his jurisdiction. The office and title slowly spread to peninsular Italy by the late Middle Ages, but was generally abolished by the start of the nineteenth century.

Notes by Stephen Sartarelli